Uncover Me

A Capture Fantasy Romance

Linda Barlow

Linda Barlow Books
Acton, MA

Uncover Me/ Linda Barlow. -- 1st ed.
ISBN:978-0-9893070-6-2

AUTHOR'S NOTE:

Uncover Me is a capture fantasy romance (romantic suspense). It was inspired by a novel that I wrote many years ago *(Hold Back the Night)*. It has been completely rewritten. The current version is much darker than the original, with stronger language and scenes intended for mature audiences.

Nick Gabriel, the hero of *Uncover Me,* is a friend of Kate, Stephen, Max, and Jeff, whom some readers may recognize from my Night Games collection of romances, but this novel is a standalone and not part of a series

Chapter 1

ELLIE

With his wind-tangled yellow hair and his tall, golden body, he looked like an ancient hero or a mythological god. But his weapon was that of a 21st century thug. Staring down the muzzle of his gun, my first thought was that my mother was bound to say, "I told you so." My second was more somber—by the time Mom had anything to say about the matter, I'd probably be dead.

She had been against the idea from the beginning. "Single women don't ride off on motorcycle tours of Turkey," she'd told me. And she ought to know; she'd spent much of her professional life in the Middle East, working on various archaeological digs.

"It's reckless," she'd lectured me as we'd dined two nights before in the rooftop dining room of her Istanbul hotel. Through the windows sprawled the lively city where East truly meets West, the only city in the world built upon two continents. In the half-light of dusk, I could see the mosques and villas that dotted the green hills of Asia across the Bosporus. "The Turks still look askance at young women traveling alone."

"I'll be fine, Mom. Don't forget that this is my adopted country."

"Even so, it's not wise. Lately I've been hearing reports of smugglers operating on the western coast, lawless ruffians running everything from guns and drugs to art objects. It's not the most sensible way for my daughter to be spending her vacation."

I swallowed a delicious stuffed grape leaf, and then poked my fork into my Circassian chicken. I love Turkish food. I'd missed it. "It's not precisely a vacation. I have an assignment to shoot some pictures for a travel website. And I've been wanting to return to the ruins I remember visiting with you—Perge, Ephesus, and especially Troy."

"Really?" Mom leveled her all-too-shrewd blue eyes at me. "You're sure you're not running away?"

Jeez! I attacked a stuffed eggplant. *Was* I running away? I preferred to believe I was finally living out my dream of being a free spirit. An adventuress. For that, I needed an adventure.

"Is it forbidden to inquire what happened to Mark? I thought you two were pretty serious."

"We broke up." I didn't want to discuss Mark—or think about him, either.

"What went wrong? You'd been together for quite a while. I thought things were settled."

"Turned out I wasn't ready to settle down. Why the big fuss? You're single. You travel the world, going wherever your work takes you. You're independent and accountable to no one. Why should you object if I do the same?"

Mom leaned over and stroked my hand. Her face was vulnerable in a manner that I had rarely witnessed. "Because it's a lonely life. I want something better for you."

Whoa, that was a surprise. I squeezed Mom's hand as hard as I could. I noticed with some alarm that her skin was older and drier than I remembered. She was pushing 50, and, as far as I knew, there was no significant other in her life. I'd always thought that she liked it that way.

"I've got time, Mom," I told her. "Please don't worry about me."

She patted my hand briskly, and changed the subject.

"I hope you've brushed up on your Turkish," Mom said the following morning as we said our farewells on the edge of a noisy Istanbul street. I was off to rent a motorcycle and Mom was heading to the airport to fly back to Ankara, where she was doing some research on the Hittite collection. "I know you used to speak it fluently, but it's been a while since you've had any practice."

"I hung out with a Turkish friend yesterday. I'm rusty, but it's coming back fast."

"Well, *iyi yolculuklar*," my mother said. *Bon voyage.* As I hugged her, stepping out of the way of a honking, careening taxi and nearly bumping into a man grilling shish kebab on the sidewalk, Mom added, "Be careful. Don't get into any trouble."

Of course not, I'd assured her. What sort of trouble could I possibly get into?

The trouble started at dawn. I'd stuck my head out of the flap of my tent and squinted at the early April sky, which was rosy with the promise of the kind of day wayfarers yearn for—warm but not too humid, breezy and fresh.

Scrambling out of the tent, I stood and stretched, gazing out toward the Aegean, enjoying the sparkling view of hills and rocks and sea. It was a pleasant change. My plane had landed a few days ago in Istanbul in a rosy-brown haze, my view of the city distorted by dust, diesel fumes and the belchings of the numberless factories that had transformed the country into a modern, industrial society. Clean air was getting to be something of a luxury in Turkey. I sucked it into my lungs, reveling in the light scent of olive trees and wildflowers.

Scooting back into the tent, I dressed, then took down the tent and stowed it with my sleeping bag at the rear of my bike. I sat down in a small olive grove to eat a quick breakfast consisting of the crusty bread, white cheese and black olives I'd purchased yesterday from a village along the road.

I would have liked to make a fire and warm some water for tea, but since I was not camped in an official campground, I decided against it. I'd had some engine trouble with my bike the day before, and dusk had fallen before I reached the campground where I'd intended to spend the night.

When I finished my quick breakfast, I checked my camera battery, and then spent several minutes checking my various lenses. I hoped to reach Troy today and photograph the ruins. After twisting the telephoto lens onto the camera body, I went to the edge of the olive grove to shoot several pictures of the grassy hills that sloped down to a peaceful, sheltered bay. What a lovely spot. The dawn sun was slowly climbing, although it was out of sight behind a hillock at present. The water was glowing apricot and gold with refracted sunlight.

I got several excellent shots. My view of the Aegean was marred only by an occasional scrubby bush or outcropping of rock. The entire area seemed untouched by human activity. Yet I knew that humans had wandered here for millennia. There were ruins all along the Aegean coastline, the remains of Greek, Roman and Selcuk Turkish cities. Not far from here, according to Homeric legend, Menelaus's army had marched to invade Troy. Warriors might well have landed here before beginning their assault on that ancient city. Their warships would have been decked out with colorful sails and fully equipped for battle.

The whimsical image had barely crossed my mind when a sail rounded the rocky point to the right of the bay and directed its course landward. I felt like a magician with the power to call up an object from my imagination and give it form.

But the illusion was dispelled as the boat drew nearer. It was real. A single-masted sailboat, it was graceful as it cut cleanly through the rough sea. A beauty. I aimed my camera at the yacht. Through the telephoto lens, I could see the figures of two men, one at the helm and the other moving about on deck, pulling in the sails as they neared the shore. The first man was dark, the other golden haired. The dark one could have been a Turk, but the man with the wavy gilt hair and sun-bronzed skin had more in common with the god Apollo.

Many modern Mediterranean guys were dark-haired. This fair-haired man might be a foreigner. Twirling the dials, I focused on him. He was in his late twenties, I estimated, with high cheekbones, deep-set eyes and an austere, yet sensual mouth. For some reason his face startled me. It wore a cold expression, yet something about its lines hinted at underlying wellsprings of emotion. A beautiful face—the sort one rarely gets to photograph, because in real life such a face simply doesn't exist. An angel's face.

But, no, the hardness around his mouth confirmed that this was a fallen angel. I seriously doubted that a dude with that face and body would ever be angelic.

He was directing operations on the yacht. When he yelled something, the other guy turned the yacht farther into the wind, decreasing the boat's forward motion. As the blond man leaped gracefully to the bow to stow the jib canvas, my camera lens followed. Although he was tall, he wasn't brawny—he was on the slim side, in fact—whipcord lean. He was dressed in faded jeans and a black T-shirt that pulled taut over the supple muscles in his chest. I couldn't help but admire his long legs and the graceful, economical way he moved.

I needed to photograph him, too. Right now, with the early-morning sun bathing his skin and the wind ruffling his hair. I had to freeze his hard, cold grace in a golden moment of time. I got a couple shots of him tying down the sail. If he'd been a model and this a professional shoot, I'd have dressed him elegantly in a flowing white shirt with an open throat and black leather pants. Pirate-style.

He strolled back to the helm to consult with the dark-haired man. The wheel turned, the boom shifted, the craft came about. It tacked in toward the rocks at the most sheltered corner of the little bay. Were they going to land? I lowered my camera. I was perhaps a hundred yards from the water, standing in the lee of a gnarled olive tree. Although I had an excellent view of the sailboat, I doubted if anyone aboard could see me, and my motorbike was out of sight behind some rocks.

I moved deeper into the olive grove. I knew I ought to get on my bike and go, but I wanted to get a couple more pictures. The sound of an engine coming from somewhere behind me startled me. There was a narrow dirt road back there; I'd ridden along it on my bike. A car was on its way down to the bay. It stopped on the slope overlooking the water, and a fat, balding man got out.

My escape route was cut off. The man from the car was signaling the yacht now, waving his arms in the air. When he got an answering signal from the gilt-haired man, the newcomer turned back to his car. Using my powerful lens as a telescope, I saw him open the trunk and lean inside, then emerge moments later with a good-sized wooden crate in his arms. He lugged it down to the shore just as the sailboat dropped anchor in the bay and sent a rowboat in toward shore.

I let a breath whistle out of my constricted chest. I must have stumbled onto a rendezvous of some sort. I had a bad feeling about this. I huddled deeper into my shelter. *I've heard reports of smugglers operating on the western coast.* My mother's words echoed in my brain. Was my golden god a thief?

The rowboat came ashore with both the men from the yacht. The blond man gestured as he talked to the newcomer; the subject was clearly the contents of the wooden container. The fat man kept casting furtive glances around, seeming anxious to be gone. But the blond man looked cool and self-possessed as he tapped the surface of the crate, indicating that he wanted it opened.

While the fat man returned to his car to fetch a crowbar, I quietly changed the setting on my camera. I was going to document this transaction. I was witnessing a crime.

Apollo, as I had begun to think of him—wrongfully, I knew, since Apollo was the god of light and truth and this man was a crook—skillfully wielded the crowbar. The crate opened down the front to reveal a dusty stone statue.

Although I was no expert, my mom was a famous archaeologist, and she had taught me a few things. The piece, a half-clad figure of a woman, appeared from a distance to be an antiquity. Roman, perhaps, considering its drapery. It was somewhat stylized rather than lifelike. It looked reasonably well preserved.

After kneeling and running his hands over its curves with more care and gentleness than he might have shown a flesh-and-blood woman, Apollo nodded to his young sidekick, who carefully resealed the crate. They turned to the fat man, who was mopping his brow with a handkerchief. A wad of bills changed hands.

"They *are* smugglers," I muttered. Having been raised by Sybil Matheson-Heath, I was furious about what I was witnessing. These criminals were removing precious antiquities from Turkish archaeological sites and smuggling them out of the country. I knew that Turkey had suffered greatly from this sort of crime. For hundreds of years, the nation had been stripped of its priceless historical relics by avaricious treasure hunters like these.

I yearned to erupt from my olive grove and challenge the men. But that would be suicidal. Clenching my fists, I assessed my adversaries once again. The youth was not particularly intimidating, but the fat man looked unpleasantly dangerous, and as for that cold sun god, there was no way I was going to tangle with him.

So instead, grimly, I used my camera. The whirr of its mechanism seemed loud, but I knew from experience that this was an illusion, induced by the adrenaline rush that made all the senses more alert. They could not hear me. They had no idea I was here.

The crate was loaded into the rowboat, and the blond-haired man stepped back on shore to confer once more with his associate. Their faces were close together, and they had both turned slightly, so they were looking roughly in my direction. I focused carefully, trying to get a clean shot, one I might later be able to blow up for the police. I'd heard that facial recognition technology was good nowadays.

Just as I was about to click the shutter, the climbing sun burst over the scrubby hillock directly behind the men. Its white brilliance poured through my lens, obscuring my shot and for a few instants blinding me.

"Damn!" I lowered the camera. I would get no more pictures from this angle.

Shading my eyes with my palms, I continued to watch the smugglers without the aid of the telephoto lens. I had to squint against the sun, which was why it took several seconds before I realized that the men had stopped conversing. They were staring at my small grove of trees. The fat man was pointing with one hand and gesticulating wildly with the other. I flattened myself in the dirt. Surely they couldn't have seen me?

Calling out a sharp command to the dark, slender man, Apollo began to run up the hill toward me. Frozen, I watched him come. I must have given myself away. But how? I jerked to my feet, my camera swinging from its strap. Sunlight glanced off the lens, and then I knew. When the sun had crested the hill and blinded me, its reflection must have flashed from the olive grove, revealing my presence just as plainly as if I'd stood up and waved my arms.

I was poised for flight, but he was close now, running with such grace and speed I knew I'd never get away. Anyway, flight would proclaim my guilt. Perhaps I could convince him I had no idea he was up to anything illicit. That I was a simple American tourist who wouldn't know a smuggler from a fisherman. That the pictures I'd been taking were innocent landscapes whose ultimate destination was a website labeled "My Trip to Turkey."

If he believed that, the golden-haired man was a fool.

Twenty yards away, he stopped and said something in Turkish. The phrase was idiomatic, but the gist was clear. "Come out with your hands up." It was then that I saw he was cradling something dark and metallic in both hands. I thought it was the crowbar. Then he aimed it, and I knew it was a gun.

Chapter 2

ELLIE

"Don't shoot!" Putting down my camera and raising my arms over my head, I stepped out from the olive grove into the sun. *"Lutfen,"* I added, the Turkish word for please. "I'm a tourist. Do you speak English? I'm sorry if I'm trespassing, but I thought this was public land."

It sounded ludicrous, but with my heart thudding and my stomach so cramped I thought I might double over and collapse before he could bother to shoot me, it was the best I could come up with. He was advancing again, his hard face expressionless, his eyes narrowed to slits as they flicked over me, taking in my appearance from my long, ill-kempt hair to my new leather boots.

His gaze lingered for an instant on my breasts and hips. As he closed in on me, I could see that his eyes were light green, the color of tropical seawater. Beautiful eyes, thickly fringed with gold-tipped lashes. Yet for all their beauty, they were mercilessly cold.

He was five yards away, then two, then one. He stopped. The gun, a large ugly pistol, was pointed dead at the center of my body. If he shot at this range, he couldn't miss, nor would I survive. "Please," I said again, lips trembling. "No English? French, then?" My French was not terrific. *"Je suis americaine."* Instinct warned me not to try Turkish—an American tourist wouldn't speak more than a polite word or two of that language. *"Je suis une touriste. Comprenez-vous?"*

"Who are you and what the fuck are you doing here?" he said in English.

"Thank god, you do understand me. It would be stupid for you to shoot me just because we couldn't communicate."

He must have found this answer flip, since he reached out, caught my wrist and jerked me against his body. My yelp of surprise died in my throat as one hand captured my arms behind my back while the other held the barrel of the gun to a point just below my left breast. His touch was both impersonal and professional. It didn't hurt, but this wasn't reassuring. If he had to kill me, he would do so swiftly, with a minimum of fuss.

"You have five seconds to explain yourself."

"I was camped here." I nodded in the direction of my pack. His English was more than excellent; it was perfect. He sounded as if he might be British, although there were American inflections, too. "I had trouble with my bike. I couldn't make it to the official campgrounds."

"You were photographing us."

"I was photographing the coastline. Not you."

"You expect me to believe that?" He kicked at my camera, which rolled over in the dirt. Inwardly I winced, and would have cried out "Don't hurt my camera," if it hadn't seemed a frivolous concern, given that he was probably about to end my life.

"That's a telephoto lens, so cut the lies."

His young sidekick had run after him and was now within hearing distance. The other man, the fat one, was following more slowly, toiling up the hill and muttering obscenities as he came.

My captor twisted my arm, and for the first time I felt a shiver of pain. "Who are you working for? The Turks? The Americans? Interpol?"

"I'm just a tourist."

His hold on my arms grew rougher. He was twisting, putting pressure on ligaments and bone. It hurt and I think I whimpered. "Where's your partner? Nobody sends a woman out on an assignment like this alone."

"Please. I'm not a cop." I could feel tears spring up behind my lashes. I squeezed them back. Courage was important to me. I knew about fear; I had suffered from occasional anxiety attacks for years. Numbing panic could grab me anytime, reducing me to a shaking, sweating wreck. But it hadn't come yet, and until it did, I would try to hang on to whatever shreds of dignity I possessed. "My name is Ellie Heath, and I'm in Turkey on vacation. I arrived in Istanbul last week—my passport's in my pack along with my camping guide, my first aid kit and my extra roll of toilet paper. I thought you were fishermen."

He barked a command in Turkish at the young man, who was regarding me with the outright masculine appraisal that had been so conspicuously absent in the cold assessing gaze of the man who held me. The kid, who looked to be in his early twenties, was good-looking. He had curly dark hair cut close around his head and a profile that wouldn't have looked out of place on an ancient fresco. His eyes were dark and liquid, full of the easy arrogance of youth.

He sauntered over to my pack and began going through it. "Here's the passport." He began reading out the information. His accent, unlike the blond man's, was atrocious, although it was clear that he must have studied some English in school. "The name written here is Helen Heath."

"Helen?" My left arm received a new wrench, and I bit back a cry of pain. "You said Ellie."

"That's what everyone calls me. My mother named me Helen. She's an archaeologist. She has a keen interest in the legend of Troy."

"Well, Helen of Troy, you're only a few miles from the site where your namesake spent her captivity. Menelaus's army could have come ashore anywhere along this part of the coast. Maybe right here in this inlet. It matches Homer's description."

I was impressed with his knowledge of Homer. I guess smuggling antiquities required some expertise in classical lit. I was also surprised by the educated quality of his voice and, once again, the accent. He sounded less British now and more East Coast American.

"Check the date and port of entry, Metin," he ordered in English.

"Atatürk Havaalani, Istanbul. Third of April."

"When's your birthday, Ellie Heath?"

"February 24."

"Year?"

I told him.

He looked at Metin, who nodded.

"The nickname is a nice touch. Along with the bit about your archaeologist mother. What's her name? Is she someone I've heard of?"

"Sybil Matheson-Heath." I didn't add that anyone who knew anything about scholarly archaeology would recognize it.

There was a low whistle from behind my right ear. So he'd heard of my mother. Maybe I shouldn't have revealed it. What if he decided to hold me for ransom? My mother was well known, but by no means rich.

"She is *cok guzel,* Nicholas, very beautiful," Metin said. He had switched to rapid Turkish, but I had no trouble understanding. "I hope you're not going to shoot her before we have the chance to fuck her."

"Stop fantasizing and examine the rest of her things," was the cold reply.

Nicholas. I concentrated on his name rather than the younger man's words, which I was not supposed to understand. Nicholas. An American who spoke fluent Turkish, as I also did. He must have lived in Turkey, too. Yet he had no qualms about stealing its archeological treasures.

The fat man had lumbered up to us now. He was demanding, in harsh, expletive-laden Turkish, that I be put to death. He picked up my camera and began punching the delete button on the recent pictures. Then he dashed the camera to the ground and battered it, provoking an involuntary protest from me. Besides the fact that I loved the damned thing, I had several thousand dollars invested in my photography equipment. I expected to be in debt to Visa for the next twenty years.

If I lived so long.

"Be quiet," ordered my captor as I protested the fat man's assault on my equipment. "Better your camera than your life."

Did that mean he didn't intend to kill me?

"She is a journalist," said Metin, holding up my press credentials. "Look."

"A journalist?" Nicholas wrenched my arms so that I stumbled and nearly fell. He caught me and pulled me around to face him. "You're a fucking reporter? Who do you work for?"

"I'm freelance," I mumbled.

The fat man was quaking in outrage as Metin translated the words on the press card. He pulled out a gun and said in Turkish, "If you don't shoot her, I will."

"Put the weapon away," Nicholas said in the same language. "She's an American. For all we know, there's a drone hovering nearby."

The thug didn't stash the weapon, but he stopped waving it and peered around suspiciously, shading his eyes to look up at the sky. Heavy clouds were moving in. The day that had started so brightly was turning dark.

The blond man returned his attention to me. "You're a journalist snapping pictures with a telephoto lens of a criminal wanted in nine countries while he's smack in the middle of his latest crime."

Nine countries? "Actually, I'm a photographer doing a fluff piece on historical sites in Turkey. I have no interest in you, no matter how infamous you are."

"I'm going to have to make certain of that." He pocketed his gun and placed his hands on my throat. It happened too fast for me to panic. I'm going to die, I thought as his strong fingers slipped around to the back of my neck, slid between two vertebrae and pressed. It didn't hurt, but I felt an odd numbness. The last thing I saw was his starkly beautiful, almost angelic, face bending over me, his gilt hair tousled by the wind. Then darkness took me.

Chapter 3

ELLIE

My return to consciousness was slow, with my brain suggesting that it might be preferable to remain blissfully blank. But I didn't. I remembered what had happened moment by moment, event by event, the images sliding in and out of my consciousness.

Even before opening my eyes, I knew where I must be. I was lying on a hard mattress, and it wasn't my dizziness that was making it pitch up and down. Something was creaking with loud, monotonous regularity; the air smelled of the sea. I was aboard the smugglers' yacht.

For several moments, I lay still, listening, feeling, sniffing the air. My wrists and ankles were bound, and I was afraid to open my eyes. I imagined myself stuffed in some dark tiny corner, locked in, unable to move, trapped. A film of sweat broke out over my body. Oh, God. I hadn't had an attack for a couple of months—not since I'd broken up with Mark, in fact—but now it was happening again, my mysterious, much-dreaded claustro-phobia.

It was dark and I was alone. I smelled the dusty earth; it crumbled beneath my fingers as I clawed at it. I screamed, but no one answered. I gasped for breath, the air burning my lungs. I screamed again, knowing I was trapped here, knowing I would never, ever get out.

Stop it! I ordered myself, forcing the nightmare images from my brain. My body was humming with panic. Fear was such a physical thing. How well I recognized the knifing cramps in my belly, the electric static of my heartbeat, the unspeakable feeling of impending doom. If this was a small, dark room I was locked in, I would die here. The absence of light was what freaked me out the most. That and the thought of suffocating in an airless place.

Eyes squeezed shut, I continued to fight the feelings. But fighting only made them worse. I wasn't supposed to fight, dammit. Why did I always forget that? The fight or flight instinct was so powerful, so immediate. By the time I noticed I was fighting, adrenaline had flooded all my cells.

Float through it, I whispered to myself. Release the fear. Just...let it go.

Relief came in the form of a shout from somewhere outside. My eyes popped open in automatic response, forcing me to face my surroundings. My panic tapered off. The room I was in was neither dark nor, by boating standards, small.

I was lying on a berth in what was probably the yacht's master cabin. There were two large rectangular portholes on the opposite wall, curtained to keep out the sun. I blinked as I looked around. The room looked Turkish. An Oriental carpet covered the tiny floor space. Copper fittings were used for light fixtures and trimming. Cabinets and bookshelves lined two of the walls. The bed where I was lying took up most of the space in the stateroom. It was large enough—barely—for two and was covered with a soft black quilt.

I sat up. My hands, bound with rope in front of me, were useless. My feet were trussed in similar fashion. My boots had been removed and were nowhere to be seen; my socks, too, had vanished. I tugged a little on my bonds, but they did not give. They were tight enough to feel uncomfortable. I moved my fingers experimentally. They felt a little stiff, but I didn't think my circulation was impaired.

"Efficient," I said aloud. I took a deep breath to calm myself. *He* had tied me, of course.

How long had I been out? What had he done to me to cause the unconsciousness? There had been no blow, no pain. Just his fingers on my neck, almost a caress, and then oblivion.

I shivered. My captor was an American who spoke Turkish. He was young, attractive and wanted in nine countries. He was so skillful in the martial arts that he could render a victim unconscious with a touch. A little more pressure would probably have killed me.

But I was still alive. Why? I saw myself as he must have seen me when he'd brought me in here—my slender body, bound and vulnerable, stretched out in the middle of his bed, my hair wildly strewn across his pillow. Oh, shit. I recalled Metin's comment about what they should do to me before killing me. Fuck me. Rape me. Maybe a small, dark corner would have been preferable, after all.

Stop it, I ordered myself. Don't jump to conclusions. Except for my socks and boots, my clothes were still intact. Maybe he meant me no harm.

I was trying to cling to this optimistic hope despite a persistent string of worst-case scenarios, when I heard footsteps outside the door to the cabin. I slid to the edge of the bed, my bare toes brushing the floor. A key turned, the door opened, and my captor strode into the room, shutting the door behind him with a thump.

His bright hair created a halo effect around his head, but he was no freaking angel. There was no innocence in his crystalline green eyes. Rather they were jaded, as if there were no vice he hadn't tried. His nose was straight, almost too perfect, but his mouth was expressive, mobile. His upper lip was thin and severe, while his lower lip was full and sulky. The combination lent a curious tension to his face—the Puritan and the libertine mixed.

"It's about time you woke up," he said.

"What did you do to me?"

He just looked at me as if this were a stupid question. Okay. I held up my cord-wrapped wrists. "Was this necessary?"

He eyed my bonds and shrugged.

"Why didn't you just shoot me?"

For the first time his gaze passed over me with some degree of masculine interest. Slowly. Thoroughly. He was smiling nastily when his eyes returned to meet mine. "Why do you think?"

I swallowed. I sought a cutting reply. None occurred to me.

He strolled over to the corner where there was a washbasin and an assortment of cupboards and drawers. He looked in the mirror, frowned at himself, turned on the taps and splashed water on his face. He proceeded to stretch and pull the T-shirt over his head, revealing a lean but muscular torso covered with golden-bronze skin. The muscles, which were well-defined without being brawny, rippled as he stretched. The spectacle made my mouth go dry.

He was already stripping. Not wasting any time. My stomach churned. From the way the boat was dancing on the waves, I guessed that we must be some distance out to sea. How many others were aboard? Would anyone help me if I screamed?

Of course not. Screams would probably amuse them.

The sound of the water splashing in the tiny sink made me aware of my parched throat. I was about to ask for a glass of water, when he caught my eye in the mirror. I fancied I saw some glimmer of emotion cross his features, but it was gone before I could analyze it.

"Thirsty?"

I nodded.

Lifting a glass from a metal ring above the sink, he filled it from a large plastic water bottle, and stepped over to the bed. I was confronted with all that lovely naked flesh. His hard belly, lightly dusted with blond hairs, was at the same level as my eyes. "Drink." He held the glass to my lips. He smelled nice—male-musky, and salty like the sea.

I sipped, and then gulped. It was warm in the cabin and my fear had made me sweat away more fluids than usual. The water caressed my throat as it went down.

"Enough." He took the glass away and sat down on the bed beside me. "You can have some more in a few minutes."

Was he being kind? Probably not. Maybe he preferred to fuck a woman who wasn't completely dried out.

Once again, I saw him as if in the viewer of my camera—still, harsh and beautiful. I wanted to photograph him. To capture, from close up, the angular set of his shoulders, not too wide, but lithe and graceful. His mobile, capable hands. Those thick eyelashes, much denser than my own, sparkling now with droplets of water. Like his hair, they curled ever so slightly. What would that rough-cut hair feel like under my fingers, those eyelashes against my cheek?

Shit. I realized the errant direction of my thoughts. Was I brain-damaged? The dude was a criminal. He'd just made it clear that the only reason I was still alive was that I'd been saved for the proverbial fate worse than death.

"Why were you there?" he asked. "Did you get a tip-off from someone?"

I realized he still thought I'd had prior knowledge of his rendezvous. "I told you. I'm just a tourist. I had no idea when I started photographing this morning that I'd be shooting anything more than sky, hills, wildflowers, and the sea."

"But when the seascape shifted to real people, you kept shooting?"

I didn't see any point in lying. "When I realized what you were doing, I decided to record it. I think it's reprehensible. If you hadn't caught me, I'd have done something to stop you."

Now he looked amused. "Like what?"

"I don't know, beyond turning the pictures over to the police. But if they'd caught you, I'd have cheered when they threw you in prison. There are strict laws in Turkey about antiquities smuggling."

"So you recognized what was in the crate?"

"Only that it looked ancient. I have no clue about the value or the date. What do you smuggle—only art objects, or drugs and illegal arms as well? Sounds like a demanding occupation, Nicholas—that's your name, right?"

There was a pause. The air of bored indifference had faded; he was regarding me as if he really saw me now. "You can call me Nick."

"And you're American, right?"

"I'm a mongrel. Part Yank, part Brit, and part Turk. I've kicked around in a lot of other countries."

"Nine of them, at least."

He raised his eyebrows.

"You said you were wanted in nine countries."

"Oh, that." He shrugged. "Perhaps a slight exaggeration. One loses count."

And what did that mean? He didn't look as if he intended to explain. "May I have more water?"

This time he tangled his fingers in my hair and held the back of my head as he tilted the glass to my lips. I choked. "Don't touch me." It was near the spot where his touch had rendered me unconscious.

He smiled nastily. His fingers came around and cupped my chin. He put the glass down and moved closer, far too close. I could feel his breath. My lips began to tingle.

I swallowed. I felt so vulnerable. I had never felt vulnerable with Mark. But Mark had never tied me up. Once or twice, I'd suggested we spice things up with a little bondage, but Mark hadn't been interested.

Jesus, why had I remembered that? That would have been different. Way different! Consensual. Unlike Mark, this man was dangerous. A criminal. He was sitting too close, touching me too much, and looking at me in a way that freaked me out.

His thumb stroked up and down my cheek. "Relax. If I were going to kill you, you would already be dead."

"What, then? Hold me for ransom?"

He seemed to consider. "Are you rich?"

"No."

"Not much point in that, then, is there?" One of his fingers brushed the lobe of my ear, making me suck in my breath. The tingles in my lips had spread to my belly. What the hell? Why didn't his touch revolt me?

Maybe I was in some sort of denial? The whole thing seemed a little unreal. I'd heard that denial was a common reaction to sudden disasters—people couldn't face that something awful was happening to them so they pushed reality away for as long as possible.

"Is Sybil Matheson-Heath really your mother?"

"Yes, but she's not rich, either. Archaeologists rarely are."

He emitted a short, cryptic laugh. I was puzzled by the storm of emotion that flashed in his eyes, but he offered no explanation.

He pushed his free hand through my hair; the other retained his grip on my chin. I wanted him to stop touching me, but I suspected that if I demanded it he would either laugh at me or up the ante somehow.

"Do you know much about your mother's work?"

"Some. She took me on digs with her when I was a child. I've read her books, and I took some archaeology courses at college."

Keep him talking, Ellie. I had read once that you should try to forge a connection if you were snatched by someone hostile, like a kidnapper or a terrorist. If you were seen as a real person, with thoughts and emotions, hopes, dreams and plans, you were harder to kill than if you remained a cipher or an object.

"I started out by majoring in archaeology, but I soon realized I'd never be in her league. The idea of crawling around in subterranean caverns, searching for potsherds, has never appealed to me." Indeed, it gave me the shudders. People who suffered from claustrophobia did not make good archaeologists. "I ended up majoring in history."

"And now you're a journalist." His voice was abstract, disinterested; his thumb had moved to my bottom lip. It rubbed gently, back and forth over the surface, sending little frissons of sensation along every nerve in my body.

"Photographer," I corrected.

His eyes turned speculative. "Are you any good?"

"Yes." I jerked my chin, trying to free myself. And failing. "Don't."

"Stop fighting me. You're my prisoner. Any rights you once had, you've lost."

Well, that pissed me off. I liked feeling angry. It felt a whole lot better than fear. "Is this the only way you can get a woman? Knock her unconscious, tie her up and toss her into your bed?"

"You're still alive. Yilmaz—that's the man I was doing business with when you interrupted—wanted to shoot you."

"Yes, but what will happen to me after you've—" I broke off, imagining all sorts of nasty things. *Dammit. Don't let him get to you. Don't give the swine the satisfaction.*

"After I've forced you to gratify all my wildest fantasies?" The dry, impatient note was back in his tone. "Don't be such a drama queen."

"I've never been tied up and raped before. Sorry if I'm over-reacting." Sarcasm. Unwise, probably, but I couldn't seem to keep my mouth shut.

His hand left my face, and then he rose and moved away from me. My relief was so strong I closed my eyes and leaned back against the wall. The boat was rocking on the waves, but the sea must be calm, because the movement was not too extreme. One thing to be thankful for, I supposed. At least I wasn't seasick.

I heard my captor cross the small room, open a drawer, then return. My eyes snapped open, and the blood drained into my toes. There was no gun this time. This time he was coming at me with a nasty, large-bladed knife.

Chapter 4

ELLIE

"Christ, you're easy to scare." His voice mocked me. "But blood-letting would mess up my cabin. Give me your hands and hold still." He slid the blade between my wrists and sawed through the rope. It took a while; the cords were thick. He then knelt, and I felt his fingers on my bare ankles for an instant before he started on the ropes there. At length they fell off and dropped to the floor.

"Thank you. I thought—"

"It was obvious what you thought."

I rubbed my wrists, which were itching from the rope. Don't act so cowed and grateful. That's exactly what he wants. It's all part of his psychological game. He intends you to be dependent upon him for water, for kindness, for life itself. Don't make it so easy for him.

Nicholas, now standing over me again, took one of my hands in his and examined it. It was scored a bit from the rope. His mouth twisted into a frown. He massaged the wrist with his thumb. It helped, but I hated him for it. Why did he keep touching me? How had I gone from being the sovereign master of my own body to having no voice while a stranger put his hands on me?

I shook back my long hair, which was falling into my face. "People will be looking for me. When I don't check in with my mother and my friends, they'll call the authorities. You won't get away with this."

He smiled thinly. "We'll see."

"The sensible thing would be to take the yacht into shore and drop me off. I'm a complication that you don't need."

"The sensible thing would be to weigh your body down with something heavy and drop you overboard. It's an option that will remain on the table while I assess what other uses I can put you to."

The uses I pictured were scary and degrading. It was nothing but bravado that kept me from curling up in a ball. "I won't be used by any man, so stop threatening me."

His eyes darkened and he grabbed me, fisting a handful of my hair. It hurt. "You're frightened and trying to cope. I get that. But you've landed in the middle of a fucked-up mess, and it's gonna get worse. Right now, I'm your best hope of staying alive, so don't piss me off. Do exactly what I order you to do, and maybe you'll survive. Defy me, and you're dead."

I noted for the first time that there were dark circles under those large eyes of his, that he was weary and not quite as much in control as he was pretending to be. An ordinary man, vulnerable, even as I was. Not a god or a hero, despite his lean, golden beauty. Not all-powerful either.

"I don't want you here," he went on. "You've no idea what a complication your presence poses. It would have been far more convenient to shoot you and toss your body into the sea. Maybe you haven't realized how close you came to endless night."

I felt the sweat break out again. He'd chanced upon a metaphor that called up my worst anxieties. So I continued to beat at him, knowing no other defense except attack.

"So I should thank you for saving my life? Am I expected to lie back, spread my legs, and express my gratitude? Is that what you mean by obeying your orders?"

He still had the knife in one hand. He saw me staring at it and his knuckles whitened around the handle. "As a matter of fact, yes," he said coldly. "If I tell you to strip, you will strip. If I tell you to spread your legs for me, you will do so. If I order you to drop to your knees and suck me off, you will do that, too, and gracefully. If you disobey me, you will be punished. If you repeat it a second time, you will be killed. Learn the rules, Ms. Heath, and follow them, or you'll soon begin to wish I'd permitted Yilmaz to put a bullet in your brain."

He grabbed the shirt he'd stripped off and pulled it over his head. Then he opened the door to the cabin and exited. I heard the key turn on the outside; I heard him stomp away. Then there was silence, except for the pounding of the sea, and my own heart.

I began to tremble all over. Then I cried.

Chapter 5

ELLIE

He did not return all day. I wallowed in a series of alternating moods—mostly scared, but sometimes angry, numb, and just plain confused because I couldn't stop remembering the way his muscles slid just underneath the surface of his smooth skin. I plagued myself with what-ifs: what if I'd stayed another day in Istanbul, what if I'd camped somewhere else on the coast? What if I'd slept a little later this morning? What if I hadn't started taking pictures? What if I'd run to my bike, started it up, and blown out of there before they could catch me?

My mind went round and round, trying to think myself out of this mess. This wasn't happening to me. This couldn't happen to me. This was all a freaking bad dream.

At some point, I pulled myself together enough to measure the boundaries of my prison.

I was securely locked in. The door would not budge and the portholes, though they opened, weren't large enough to crawl through. Anyway, the cabin was in the extreme bow of the sail-boat and the windows opened onto the churning sea.

One door did open, though. It led to a toilet. The head, as I supposed they called it aboard ship. I was glad to find it. After neglecting to ask him for it earlier, I'd been anxious over the possibility that I might be locked up somewhere without one.

I used the sink in the cabin to clean up a bit. I pulled off my sweaty clothes and scrubbed myself. The water was plentiful and hot; it revived my spirits. Wishing I had clean clothes to change into, I donned my underwear and jeans and looked sadly at my top. Lying bound on that bed in a sweat of panic had resulted in two dark patches under the arms. I wondered what he'd done with my pack, my camera equipment, my cell phone and my rented motorcycle.

Despite what I'd claimed about the people who would be looking for me, I didn't think anyone would even realize I was missing. I'd told my mother I'd try to give her a call in a week or so when I reached the city of Izmir, but Mom was often in a location where both cell and internet coverage were bad, so she wouldn't be worried when she didn't hear from me.

Disgusted with myself for my folly, I flung my shirt into the sink and scrubbed it, then opened the cupboard doors in search of something else to wear. Ruthlessly I pushed aside hangers and rifled shelves. He was irritatingly neat. His shoes were lined up, and his shirts all looked as if they'd been freshly washed. Belts were hanging from hooks. His clothes were simple and casual—mostly T-shirts and jeans, bland and muted of color—but they were of good quality.

The shirts had no tags. In fact, none of his clothes, including the leather jacket and the bad-weather gear, had labels of any kind. Maybe they'd all been removed to make it difficult for anyone to identify him if he was captured.

The only frivolous item I found was a pair of black leather pants that obviously went with the jacket. I took them out and ran my fingers over the buttery-soft leather, imagining them molding to his lean, muscular legs. I flushed as the fantasy briefly veered in the direction of X-ratedness. I squelched it. What was the matter with me? In the year I'd been with him, Mark had never inspired such thoughts.

Disgustedly I thrust the trousers back on their shelf.

My captor's shirts were huge on me, but I pulled on a faded blue one, anyway. Then I abandoned the closet and went through his drawers.

I didn't know what I hoped to find—personal papers, passports, newspaper clippings about his crimes, something that would give me more of a handle on who he was and what he was up to—but I had little luck. The three drawers, which were lined up vertically right next to the bathroom door, only confirmed that he was neat, simple in his tastes, and likely to remain a mystery.

In the top drawer, I found various toiletries, all Turkish brands. A toothbrush, comb, bottle of aspirin and other medical supplies were also in the drawer.

The bottom drawer contained two clean towels and a long, slim, rectangular case. My pulse leapt as I pried open the case, wondering if he'd been careless enough to give me access to a weapon. If I found a gun, I would use it, dammit. I knew how.

But the case contained the segments of a delicate, silvery flute, each piece nestled in a blue-velvet lining.

A flute. I tried to picture him playing it. My imagination was usually vivid, but here it failed me. "Stolen, no doubt," I said aloud, and closed the drawer. Maybe it was a freaking antique.

Frustrated, I checked out the rest of the room. There was a desk built into one corner, with a laptop packed away underneath it. It worked, but was password protected. There were several books neatly lining the bookshelves. Paperbacks, mostly. The more literary volumes included the works of Homer—in Greek, no less—and some Latin poetry. Could he read Latin and Greek?

His popular fiction included novels by such writers as George R. R. Martin and Ken Follett. There were also five or six books by a writer I'd never heard of, Stephen Silkwood. They appeared to be historical mysteries. All the volumes were well-thumbed.

So he liked to read. So what? I took down a collection of poems by Coleridge, which fell open in my hands to one of my favorite poems, "Frost At Midnight." I read it silently, feeling the nameless sorrow that the poem invariably induced in me. Why did it disturb me that an international criminal engaged in the despicable business of stripping a country of its priceless historical relics should own a volume of poetry?

I flipped to the front of the book. It was inscribed in a feminine hand: "To Nicholas. Happy twenty-first birthday, my love. Forever... Elizabeth." At the bottom of the page the same hand had written, "Penshurst College, Rolling Meadows, Massachusetts."

Curious now, I closed the book. The short inscription had told me a lot. His birthday, his age, the name of his college, whom he'd been fucking back then. What had happened to Elizabeth? Did she know her college sweetheart had grown up to be a thief?

What else would I learn, I wondered, from possible inscriptions in the other books?

Half an hour later, I had my answer, although it didn't help much. He had several inscribed books. He must know the mystery author, Stephen Silkwood, since Silkwood had autographed each of his books with a different cheerful insult. Two other volumes also bore messages: a volume of Shakespeare's plays, which young Nicholas had won as a prize for special achievement in prep school, and an archaeology text, which said merely, "Dear Nick... good show! Granddad." Several of the books had his name written in them—Nick Gabriel—in a dark, angular hand. So Gabriel must be his last name.

The rest of the day passed uneventfully. The cabin refused to yield up any further information, unless I was interested in sea charts and shipboard navigation, which I knew nothing about. I started to read one of the historical mysteries, which turned out to be set in 16th century England during the reign of Queen Elizabeth Tudor. It helped distract me from the near-constant worry about what was going to happen to me.

At sunset, I was considering pounding on the door and demanding something to eat—he had yet to feed me—when I heard footsteps approach the cabin. I tried to psych myself up as the lock was disengaged. This time I was determined to keep my emotions under control.

But it wasn't Nicholas Gabriel who unlocked the door and entered the cabin. It was the younger man, Metin.

"Greetings," he said in heavily accented English. "I bring food."

"Thank you. I thought maybe you guys were planning to starve me."

He came in, kicked the door closed with one booted foot and looked for a place to set the tray. He seemed reluctant to put it on the desk with the charts. He finally placed it on the end of the bed.

I, meanwhile, had stepped casually toward the bathroom. I'd noticed a latch on the inner door. Metin was cocky and far too handsome for my liking. Medium height and slender, he was fit and strong. His skin was dark and his teeth a blinding white in contrast. He wore a mustache that gave him a rakish air. He was dressed in the regulation jeans and T-shirt.

He had been the one to suggest fucking me, and I didn't like the look in his eyes now. He didn't frighten me quite as much as Nick did, but he was a male, possibly armed, definitely dangerous.

"You are well?" he asked.

"Fine. Your name is Metin, right?" It seemed politic to be friendly. He was young; maybe I could gain his sympathy.

"Evet. Yes. And your name is Ellie."

"That's right." I tried a smile, to which he responded with a grin that made him less sinister. "If you're down here, who's sailing the boat?"

"Nick is at the helm." Ellie noted that he referred to Nick with respect. "It only requires one when we are not under sail."

"So we're using the engine?" I had known that, actually, from the noise. "I thought so large a yacht must possess crew of at least three or four men." I smiled at him again. "I don't know much about boats."

Metin nodded as if it were to be expected. I was a female, after all, and a foreigner. "Oh, no, it is just the two of us. When
the sails are extended we must both work, but tonight Nick will
direct our way until it is his time to sleep. Then I will work the
boat until morning."

"When will it be his turn to sleep?"

Metin pulled a cell phone out of his pants pocket and checked
the time. "One hour from now."

One hour's respite. That was all I would have. I bit my lip.
That was why I hadn't seen Nick all afternoon; he was taking his
turn at the helm so he'd have the night free to "sleep."

I looked up to find Metin watching me, his dark eyes filled
with curiosity and something that looked like compassion. "You
are afraid from something?"

I felt a rush of irrational affection for the young man. He was
friendlier than his captain was. "I guess I am."

Metin was shaking his head in surprise. "How can that be?
All women admire Nicholas. He is very much a man."

This didn't offer much consolation.

"You must become his woman, but where is the terror in
that? You are not so young," he added dispassionately. "And you
are American, so you must be—" he hesitated here, clearly
searching for the right term "—making sex with many men."

I wasn't sure whether to be insulted or touched. I no longer
sensed any threat from him. His precious Nicholas must have
made it plain that I was *his* woman. And Metin seemed eager to
put my fears to rest.

"I don't know where you get your ideas about American
women, Metin, but I don't go around making sex with many
men."

He looked skeptical. "You travel alone, without a male relative's protection."

I could feel myself flushing. Damn sexism, anyway. "Men travel without a relative's protection, don't they? Why shouldn't women be free to do the same?"

Now he looked as though he were barely resisting laughing at me. He controlled himself, though, and said, "Americans are more easy about these things than Turks."

"Look. I am not your friend's woman. I am my own woman. I do not choose to share myself with him or anybody else. Can you understand that?"

He looked doubtful. "If you are not Nick's woman, he will not be able to protect you from the others."

I stiffened to attention. "What others? Where are we going?"

The young man's smile vanished and a guilty look replaced it. "You will pardon me. It is not permitted for me to tell you."

"Metin, please! Who are these others? Where are we going?"

He quickly retreated to the door. "*Afiyet olsun,*" he added, the Turkish for *bon appetit.* Then he fled, locking the door behind him.

Frowning, I sat down to my supper of bread, cheese, fruit and hot, strong tea. I was hungry, so the food tasted good, but when I finished, the butterflies in my stomach started up again, giving me indigestion. One hour. I waited, begrudging each minute as it passed by. *You must become his woman, but where is the terror in that?*

Why did those simple words sound like a prophecy of doom?

Chapter 6

ELLIE

I stiffened at the sound of the key in the door. It was dark in the cabin. I had switched off all the lights, with the exception of the overhead lamp in the toilet, which showed under the closed bathroom door. The water in the sink was running; he would probably hear it as soon as he entered the room. For a few seconds he would assume I was in the head, and during those few seconds, I would act.

The door swung inward, hiding me where I stood flattened against the wall, holding *The Complete Works of William Shakespeare* high over my head. It was the only weapon available. He'd taken the knife with him and I had not been able to find his gun. The volume was heavy; my arms were aching. But he was fit and strong, and I was worried it wouldn't be heavy enough.

He entered and slammed the door. Aiming at the golden glint of his hair, I brought the book down with all my strength. Quick and alert, he pivoted. Shakespeare struck him on the shoulder and crashed to the floor.

He was cursing as he grabbed me, spun me around and jammed me, face first, against the wall. He twisted my arms behind my back, which fucking hurt. I must have yelped with pain. The boat rocked, which pressed his body into mine from behind. As we rolled over another wave, I felt him grow aroused. It was impossible to mistake the pressure of a stiffening cock against my ass.

Oh God. Big, pathetic mistake. Too bad I had never learned kickboxing or Tae Kwan Do.

"Giving me an excuse to punish you?" he asked.

"Do you need an excuse?"

"No." The painful pressure on my arms changed, but did not ease. He shifted so that one of his hands smashed both of my wrists together. With the other hand, he reached around to the front of my body. His grip closed over one of my breasts. He explored, caressed. His fingers were strong and warm, and their touch sent a current through me. My heart throbbed as my breast expanded to fill his palm.

Dammit! I wanted to scream with fury at my dumbass body's weakness.

"Stop it," I said, trying to keep my tone icy.

"You're going to have to get used to me touching you. I'll be doing it a lot."

"No." I writhed against the wall, attempting to free myself. Uselessly.

"Yes." His fingers rose to my chin and tipped my head back. He pressed his face into my hair. "My advice is to relax and accept it. Because you're going to lose this battle."

Oh, God. I had this weird instinct to surrender. Lean into him. Allow his hands to do whatever they wished. I could feel a softening inside me as my core came alive. Did I seriously have *chemistry* with this jerk? What was wrong with me?

It must be because of not having a damn orgasm for a while. Jet-lagged and traveling, I hadn't gotten myself off for, jeez, I didn't remember how long. This horrible man had a body that was attractive to me. I'd thought him super hot from the moment I'd first caught a glimpse of him through my telephoto lens. It was one of those odd physical things. Hormones don't have a conscience. Or a lick of good sense.

He turned me around and flipped on the overhead light. I was panting, while his chest still rose and fell at a normal rate. If his shoulder hurt, he didn't betray it. Poor Shakespeare was more damaged than he was.

"Where were you going to go? Over the side?" His hands tightened on my shoulders; he shook me slightly. "We're nowhere near land. Even a trained long-distance swimmer wouldn't have a chance."

"I was hoping to convince Metin to put me ashore."

"Forget it. He's loyal to me." His tone was scathing. "Besides, no Turk would touch the woman belonging to his *kardesh*—his good friend, his brother."

"I don't belong to you."

"Wrong," he said, picking me up bodily and swinging me toward the bed, "like it or not, you do."

He dumped me unceremoniously, then stood back and did some stiff circles with his left shoulder. "Fuck. What did you hit me with?"

"*The Complete Works of William Shakespeare.*"

He snorted a laugh. "Shall we read *The Taming of The Shrew* together?" He picked up the volume from the floor and stuffed it back on the shelf. Then he locked the door and jammed the key into the front pocket of his jeans. "Turn off the tap. This is a boat, not a bloody hotel. There's no water to waste."

"Do it yourself."

He grabbed me again and marched me to the sink, his arms brutally strong around my struggling body. "Do it," he ordered harshly, forcing my head down until it was just above the tiny sink. Water from the open tap splashed in my face. The basin was full. He pushed down until my nose and mouth went into the water. Terrified that he was going to hold me under, I flailed around with my one free arm until I found the tap. I shut the water off, trembling, desperately afraid now of what he might do next.

He jerked my head up and dragged me away from the sink. I gasped, shaking myself like a wet pup. He shoved me at the bed. I stumbled and fell upon it. I righted myself quickly, brushing at my eyes where tears had formed. I was *not* going to let him see me cry.

He stood beside the bed, his legs a scant inch from my knees. The boat was riding the waves with more motion now, but he was obviously at home with the heaving of the sea. I noticed that he had impossibly long legs. I followed their lines up past his slim hips and flat belly. He was now wearing a loose sweatshirt with his jeans. The sweatshirt was old and ragged. It had once had long sleeves, but they'd been hacked off at the elbows, making him appear tough and uncompromisingly masculine. I glanced up at his face. His eyes were narrow slits of green, his cheeks rough with the faint gold stubble of his beard. His aura of power had never been stronger. I felt a curl of fear.

"Don't push me." Each word was clipped off, separate.

Gathering my battered courage, I said, "Or you'll waterboard me?"

He shook his head. "I'm trying to figure out if you're stupid, crazy, or just incredibly stubborn."

"I got kept after school a lot when I was a teenager for defying authority. It's a personality flaw."

"I'm not the fucking high school principal."

He sat beside me on the bed, angling his body so he was facing me. I tried to slide away from him, but there was nowhere to go.

"How old are you?"

"You saw my passport."

"Give me a fucking answer when I ask you a question."

"Twenty-three."

"You look younger."

"I'm not. I graduated from college last spring."

"Okay. There are a couple of things I need you to understand."

I waited.

"When we reach our destination, we'll be meeting with some associates. You'll be expected to behave in a certain way."

"Meaning what?"

"Let me demonstrate."

He stood again, hovering over me where I huddled on the edge of the bed. The cabin was so small that there was nowhere else for me to go, especially with him in it. He dominated the tiny space, making me want to curl up and find an unobtrusive spot in a corner somewhere. He wasn't threatening me with a gun or a knife now, but I still felt like prey.

He removed the belt from around his waist. It wasn't made of leather, but of some ropey macramé. I thought he was undressing for the expected sexual assault, and my tension skyrocketed. But he threaded one end of the belt through the buckle, made a loop, and, in a swift and unexpected move, slung it around my neck and tightened it.

I froze. What the fuck?

"Get on your knees," he said, pulling up on his end of the belt. It was not so tight that it cut off my air, but the threat was there. I had to stretch my neck, moving in the direction he moved the belt. "Kneel up. On the bed."

My hands had flown to the rope material, trying to fight his control, but the angle was wrong. I couldn't get purchase. My palms turned slick with sweat, and I felt panic come roaring up again. This couldn't be happening. Was he going to strangle me? I couldn't deal with the thought of not having enough air. It was my absolute worst nightmare.

"It isn't hard," he said, his voice wintery cool. "Tuck your legs under you and kneel up. Show me you can obey a simple command."

Was he crazy? Some kind of psychopath? I realized I could still breathe, but I felt like an animal in a choke collar. Humiliation washed over me.

Clumsily I knelt. The dipping and rising of the boat confused me and I nearly toppled sideways as I tried to rise on my knees. His hand on my shoulder steadied me. When I managed it, the pressure on my throat was much less, but I was trembling.

"Good girl," he said, and lowered his arm, releasing the tension in the rope.

My hands tried again to remove it from around my neck, but he pulled it taut again. Oh God. I couldn't deal with this. I couldn't stop shaking.

"You will obey me. Drop your hands or I'll bind them behind your back."

I did it. As long as I could breathe, I'd freaking do anything.

"That's right. Not so hard, is it?"

"Please don't choke me," I whispered. I hated myself for saying it. It felt like begging. And it showed him that I had a weakness he could exploit.

And exploit me he did. I felt his free hand move over my hair, then under it. Along my shoulders and down my spine. His touch was light. It didn't hurt. In fact, as he continued to slide his hand around, I realized it was seductive. He kept it up, and I was horrified to feel a sweetness begin in the pit of my belly as he stroked me. I closed my eyes, afraid he would read my reaction there.

What was *wrong* with me? I couldn't get my mind around it. Everything seemed fuzzy and unreal. No one had ever hurt me, bound me, knocked me unconscious, or tightened a cord around my neck before. I knew such things, and worse, happened to women the world over. I hadn't appreciated how fortunate I'd been never to encounter a man who wanted to hurt or control me.

I'd had fantasies about such things, though. Safe unthreatening imaginings that could be banished back into the dark place from which they emerged. I'd talked about sex with enough friends to know that other women shared my fantasies of being swept away by rough, tough, masculine guys who wanted me so badly that they would break social and ethical conventions to get me in their bed. I'd even urged Mark, my last boyfriend, to be a little more adventurous in the bedroom. He'd tried, but his heart hadn't been in it.

"I'm not going to strangle you," Nicholas said, "but I want you under my control." He loosened the belt slightly, but he did not remove it. "There isn't time to do this slowly. We are about to enter a realm where your only safety will lie in how convincingly you can demonstrate your devotion to me."

I shook my head in silent denial.

"Get used to it."

"I can't." I was horrified by the sound of my own voice, which came out as little more than a whimper.

"You will. Now sit any way you feel comfortable, but do not touch the belt."

"Why are you doing this?" I was shaking again, and I hated it. His belt hung like a leash from around my throat. "What kind of freak are you?"

"It's not about me. It's about you learning to survive. You can bend or you can break."

"You can't break me."

"Of course I can. I'm bigger, stronger, and a whole lot nastier than you."

"It doesn't matter. I'm a free human spirit, and nothing you do to me can change that." *Except choke me. Or lock me up alone in a small, dark place.*

He snorted. "Right. I don't know what world you've been living in, but freedom is a luxury known to few people on this planet. Political freedom, economic freedom, religious freedom—how many people living today are fully endowed with those supposedly fundamental human rights? Not as many as you'd probably like to believe. Slavery still exists—you knew that, right? Do you have any idea how many millions of people, mostly women and children, are trafficked every year?"

Was it a rhetorical question? "So...are you pro or con?"

He stared at me. His beautiful muscles were tense and a tendon spasmed in his jaw.

"Because," I looked down at the macramé belt hanging from my neck, "you're treating me like a sex slave."

His lips curled down. "Except for the sex part."

What did he mean? Hope flared in me. "You grabbed my breast."

"Yeah, I know, but I don't fuck unwilling women. If you're afraid of rape, you can relax. That isn't gonna happen."

I felt a little woozy as relief washed through me. For hours I had been trying to tell myself that maybe it wouldn't be so bad...maybe he wouldn't hurt me too much...maybe I'd be able to close my eyes and pretend I was somewhere else.

"Don't look so relieved. It doesn't mean I won't fuck you. It just means you'll enjoy it when I do."

"If you think you can convince yourself that I'm willing when I'm not—"

"Don't pretend you don't respond to my touch. I hate liars. Anyway, you haven't heard the bad news yet."

"So what's the bad news?"

"One of these men we'll be meeting likes to take things away from me; it's an old habit of his. Anything I value, he wants. Including women."

"I have no value to you."

"There's the Catch-22. You're with me, so you must have value. This will make you irresistible to my cousin Nigel. His soul, if he has one, is blacker than hell."

"Your cousin?"

"I come from a fucked-up family. They don't trust me much, and they'll trust you even less. I can only see one way to make you seem both valuable to me and no reasonable threat to them." He tugged on the free end of the belt around my neck. "Meet my new sex slave. Discreet, obedient, loyal, and abjectly submissive."

Chapter 7

ELLIE

"I can't pretend something like that."

He tightened the belt a little. "Who said anything about pretending? You are going to learn a few new skills. We don't have much time. If you have half the smarts I'm giving you credit for, you'll follow my instructions and learn fast."

After getting captured as easily as I had, I wondered why he was giving me credit for any smarts. It felt to me as if I hadn't done anything sensible or intelligent for weeks. Except maybe for hiding my knowledge of Turkish.

"So, what? The place you're taking me is some sort of sex den?"

"My cousin Nigel is interested in human trafficking, among other unsavory activities."

"Your cousin is a trafficker?" I heard the horror in my own voice. I knew human trafficking was still a huge criminal enterprise, despite the international laws against slavery. I had thought antiquity trafficking was bad enough, but what he was talking about now was even worse.

"I believe it's a sideline of his, not his main business."

"And you? Do you traffic in human flesh, too?"

"I'm sure I could find a buyer for you, if you give me any trouble."

I was running out of sharp retorts. *I've got to stay strong.*

"In the past, I've never appeared in front of Nigel with a slave of my own," he continued. "He has taunted me about it for some time. He's convinced that I like to abuse and degrade women. He's sociopathic, so I must be, too. Sooner or later, he has often said, my true nature would emerge. So I am going to let it."

"That's why you didn't kill me? So you can let the Sociopath Within come out to play?"

"You're getting it. Your devotion to me is limitless, and in return I extend you my protection and don't treat you too harshly. Unless you disobey me. That would require punishment."

The thought darted across my mind that in some circumstances, the scenario he was outlining might actually be hot. If I were home and safe and with a sexy man whom I loved, I could get into this sort of thing. But with a stranger who had pointed a gun at me, knocked me unconscious, tied me up and kidnapped me? I don't think so.

"I can't do this. Please. Can't you set me ashore somewhere? I will keep my mouth shut about you, I swear."

He shook his head. "No."

I won't cry, dammit. I won't give the creep the satisfaction.

"But you can do this. You're no coward—you've proved that much already. And it'll only be for about ten days. At the most, two weeks. After that, if everything goes as planned, I'll set you free. In the meantime, you'll just have to play the game you've stumbled into. Play it well, and you'll survive. Fuck it up, and you'll die, and probably take me with you."

"If I die, you can count on me taking you with me."

He laughed. "I don't think you've got the submissive mindset down yet, Ms. Heath. Shall we see how tightly I have to wind this rope around your throat until you do?"

I shuddered. "What do you mean by the submissive mindset?"

He looked at me hard before answering. "Most people have played around with this sort of thing. Or at least read about it. Or watched porn on the internet."

I had of course. Read about it, at least. It was hard to avoid—books, TV, pop music. When I just sat there, silent and embarrassed, he said,

"No? Please don't tell me I have to explain this to a 23 year old college grad."

"I get the general idea. It's the practical experience that I lack."

"Well, to put it in terms my nasty cousin would understand, I own you. You bow, scrape and defer to me. You obey my orders without a word—or a look—of protest. No more fucking sarcasm. You are sexually available to me at all times. If I'm rough with you, you enjoy it. If I punish you, you thank me for causing you pain. If I tie you up and whip you, you come. Unless I deny you permission to come, in which case you suffer."

I experienced a moment of horror as my body reacted with a thrill of excitement to his description. It was something about his voice. It was low, a bit gravelly and hot as hell. A weird memory struck me of reading an erotic romance about a woman kidnapped by a brawny Scottish pirate who did some of the things he had just mentioned. It had been full of sensual love scenes that had rocked my world when I'd discovered the book at age sixteen.

"I'm not into that," I tried.

"I don't fucking care if you're into it or not. That's your role for the next couple weeks. Since you seem to be having trouble with the concept, we'll have to practice."

I wondered what the hell that meant.

"Strip," he said.

Oh god, oh god. I clung to what he'd told me a few minutes ago. No rape. "You said you wouldn't—"

"Do it. You have to learn to obey any order I give you without argument or hesitation. That's what slaves do."

"I'm not your fucking slave."

He tightened the rope around my neck. "The subject is not open for debate. I see you're wearing one of my shirts. Take it off."

The thing around my neck was just too much. I started to unbutton the shirt, saying to myself, it's better to be humiliated, even raped, than killed. I have to stay alive. I have to escape. He said that if I do what he tells me for two weeks, he'll let me go. He said he wouldn't rape me.

I know. I was allowing him to frighten and intimidate me. To dominate me. But when someone tightens a cord around your neck, it's difficult to remain defiant.

I took off the shirt. I was still wearing my bra, my jeans, and my panties.

"Keep going." His voice was cold. So were his eyes. That was good, right? He didn't look as if he were bursting with lust.

For the first time ever, I was glad that my breasts were small and unimpressive. I'd never been proud of my body. It was ordinary. On the thin side, which I'd always liked because it meant I didn't have to go on diets all the time like most of my friends. I could stuff myself with pizza and chips and yummy desserts because I had a fast metabolism or something. I could eat and eat and hardly ever gain a pound.

My hair was good—long and fiery red, a color I used to hate but had grown to appreciate in recent years. My features were regular and balanced enough to pass for okay-looking. Or at least, so my best friend Katy always told me. "You're not super-model stunning, but your face is really nice," she used to say. "You should do your makeup, though. Your eyes are stunning when you spend some time on them."

Needless to say, I wasn't wearing any makeup. Anyway, the creep wasn't looking at my face.

I removed my bra next, because the thought of removing stuff below the waist really freaked me out. I did it awkwardly, blushing and feeling ashamed. I didn't know this guy. He had knocked me out, tied me up and kidnapped me. He'd threatened me with a gun and a knife. He'd put a noose around my neck, and now he was making me strip.

"Faster. Christ, you're acting like a virgin who's never taken her clothes off before."

I stiffened, ricocheting back to something Mark had taunted me about. We'd had a fucked up sex life during our year together. I don't think either of us was ever satisfied. I thought he was pretty vanilla and boring in bed, and my attempts to encourage a little more adventure had been ignored. But he hadn't been happy with me, either, although he never said why. He used to taunt me sometimes by making cracks similar to what Nick had just said...implying that I wasn't very sexy. Or that I was too shy.

Maybe I *was* a little modest, but I wasn't ashamed of my body or anything like that. I just wanted a man who would take charge. How could I strip if I wasn't turned on?

"Well? Do I have to get my knife and cut those jeans off your body?"

I undid my jeans and slid them down over my hips. "Why are you doing this?" I asked, feeling truly miserable.

"It amuses me," he snapped. He sounded either angry or sarcastic. I wasn't sure which.

"I don't take off my clothes for men I don't even know."

"You do now," he said, yanking the rope around my neck again.

Dumbass. As I forced down the jeans, my panties started to go with them. What the fuck...they were going to be next anyway. I pushed both pants and panties down my legs and over my feet. They fell to the floor. I hunched up, arms around my middle, hating the man at the other end of that rope.

"Good," he said. He pulled me close to him by means of the rope. I froze, expecting him to start pawing at my naked body. But instead, he loosened the macramé belt and removed it from my throat. I sagged with relief. He tossed me a blanket from the foot of the bed. "Now lie down on the floor and go to sleep." He gathered up my clothes and tossed them into one of the drawers with a lock on it and locked them inside. By the time he had finished doing that, I had wrapped the blanket snugly around myself.

"I need to use the bathroom before I sleep."

"You can use it when I'm done, slave."

When it was my turn, I dawdled in the head for ages, treasuring the only privacy permitted to me. I kept the blanket wound around me; no way was I letting it slip.

When I returned to the cabin, Nick was lying on the bunk. He was still wearing his jeans, I was glad to see, but no shirt or shoes. He had tossed a pillow to the floor beside the bed. When I lay down there, I took up most the space left in the small cabin.

He reached up and switched off the overhead light, then glanced at the head door, which I'd left ajar. "You left the light on in there."

"I can't sleep in total darkness."

"Why not?"

I wasn't about to reveal my claustrophobia, my desperate need to hold back the night. I felt weak enough in his presence as it was. "I just can't."

"Well, I can't sleep with light in my eyes." He started to get up.

"Please. It's not bright." I scuttled over to the head door and closed it until it was only open a crack. "Is that better?"

He hesitated, and then cursed under his breath. "You're a real pain in the ass."

For some insane reason I heard myself say, "I guess if we were lovers, we'd fight."

"If we were *fucking*," he retorted in a smooth-as-liquid voice, reducing the word "lovers" to it most basic meaning, "I'd be content to leave the light on. In fact, I'd insist upon it."

Cheeks burning, I buried my face in the pillow. *If we were lovers?* What the fuck was I thinking?

"Go to sleep. No escape attempts. I haven't bound your arms and legs again, but I will if you so much as stir from the spot where you're currently lying. I want a peaceful night. No more idiotic attacks with William Shakespeare. I'm a light sleeper, and I'll know if you try anything."

I rolled over with my face turned away from him. I was certain I would be lying awake all night, reliving every horrible moment of my captivity, but to my amazement, I fell asleep and didn't wake up until morning.

Chapter 8

ELLIE

I was alone in the cabin when I woke. The boat was pitching more vigorously than it had been the night before. I sat up. The blanket must have slipped off me during sleep, since I was only half covered. Either that or he had uncovered me to look at my body. I imagined him doing so, while I was unconscious and unable to stop him, and I felt myself flush.

It wasn't an entirely unpleasant feeling. Instead of remembering how he had forced me to strip and threatened to strangle me, the first thing I thought of was how built his body was. How honed his face. How sexy his voice was. And once again I grew angry with myself for having such thoughts about the man who was holding me captive against my will. Did I have Stockholm syndrome? How long did that take to set in? I didn't think you could come down with Stockholm in only 24 hours, but what did I know? Maybe I was just weak and pathetic.

My clothes, which he had taken last night, were still locked away. Even my own shirt, the one I'd washed and hung to dry on the towel rack under the sink, was nowhere to be seen. Worse, I discovered that he had locked all the drawers and cupboards where he kept his own clothes. He had left me nothing to cover myself with except the blanket.

Bastard. The blanket was wool, scratchy and hot. We were in the Aegean, and the air was already feeling warm and humid. Was he planning to keep me naked?

At least he hadn't raped me. So far, he'd kept his promise about that.

I used the bathroom and washed as best I could at the sink, wishing for a shower. Then I had nothing to do. I could vaguely hear voices on deck—the men talking among themselves—but I couldn't hear what they were saying. My stomach growled. I hadn't eaten much in the past 24 hours and I was hungry. There were several water bottles on the shelf over the sink so I helped myself. I was surprised at how thirsty I felt, but I suppose being scared out of my wits had contributed to that.

I tested the door just to make sure I wasn't free to wonder up on deck. Nope. Locked.

Fortunately, the books weren't locked up, so I found the historical mystery I had started reading yesterday and fell into Stephen Silkwood's Renaissance England world. The story was good, if rather violent. I kept turning the pages until I heard steps outside the door and the sound of the key in the lock. I wrapped the blanket more securely around me as my captor entered the cabin.

He was holding a tray of food. I smelled hot coffee, which made my mouth water. "Hungry?" he asked.

"Yes."

"Yes, Master."

I rolled my eyes and repeated the words, "Yes, Master."

He set the tray on the end of the bed where I was sitting. "What's your name?"

"I told you my name. Have you forgotten it?"

"Wrong answer. You're a slave. You no longer have a name. Drop the blanket. Fold it neatly and lay it on the bed. You are not permitted to use it in place of clothing."

I clutched the blanket to me. "Where are my clothes?"

He pulled something from the pocket of his pants. It was a couple of pieces of rope, roughly woven into a circle. "This is all you will be wearing today."

It was a collar. Probably handmade. When I just stared at it, he grabbed me by the hair—my long thick hair made this easy to do—and dragged me to my feet. He ripped the blanket away from me. While I struggled with the idea that he was now looking at my naked body in the full light of day, he took advantage of my frozen stance to twist the rope collar under my hair and tie it in back. It fit me tightly, and I bucked under his hands, beginning to panic even as I told myself that I could breathe fine and to calm the fuck down.

"Next time I give you an order, you will obey me instantly or be punished. Do you understand?"

"Fuck you."

He slapped me lightly across the face. My hand flew to my cheek and I backed away from him, more angry than hurt. No one had ever raised a hand to me before. I'd certainly never allowed any man to strike me!

"Are you crazy?" I shouted. "Some kind of psycho abuser? Don't you ever fucking hit me again!"

He grasped a bunch of my hair in his hand and forced me to my knees. "You forget yourself, slave. Either we do this my way, or you go overboard with a weight bound to your feet. I don't have time for your bullshit defiance. We're going to spend the day curing you of it."

He went to the door and yelled out for Metin. I heard footsteps approaching and, to my horror, Nicholas opened the door and let the younger man into the cabin. I was kneeling on the floor, naked, and he allowed Metin, who had been kind to me, to see me like that. Well, maybe he couldn't see me too well, because Nicholas had placed himself between me and the door, blocking the other man's view. I stared at the floor, afraid to see if Metin would try to look. "My slave isn't hungry, after all," Nick said. "Please remove her tray."

I wasn't sure which was worse, being deprived of my coffee and the traditional Turkish breakfast of bread, white cheese, fruit and jam that had been on that tray, or the shame of having been naked in front of another man. Either way, I pretty much wanted to die.

"You'll eat when you learn to obey," Nicholas informed me.

I was beginning to hate Nicholas Gabriel. "From a psychological point of view, this is not the right way to deal with me," I informed him. "I don't respond well to people pushing me around."

"You don't get it, do you? What you like or don't like is irrelevant. Your thoughts and feelings are of no interest to me. Your sole reason for existing is to obey me and please me. Your body is no longer your own."

"But...it's all an act, right? You don't really believe that?"

"*You* have to believe it. That's what counts. You have to believe it so utterly that you don't make any mistakes. You have to be conditioned to believe it. Am I getting through to you yet?"

He was. It's a game, I told myself. He had written this part for me, and now he wanted to rehearse.

"If you fuck up, you die," he reminded me.

Intellectually, I understood, but my instincts told me there was something more going on here. "If it's an act, why do you look like you're enjoying this?"

He stared at me in silence, and I thought I saw something kindle in his eyes before that cold control stamped it out. "I have a lovely, naked woman kneeling at my feet. What's not to enjoy?"

* * *

He informed me that I was being slave-trained. That this was usually a much more lengthy process, so I would have to endure a crash course. Apparently we would be meeting his evil associates tomorrow. I had one day to learn to act like a broken woman with no will of her own and no fight left in her.

He was ruthless. I told myself that it was like boot camp—designed to be just short of unendurable. He was the harsh, angry drill sergeant who was teaching me to be a soldier. To follow orders. To survive.

"Eyes down," he said, pointing at the floor. "You don't look me or any other man in the face unless I give you permission."

Jeez! I bowed my head. I was not cut out for this.

I heard him moving, and lifted my head enough to peek at what he was doing. He got a leather belt from his cupboard and a long piece of cloth. As he turned back toward me, I quickly pressed my forehead against the carpet.

He pulled my face up by sliding his hand into my hair and twisting. He wrapped the cloth around my head and eyes several times before tying it off. "I'm going to teach you to respond to the sound of my voice. The blindfold will prevent any distractions."

The cloth was completely opaque. I couldn't see a thing.

"The rules are simple: You do what I tell you to do with all possible speed. If you don't obey, I will hurt you. If you don't obey quickly enough, I will hurt you. If you make a mistake, I will hurt you. If you complain, I will hurt you. If you speak without permission, I will hurt you. Is that clear?"

"Crystal," I snapped.

He slapped my thigh with the belt, and I yelped. It stung. Because of the blindfold, I couldn't even see if he had left a mark.

"What mistake did you just make, slave? You may answer."

"What mistake did I make? I took a few pictures of a beautiful dawn sky."

"Jeez, you are asking for it. Answer the fucking question."

I sighed. "I didn't call you by your lordly title of, what was it? Oh yeah...Master."

He struck me again. When I cried out (more out of protest than pain, since it didn't hurt that much) he said, "Don't scream. One more sound and I'll punish you much more severely."

He opened the door and took me out to the main salon of the yacht. I inquired nervously where Metin was, since I was still naked, and he assured me he was at the helm and would not see what was happening. Since I'd been unconscious when he'd brought me aboard, I didn't know the layout of the salon, but it seemed a lot larger than the sleeping quarters.

In rapid succession, he made me crawl, walk, move three paces. Stop. Move four paces to starboard. It took me a few moments of trying to focus on the vessel's forward motion before I figured out which side was starboard. Turn. Crawl four feet forward on my belly. Stand. Walk in a circle. Crawl in a square. Walk to the port bulkhead wall. Go to him and kneel.

Blindfolded.

The slightest mistake, hesitation or confusion was punished with a smack from the belt. Once I turned right when he'd told me to turn left. My circle, he said, wasn't a circle. My square wasn't perfectly square. When he twirled me around four times before he told me to find the port bulkhead, I got disoriented and went starboard instead. I crawled five feet, not four. When I objected that it was impossible to know how many feet I'd crawled while wearing a fucking blindfold, he whipped me twice—once for the complaint and the second for failing to address him correctly.

His voice as he commanded me was unfailingly calm and even. He sounded in control of me, of the situation, and of himself.

There seemed to be no order to the locations on my body where he struck me, but soon I felt the stinging all over—my thighs, arms, upper back and buttocks. It was mildly painful. He wasn't hitting me hard, but it was a bitter reminder that he now had access to my entire body.

"Why are you doing this?" I shouted at one point. "It's stupid and pointless."

"I want you conditioned to respond to my voice." He said this in a different tone from the one he was using to harass me. "It might save your life."

What the fuck did that mean? I wanted to call bullshit on that claim, but he kept me too busy as the orders came fast and furiously:

"Head down!"

"Kneel."

"Crawl."

"Don't speak."

"Don't make a sound."

"Don't shed a tear."

"Stand up."

"Bow your head."

"Kneel down."

"Kiss my foot." Eew, I thought, but it was fine. He smelled clean and kinda good.

"Don't cry out when I hurt you."

"Don't say a word unless I give you permission to speak."

I lost track of how many orders he'd given me or how many times he'd punished me. So, of course, he asked me how many instructions I'd received and ordered me to answer. When I guessed wrong, he whipped my ass harder than usual and told me I had to keep count from then on.

At some point, I began to balk. I just couldn't take it anymore. He punished me for resisting and gave more orders, demanding things that were harder all the time. I couldn't remember which was the port side, and because he spun me around after every attempt to locate it, I got more and more confused. Just as I was about to collapse from stress and exhaustion, he knelt beside me and stroked my hair. "You're doing very well. Don't give up now, Ellie." It was the first time he'd called me by my name since he'd told me I no longer had a name. "Just a little longer. A little more practice and I'll let you stop."

Being told that I was doing well helped to calm and center me. I recognized what he was doing–this was a trick, a way to control me, a way to make me want to please him. But I could feel it working on my emotions anyway.

The next time I came to the edge of my endurance, he caressed my shoulders and told me to breathe slowly and deeply. To focus on the sound of his voice. I could get through this, he encouraged me. I was strong, and I was doing well.

He gave me water, and held my head while I drank it.

Then he told me to find the port bulkhead.

At last, unexpectedly, he interrupted me in the middle of a ridiculous task where I was supposed to build several levels of plastic mugs into a tower without allowing any of them to fall. My hands were shaking as I tried to concentrate. The weather must have deteriorated because the boat was bobbing merrily on the waves. This wave action kept toppling my pathetic tower.

"I'll make it easier," the sadist offered. He untied the blindfold and unwrapped it from my eyes. The sudden light dazzled me, but he gave me time to adjust. He allowed me complete the task with the help of my vision, making me feel so absurdly grateful that I actually thanked him.

This time the punishment for speaking without permission was only a light pat on the top of my head. Good puppy. But he soon started giving commands again. It should have been easier without the blindfold, but I was so weary that I couldn't concentrate.

At some point, tired, thirsty, hungry, and emotionally over-come, I curled up in a ball and stopped responding to him. I heard him move and felt the bottle of water applied to my lips. I drank. When some dribbled over my trembling chin, he wiped it away.

"We'll take a break." He picked me up off the floor and car-ried me back into the stateroom, where he bathed my face and neck with water from the sink. Confused and trembling, I didn't raise a protest, lest he change his mind.

He didn't, though. "Lie on the bed and try to calm down."

I complied, curling up in his bed. He tossed the blanket over me and left the cabin, locking the door behind him.

Once again, I cried.

Chapter 9

ELLIE

Thinking it over while I was alone, I was thankful for one thing: Despite my nakedness, I hadn't been forced to do anything sexual. Maybe being forced to obey commands and being whipped on my bare ass when I failed was erotic in some context, but it didn't feel as if he was sexually abusing me. He didn't touch me any more than absolutely necessary. He didn't make any humiliating comments about my body. If he was aroused by anything he was doing, he didn't give any hint of it. He was wearing loose trousers, so I couldn't see if he was erect. Anyway, I was supposed to keep my gaze on the floor.

So even though I had accused him of enjoying this whole thing, I wasn't sure I really believed that. He did not give off many emotional signals. He continued to seem frosty and mechanical. I wasn't sure if that meant he really was cold or if he was just extremely good at keeping his feelings hidden. I suspected the latter.

I had examined my skin anxiously, after he left, expecting to see welts and bruises. But the damage was superficial—there were only a few red blotches, and those were fading rapidly. He hadn't touched any vital areas. He hadn't struck my breasts or ribs or belly or kidney area, nor anywhere on my head or neck. He knew how to cause pain without causing injury. He was, I realized, a master at this.

He left me alone for maybe a couple of hours. It was hard to judge how much time was passing. The day was windy and cloudy, so even though I had a porthole to look through, I could only estimate that it was now afternoon.

When he returned, he brought another tray. This time I was docile, saying nothing and keeping my head bowed. Having eaten nothing all day, I was famished. He placed the tray on the end of the bed. "Thank you, Master," I said, playing his game. Or was that a mistake? Was I not supposed to speak?

"You may eat."

He wanted me dependent upon him for my most fundamental needs. If he was pleased with me, I'd have food, water, sleep, relief from pain. If he was not pleased, I'd probably have none of these things.

Still, I didn't waste any time in grabbing a peach and biting into it. I almost wept at the divine juicy flavor. Turkish peaches are the best.

There was ample bread, cheese, fruit, yogurt and a large mug of strong, black coffee. It tasted fresh-brewed. I gulped it down as I ate.

"At least you haven't lost your appetite," Nicholas said.

"It's delicious. *Ellerinize saglik*," I said automatically, then panicked. I wasn't supposed to speak Turkish.

"How much Turkish do you know?" he instantly demanded.

"Just a few polite phrases. I have a traveler's phrase book somewhere."

"You said that accurately. Can you translate it?"

"Um..." It had already become difficult to lie to him. Was that related to the "training"? "Something about hands? I know it's what you say when the food tastes good."

"Health to your hands. It's something you say to the cook. Or to someone else who creates something by hand."

"I know *el* means hand," I volunteered. "But the extent of my Turkish vocabulary is pathetic. It seems like a difficult language. I studied French in school, but Turkish isn't a romance language, right? I rarely hear words that sound at all familiar." Desperate to get the focus off my knowledge of Turkish, I added, "How did you learn Turkish?"

"My mother was half Turkish, and we lived there when I was a child. It was my first language."

"Your English is perfect."

"I'm bilingual."

"That's cool." The food was reviving my spirits. "I've always envied people who were raised to speak more than one language." I remembered the Greek and Latin tomes. "Do you speak other languages, too?"

"Yes. Several. *Bana bak.*"

Shit. He had just ordered me in Turkish to look at him, and it had almost worked. I happened to be looking down at my food when he said it, and my inner alarm bell was still stronger than my "conditioning." "Huh?" I said, keeping my eyes averted. He was fucking testing me.

"I told you to look at me."

I screwed up my face. "How am I supposed to obey an order if I don't understand it? Is it a trick? May I look at you or not, Master?"

"You may."

So I did. I couldn't make out what his expression meant, though. He seemed puzzled, and possibly amused.

"You're doing well," he said some time later, after he had once again gone through the drill from this morning. "You learn fast."

Again, his praise made me feel good. I tried to suppress the feeling. All he deserved from me was hatred and revulsion. His freaking assessment of how obedient I was learning to be couldn't be allowed to affect me.

"It's not exactly hard," I snapped. "Repulsive, but not difficult."

I waited to be struck with his belt for disrespecting him. Instead he put his hand under my chin, lifting my face up to look at him. I was kneeling naked on the floor of the cabin, as usual. He was standing over me, also as usual. He was wearing loose pants made of some light, synthetic fabric that had lot of pockets and would be convenient for hiking or trekking. No doubt they dried extra fast and protected against the wind. On top was a black T-shirt with a smoky picture of some rock band I'd never heard of. His feet were bare.

Since I hadn't been permitted to look at his face for some time, it had been easy to forget how attractive he was. It seemed wrong to me that such a beautiful face could mask such a cruel heart. His eyes were an unusual pale green, with thick lashes. His mouth was sinfully tempting. Unlike his pants, his shirt was tight, and I could see the ridges of his chest and shoulder muscles beneath it, and even a hint of abs.

"You have a beautiful body," he said. I'd been thinking the same about him. "Is it really repulsive to show it to me?"

The question startled me. I'd never thought of my body as beautiful. For about two seconds I was pleased by the compliment. Then I remembered that this was all acting, lies and manipulation.

"It's repulsive to be forced to strip and to parade around in front of you naked, yes. Plus, you let Metin in. You let him look at me."

"He didn't see much. But where we're going tomorrow, there will be lots of unpleasant men looking at you, so get used to the idea."

My mouth went dry. "You're not going to drag me around naked on a leash in front of them, are you?"

"Not if you behave yourself. But I want you to keep that image in your mind. Act as if I *were* dragging you around naked on a leash. I want you to respond instantly to any commands I give you. Basically, I need you remain in a very submissive state of mind." He added wryly, "If that's possible."

"It's not my fault that the word 'submission' is alien to my personality."

He stroked his thumb over my lips and a flash of heat shot through me. I hadn't felt much of that today, for which I was grateful. Some women might be turned on by being humiliated and roughly treated by dominant males, but I didn't think I was one of them. I had felt more pulses of attraction for this man *before* he'd started ruthlessly training me.

"Look," he said. "Most of the men we'll meet tomorrow haven't seen a woman for weeks. You're young, pretty, desirable. You're a stranger, an outsider, a woman they can't trust. What we are trying to do is reduce the threat factor associated with you. You get that, right?"

"Can't I just stay on the boat? Hide? Can't you make sure nobody sees me?" Even as I suggested this, though, I shivered a little. What if he locked me up alone here for hours? I would go mad in such a small, enclosed space.

"We're going to be there for at least a week, and the boat won't be secure. Metin and I will have to go ashore. Anyone could investigate the boat, find you, and..." he allowed his voice to trail off.

"Who are these people?"

"Art thieves and antiquities smugglers." His beautiful mouth twisted. "Unless it's plain that I can control you, they're going to demand your blood." He paused. "Only you and I will know that you're a free human spirit."

I bristled, but there was no mockery in his repetition of the words I'd used yesterday. "I don't want to break you. That's really not my style."

"You could have fooled me."

He said nothing. His expression had closed down again, and his hand had fallen away from my face.

"Tell me about this island we're going to. Is it your headquarters, your smugglers' den?"

He moved away from me, and began pacing back and forth across the small cabin. "It's a barren Aegean island. The Turks claim it as part of Turkey, but there are no settlements there currently. Except for my family, it's uninhabited."

"Your family? You mean your cousin?"

"My cousin and my grandfather." His tone had stiffened. "Granddad's old now and not in good health, but he's the despot of Altinyunush Adasi—Golden Dolphin Island. He owns some land there and an old villa that was once a vacation spot for some 20th century tycoon. After an earthquake decimated the island, the place went unoccupied until Granddad turned it into his compound."

"Your grandfather is a smuggler?" I pictured an aging Bluebeard in a cave full of booty, grinning diabolically as he defied society by raising his sons and grandsons to follow in his piratical footsteps.

"He's an archaeologist. Have you heard of Sir Avery Lindstrom?"

"Sure. He was one of the great archaeologists of the last century. You don't mean that *he's* your grandfather?"

"Yeah."

Holy shit. "Didn't he die a couple of years ago? I thought he'd been killed in an accident trying to excavate some tombs in South America. There was a cave-in, wasn't there?" I didn't follow the careers of all archeologists, but Lindstrom's story had stuck in my mind because it called up my own terror of being trapped in a dark, airless place.

"He was injured, but he didn't die. Granddad's legs are crippled now, but he's still alive. How much do you know about his work?"

"My mother would know more than I. She's probably met him. What I remember is that he was interested in the Mycenaean Greeks and the Minoan culture of Crete. Didn't he write about the excavations at the royal palace of Knossos?"

"Yes." He raised an eyebrow at me. "I'm surprised you know that. How much archaeology did you study?"

I shrugged. "I'm interested in the history of archaeology. And I learned a lot from hanging out with my mom."

"Well, like your mother, Granddad is fascinated by the Trojan War. He believes there are still some undiscovered artifacts from the destruction of Troy."

"Wasn't the site of Troy fully excavated in the 19th century?"

"It's not that site he's interested in. You've read Homer, right?"

I nodded.

"Remember the legend of the great storm after the fall of Troy? It resulted in the dispersal of the Greek armada."

"It took Odysseus another ten years to get home."

"Right. Our local legend is that one of these ships, complete with its plunder, ran aground on a small Aegean island. No one knew which island, and no one's ever found the site." He paused. "Until now."

"Oh, please. You're not suggesting—"

"Yes. At least, my grandfather thinks so. He believes that Golden Dolphin is the island."

"But the legends of Troy are just that—legends. I mean, we know the city existed and all that, but archaeology has never proved that its destruction occurred on the massive scale suggested by Homeric epic. In fact—"

"I know the historical problems involved," he interrupted. "It's a dream, of course. But many of the greatest discoveries of archaeology have been inspired by people's dreams. If Schliemann hadn't pursued the legends of Troy so ardently, we'd still be thinking it was a fictional city."

His face had become unusually animated. I blinked at him, recognizing that I was catching a glimpse of the human side of Nicholas Gabriel at last. It made me all the more curious about him. "Are you an archaeologist, too?"

His eyes looked full into mine for a long moment before those golden lashes came down and curtained them off. "I'm a vagabond."

"Do you own this yacht?"

"No. My friend Max owns it. But I live onboard. I sail around, smuggling art objects, ripping people off, kidnapping women and generally wreaking havoc wherever I go."

"A vagabond and a pirate."

"Right," he said, and sat down on the bed, stretching his long legs out in front of him and leaning his back against the wall.

"Has your grandfather actually recovered any Trojan artifacts?"

"I don't think so. But he's still looking. He closes down the dig for the summer, though. Too many tourist boats sailing around as the weather gets warmer."

"Why does that matter?"

He just looked at me.

"The dig is illegal? The Turkish government doesn't know about your grandfather's theories?"

He nodded. "They would lay claim to the site if they had any idea what we were seeking."

"If this island is part of Turkey, the excavations belong to the Turkish people."

"My grandfather doesn't see it that way."

"They intend to suppress the discoveries if they find any-thing?"

Nick inclined his bronze head.

Wow. Sir Avery was a crooked archaeologist. Who would have thought it?

Schooled by my mother in the ethics of modern archaeology, I had nothing but contempt for the avaricious few who viewed the science as nothing more than a means of unearthing coins, plate, pottery and precious stones. That Sir Avery Lindstrom should be one of these thieves appalled me. "You're keeping the stolen objects on this island?"

"A few, yes. Until we find buyers. The world is full of wealthy private collectors who are prepared to pay lavishly for genuine antiquities. Nigel takes care of that end of things."

"And you do the actual stealing. What did Sir Avery give you the book for—robbing your first tomb?"

He looked blank.

"'Good show! Love, Granddad,'" I quoted.

He looked over at the bookshelves, and then smiled grimly. "You've been busy, I see."

"I invaded your privacy, yes." I was angry. For some reason I'd been cherishing the faint hope that despite everything that had happened between us, Nicholas Gabriel wouldn't turn out to be greedy, immoral and rotten. It was an affront to nature that his beautiful body was so corrupt. "I poked through every-thing—books, drawers, the lot. Before you locked them all."

He rolled his eyes, unimpressed with my initiative.

"Why aren't you angry? I would be if someone searched my room."

He shrugged. "If I were you, I'd have done the same."

I turned away, hating him as much for his patience and his tolerance as for his ability to scare me. Nothing about him fit. He was a devil with the face of an angel. He was a pirate with a classical education. It made no sense.

It struck me that for once we had actually had a normal conversation. He had answered my questions and spoken directly, maybe even honestly, about what was going on. He hadn't snapped at me or ordered me to call him Master even once.

"Why don't you just let me go?"

"You know too much."

"You didn't have to tell me about your grandfather's criminal excavations."

"You knew too much as soon as you saw me collecting that statue." He touched my hair, running a long strand through his fingers. His face was set, his eyes weary. "You could try trusting me."

"Why the hell would I trust you, after everything you've done to me?"

For an instant, I thought he was going to give me a reason, then something altered in the green depths of his eyes and the chance was lost. "We haven't even done the hard part yet," he said.

There was something about the way he said it that warned me. Uh oh. Now what?

"I know this sucks for you, but we need to have sex."

My stomach sank. "Wow. That's the most romantic proposition I've ever gotten. Can I have my cell phone back so I can text about it to my friends?"

"I'm glad I haven't shattered your sense of humor." He looked me over—me in my naked glory—more appraisingly than usual. "If we had met in normal circumstances, this might have been different. You're a bit young for me, but you're smart and you're gutsy."

"I thought you hated gutsy. Obedient and passive seems to be your thing."

He rolled his eyes.

"I'm not having sex with you. Not willingly. If you starve me, strangle me, whip me or tie me to the bed, it'll be rape, which you said you wouldn't do. I draw the line at fucking a psycho kidnapping dickwad who makes me strip, kneel, crawl and call him Master."

I seriously expected retribution for that crack. Instead, he leaned forward until his mouth was poised just over mine. I could feel his warm breath dampening my lips. Heating them. "Liar."

"I'm not lying."

"Yes, Ellie. I think you are." He slipped his fingers into the hair at my nape and held my head still. His eyes gazed into mine, then closed, those thick golden lashes a pale contrast to his sun-tanned skin. He tilted my head back so my mouth came against his. And then he kissed me.

Chapter 10

ELLIE

I struggled. I pushed at his shoulders; I tried to hold him off. He persisted. He held me, let his strength sink into me. Then he deepened the kiss, and I got the feeling I was doomed. His lips crushed mine. For some absurd reason, I yielded. He wasn't really forcing me, but I stopped fighting him.

I know. There's no excuse for me. I'm pathetic.

Our mouths melded. They seemed to fit together perfectly. Warm, fragrant, sweet. No, not warm—hot.

I was shivering, but not with fear, when he raised his head and whispered, "You have the sexiest mouth." He ran his tongue over the moist surface of my lips. The muscles in the pit of my belly convulsed. "This time open it for me." Holding my head still with both hands in my hair, he took me like the pirate he was, with confidence, authority and passion.

I parted my lips as his sinuous tongue invaded and explored. I met it with mine, shifting as the tips of our tongues touched and rubbed gently against each other. Desire exploded in me, making my nipples swell and my pussy slicken. Fuck! I'd felt an attraction from the moment I had first seen this golden god on the deck of his sailboat. All I could think of now was how much I wanted to tear off his clothes and offer myself to him.

He hadn't been touching any other part of my body, but now he slid his arms around my waist and pulled me astride him, trapping my hands against his chest while his mouth nuzzled my ear. I was no longer protesting. Not one peep. My body was pressed to his from shoulder to thigh. He rubbed himself to my belly, hard as steel, and proving that there was nothing cold-blooded about this, after all.

I hadn't been able to tell before if he was aroused by all the kinky shit, but there was absolutely no doubt about it now. His cock felt huge. Magnificent. Tempting. But, dammit, was this the way it was going to happen? Was I going to cave in for a criminal? I hadn't even put up much of a fight.

"Wait. I really don't think—"

He stroked his hands down along my sides, then up, pausing with his splayed thumbs just under my breasts. He didn't touch them, not quite. But his restraint increased my need. Between my legs, I was sopping wet for him.

"Ssh," he said. "Don't think."

Unlike some, this was an easy command to obey. In his arms, feeling his blood beating steadily beneath his supple skin, the last thing I wanted to do was think. He kissed me again, demanding and hot, his tongue plunging deep. I responded. While our mouths eagerly assaulted each other, I dipped my fingers into the tangle of gold at his nape; it felt both soft and rough against my fingertips. I pressed rhythmically, like a cat, until he made a low sound of pleasure.

There was something between us. Something relentless, something powerful. Something I'd fantasized about and yearned for, but never actually experienced. Something a little bit cruel.

His fingers closed over my breasts. He rolled one of my nipples between his thumb and his forefinger. He tugged on it. He squeezed. He was being rough now, but I didn't mind. His face was flushed, his skin damp. I could feel the wild thunder of his heartbeat as my fingers caressed his throat. No cold Greek god now, Nick Gabriel was warm flesh, hot blood. I wanted him.

He pushed me off his lap and laid me down across the bed. Then he knelt over me, straddling my body. The sight of him looming over me excited me so much I had to close my eyes. He touched my breasts again. Gently now. Carefully. With skill. Strong, callused fingers whispering over my soft, sensitive flesh, giving too little, making me arch and seek and strain for more. I flexed my knees, unconsciously parting my legs. Blindly I reached for his shoulders, trying to pull him down atop me.

"Just a second," he said. "I'll undress."

His statement was really a question, I knew. The subtle question sophisticated men ask sophisticated women, expecting to be answered with an eager nod.

But I wasn't that girl. I wasn't subtle or sophisticated, and he was my captor. Passion or no passion, he wanted this because it was convenient for him to be fucking his slave. No doubt it would make him look manly in front of his criminal friends.

Why should I subject myself to that? He didn't know me or care about me. He wouldn't be tender or kind. He was a smuggler!

"No," I said, letting my hands fall away from his body. "I can't."

He slid down a little and lowered his mouth to my breast. He tongued my nipple. He sucked and nipped the tender flesh there until I writhed and cried out.

He raised his head. "Let me, Ellie." His voice was low and lazy. "No acting necessary—it's better this way."

"No." I twisted vainly, trying to escape him. "This is all wrong. You're my captor, my enemy. I shouldn't be feeling this for you."

"Ellie—"

"I mean it. This can't be real. It's Stockholm syndrome."

"I don't give a fuck how you define it." His voice was rougher now. He slipped one hand between my legs. "You're wet for me. That's all the reality I need."

"Please don't. I'm saying no."

His eyes turned very green, and for a moment I thought he was going to insist. I tensed, waiting for him to cross the fragile line between civility and savagery, seduction and rape. It happened all the time, I knew. On lonely roads, in dark hallways, on soft couches after a pleasant first date. It could be a man you knew well and trusted. How much more likely was it to be a pirate who had taken you prisoner at gunpoint.

Nick shifted, pushing up on his strong arms and gazing down at me. He seemed to be trying to figure me out. Then his expression altered, becoming the same cold one with which I was so familiar. There was a cruel twist to his lips. "I promised no rape. But I haven't forgotten the "psycho kidnapping dickwad' crack. That was disrespectful and deserves punishment."

Maybe because I was already aroused and trying so hard to resist my own impulses, the idea of punishment didn't sound as awful as it had earlier in the day. I flashed back to the way it had felt when he had whipped me with his leather belt. Once I had grown accustomed to it, the sting had died down and a kind of sexy warmth had remained.

"Fine. Go ahead. I'm going to keep telling you what I really think of you even if I get whipped for it. *Master.*"

"Kneel here, with your chest on the bed."

I did it. I knelt on the floor with my belly and chest pressed down on the berth that I considered his bed, since he had slept there last night while I had lain on the floor, naked and clutching my blanket.

I closed my eyes when I heard him step behind me, waiting for him to strike me with the belt. But that wasn't what happened. Instead I felt his hand on my ass, caressing me gently. I was about to object that I wasn't doing any more damn sexual stuff with him when he lifted his hand and then brought it down on my butt with a loud crack.

"Ow!"

"Don't make a sound," he warned in that harsh drill sergeant voice. Then he spanked me again. And again. And again.

I had never been spanked as a child. As an adult, I'd fantasized about it during vanilla sex with a couple of boyfriends. But I'd never fantasized that it would hurt so much. He hadn't really hurt me with the belt. It had seemed scary because it was, like, a freaking belt. I guess he hadn't swung it hard.

This was different. Now he *was* hurting me. He kept changing the spot where he struck me, adding new areas of pain to the mix. I'd never realized there were so many different spots available for punishment on my buttocks, but he kept finding new ones. Weren't people supposed to have a safeword for stuff like this? I guess there were no safewords when you got yourself kidnapped.

Each blow left a stinging sensation on the skin and, deeper down, a sort of ache. He had told me not to cry out, and I tried not to. Less because of the order than out of pride. Wasn't he getting tired? When was it going to end?

In my effort not to scream or whimper or cry, I responded to each slap by arching away from his hand, a movement that drove the inside of my thighs against the frame of the bunk. When he found a spot down on the underside of my bottom, near the place where it met the tops of my thighs, his spanks drove me up in such a way that my pussy, which seemed unaccountably damp, and my clit were being pressed into the mattress and my own movements added to the pressure there. My ass felt warm and warmer still, and my clit began throbbing with the need for more pressure, more stimulation.

As my arousal intensified, the pain from the spanking faded. I wasn't even sure if he was still hurting me, or if his hands were caressing me instead. My heart was rocketing in my chest and my breathing had turned quick and light. Images of him fucking me—maybe even in the ass, where I was still a virgin—filled my consciousness. I wanted his cock in my pussy, soothing the fire he'd started. In my ass, hurting me. In my mouth, driving into me while I knelt naked before him and endured whatever punishment he felt like dealing out. I didn't even mind the rope collar around my neck, which wasn't tight enough to restrict my breathing. It marked me as his. I was his slave and he my master, and, in my spiraling excitement, that was okay with me.

The hand that was spanking me slipped between my legs and found my wetness. Yes, yes, I thought, touch me. Release me, free me, make me come.

"No," I moaned, as his thumb flicked the engorged bud that was my clit. At the same moment, one of his fingers was slipping into me, sliding in easily because of the slickness there. "I don't want...please, no, please stop."

"I don't believe you," he said. His voice had lost its usual cool inflection. I realized he was kneeling on the floor behind me. He was still dressed, but I could feel his erect cock pressing against my ass, just as I had imagined it.

"I. Don't. Want. This." Each word was a monumental effort to force out. Because I did want it. Oh so very much.

He stopped. His hand disappeared from between my legs, and the other hand, the one that had been spanking me, ceased that activity, too.

Oh god, oh god. I groaned in frustration. My hands were clutching the sheets on the bed, all but tearing them off the mattress. I had been so close to coming that stopping made my sex ache and vibrate with tension, practically screaming with a voice of its own, "why, why, why?"

My captor pushed away from me and stood up. A moment later, I heard him leave the cabin and lock the door behind him.

I dragged myself up on the bed and lay there, legs pressed together and twisting in frustration and misery.

I was weak. But I'd said no in the end, hadn't I? Was I weak or was I strong?

I didn't know.

He had stopped. Was that cruel or kind?

I didn't know that either.

I didn't know anything anymore.

Chapter 11

NICK

Fuck.

Up on deck, I stared at the gray sea and tried to regulate my head, which was churning with violent and erotic thoughts. I'd already given up attempting to master my cock. I considered diving into the sea for a swim, but the water wouldn't be cold enough to dampen my fires.

Ellie Heath. If there was a highway to hell, I was cruising down the fast lane. Maybe Nigel was right about me, after all.

I hadn't thought myself capable of doing some of the things I'd done to her. Worse, I'd been reveling in it. The more I handled and dominated her, the more I wanted to master her, break her, hurt her. Make her my slave in truth.

The dark energy just kept rising from somewhere deep inside me. It fizzed through my brain like champagne. It made me feel absurdly powerful to see her crawling at my feet. Naked. It made my dick painfully hard and left me amazed at my restraint.

Why I hadn't fucked her yet was a mystery to my horny body. My mind knew why—I'd been stupid enough to make that promise.

Not until you beg, captive mine. Which you will very soon do.

But my mind was slowly losing this battle. And that scared the shit out of me because it almost never happened. Mind over body—that had always defined me. I'm good at controlling myself. Locking down any stray antisocial feelings. Being the good boy my fucking bastard cousin Nigel so blatantly was not.

Ever since finding Ellie Heath, of the glorious red-gold hair and the purple hyacinth eyes, I'd been aflame. I didn't have a clue why this should be so. Nothing about it made sense.

Meet sexual sadist Nick Gabriel. Was there a monster in every man?

I'd always had extreme fantasies. I'd played around with kink with many of my former lovers, but that had been consensual. Ordering someone to bare her ass so I could spank it would be done with a safeword in place. It would be followed by mutual orgasms and laughter.

This was different. This was something I'd never intended. Ellie's sudden appearance was wrecking all the plans I'd worked so long to achieve. She was a wild card thrown by the laughing gods in the final stages of the game. *You think you've got everything figured out? Deal with this, sucker.*

So I'd had to improvise. And, fuck, before I could even think it through, it had roared out of control. I was supposed to be calm, cold, and in tactical mode. Instead, I was finding perverted pleasure in humiliating some innocent bystander who'd had the bad luck to stumble into my melodrama with my fucked up family.

And everything I'd done—the rope around her neck, the beatings, the commands I'd insisted she obey, the sexual groping—had sent sick waves of exaltation through me. Maybe I'd never known how it felt to have all boundaries lifted. No pesky social restraints. Total freedom. Man. Woman. See. Want. Take.

The thing was, I liked Ellie. She wasn't my usual type, but she was brave. Intelligent. Hilarious, at times. Some other woman might have cracked by now, but she'd kept it together. I admired her for that. It didn't prevent me from wanting to break her down, but I had to give her credit—she wasn't making it easy.

In normal circumstances, I might even have hung out with her. Tried for a hook up, maybe more. If things had been different, I don't think she'd have refused. There was chemistry. Hell, she was close to being willing, even now. I could have taken her a few minutes ago. The lips of her sex had been puffy and wet. She'd forced out that "no" from sheer gritty determination. And it had just about killed me to stop.

Today had been rough on her. But I'd gotten her close to where I needed her to be. Which was good, because we were running out of time.

I had to cool down. Thinking about dominating and fucking Ellie was not what I needed to be doing right now. If I got careless and screwed up, people would die.

I needed to focus on Nigel.

If I had to use Ellie to bring him down, then use her I would.

Metin came somewhat hesitantly to my side. "How's it going?"

"Fine." I looked into his curious, slightly envious eyes until Metin's gaze dropped.

"Your girl—she is okay?" he asked.

"She will be." *I hoped.*

"She is afraid. Foolish woman." He seemed less callous than he was trying to sound.

Fuck. Metin had never been too good at disguising his basic decency. He probably had a lot more of that quality than I did.

Metin hesitated. "You aren't—" He paused, probably deciding which question he was brave enough to ask "—hurting her?"

I *am* fucking hurting her. "Have you ever heard a woman complain after she'd been with me?"

Metin considered. "You haven't been with a woman since I've known you."

Whoa. Was that true? I'd known Metin for six months. Surely... I thought back. Fuck. The kid was right. No wonder I was walking around with a dick too swollen for my jeans.

This whole mess was turning out to be a lot harder than I'd anticipated.

Chapter 12

ELLIE

I awoke with the sun in my face and a low male voice whispering in my ear. "Wake up."

I blinked into Nick's vivid green eyes. He was clean-shaven and his breath smelled faintly of toothpaste. In the full light of day, he was even hotter than he'd looked yesterday. He was dressed in blue-jean cutoffs and a black T-shirt. Tall and tan, he seemed to explode with sexy goodness. His gilt hair shone; his eyes reflected all the mysteries of the sea.

My sex clenched in that unpredictable but delicious way it tended to do when he was around. I glared down at my body as if it were my enemy. My pussy didn't care that he was a smuggler and a thief. My hormones had no shame, no self-respect.

He had left me alone all night. He'd never returned to the cabin after that abortive attempt at sex. Metin had brought me supper and, later, taken away my tray. I'd seen nothing more of either of them after that. I'd finally gone to sleep, leaving the light in the head on and its door fully open.

"I'm leaving it unlocked," Nick said. "You can come out when you're dressed." He nodded at a bundle on the floor. "You'll find your things here."

"My pack?"

"Your camera's there, too. Undamaged, I think, except for a few dents."

I pulled out the camera and examined it as tenderly as I might an injured puppy. "Thank you."

He ignored me and left the cabin. As he closed the door behind him, I took my camera and went to the porthole to look out into the bright iridescence of the new day. I saw no sign of land. We were well out in the Aegean Sea, whose name conjured up visions of the ancient world.

The water sparkled liquid gold under the radiance of the rising sun, and the morning had a hazy, timeless quality to it. For an instant, I felt transported to another century. I seemed to know these waters intimately, as if I had sailed them myself in the Golden Age with the heroes and warriors.

But no. There was nothing heroic about this voyage.

Ten minutes later, dressed in the fresh jeans and dark blue top I'd taken from my pack, I grabbed my camera and left the cabin where I'd been imprisoned. I could hear men's voices out on deck. Passing through the far end of the salon and up several steps, I saw Metin at the helm and Nick in the bow, doing something to one of the sheets that controlled the jib. One blond head and one dark against the bright-blue sky. My captor must have sensed my presence. He beckoned, and I went out, grateful that I wasn't to be locked up below all day.

The fresh air assaulted me, rushing to fill my lungs and wreak havoc with my hair. Spreading my arms out wide, I inhaled deeply. There were worse fates, I decided, than being snatched away on a yacht.

I shaded my eyes to stare across the deck. The sails were puffed full of wind; the sea creamed beneath the prow as the yacht skimmed over the sea with all the grace of a great white bird. I noted the boat's name stenciled on a life preserver. *Voyager,* she was called. As the sun rose higher in the eastern sky, its radiance bathed the entire vessel, tipping the slender top of the mast with amber. My imagination let loose again. I was on a mythical ship, sailing Homer's wine-dark sea; my fate was in the hands of Poseidon, the fierce god of water, wind and waves.

"Is it okay if I take a few pictures?"

Nick nodded.

I got several fast shots of the wind-filled sails and the glowing mast before the light changed. Then I moved about the boat, shooting from several different angles, losing track of the time, concentrating all my energy on my task.

I whirled to the touch of Nick's hand on my shoulder. "Getting any good shots?"

"A few. The light is excellent. Look." I pointed at the foamy spray that rose before us each time the bowsprit rode the curl of a wave. "Can you see the color refraction as the sun pours through the spray?"

"Yeah. Like hundreds of rainbows. Can you capture that?"

"I can try." I leaned over the rail, focusing on the swirling colors. The rocking of the waves made it difficult for me to hold my camera still. My arms were beginning to ache with the effort. Still I shot, leaning over some more as I shifted the camera to get a new angle.

"Watch it," Nick said sharply as a gust took us and the yacht rocked, nearly sending me off balance. I felt his hands grip my waist. "I don't want you falling over the side."

I turned, feeling his hands tighten on me as I rotated. My stomach muscles flexed and the desire lurking under the surface fluttered. "Thanks." Jeez. Stop thanking him. He didn't deserve any thanks from me.

For several seconds he continued to hold me, not exploring, not caressing, just letting me feel his heat. At last, he allowed his hands to fall back to his side. "You seemed totally absorbed, as if you could see nothing but the images in your lens."

"I get that way. I love taking pictures." I was speaking fast, nervously. "Seeing an image the way no one else sees it. Capturing it."

"I'd like to see your work."

"Sorry, but your associate back on the Turkish coast deleted all the pictures I'd already shot."

"True." He was looking speculative now. "Have you ever shot for your mother? Photos of the artifacts recovered on digs?"

"Now and then. I've never specialized in that kind of work, although I suppose it's what inspired me to take pictures in the first place. As a child, I used to pore over those beautiful color photographs of King Tut's golden mask and the frescoes on the gates of Babylon." I paused. "Why? You want pictures for your smuggler's scrapbook?"

I expected him to take offense at my non-submissive tone, but he just shrugged it off. It wasn't easy to needle him.

My first sight of Golden Dolphin Island came several hours later. It was little more than an arid hunk of rock. Stark and gray, it rose in masses of volcanic rock against the blue sky. Here and there, I saw some olive green or yellowish scrub and a few scrawny trees and bushes, but for the most part, the island was bleak and uninviting. "It looks forbidding," I said.

"It is forbidding," Nick returned with a distinct edge to his voice.

"Have there ever been any significant settlements here?"

"Not recently. Fresh water is sparse, so not much grows."

"Is the island recorded on any ancient charts? How do you know it's been here long enough to have anything to do with the Trojan War? Maybe it was thrown up by volcanic activity in later years."

"No, it's been here for eons. The Greeks of the fifth century B.C. had a name for the island—Worthless Rock."

"But the Turks called it Golden Dolphin Island? Why?"

He shrugged. "I've no idea."

He seemed edgy as we approached the island. He hid his feelings well, but I had little to do to pass the time except observe him. His face became more drawn, his conversation more terse with each passing minute. It did not help my own peace of mind to know that he was ill at ease.

The sails were down as we entered a narrow bay. Metin was at the helm. Nick touched me on the shoulder. "Come with me," he said, waiting for me to stand and follow.

We descended to the stateroom. He closed the door and turned, close to me—too close, as he so often seemed to be. Why did his big body generate such warmth? And why did my own respond with such hunger every time he looked at me?

"Listen." His hands came down on my shoulders. He adjusted the rope collar around my throat. "Your life is in danger here. If you decide to do anything stupid—like try to escape—I'll be hard put to save you."

I didn't say anything. If I saw a chance to escape....

His fingers tightened. "You do want to keep on living?"

"Of course I want to keep on living."

"Then remember your training. Follow my orders. Act submissive. Swallow your protests even if I tell you to do something you hate. This will be tested, you can count on it."

"Do I have to pretend to be some dumb bimbo? Never to have heard of your grandfather's work?"

"We'll stick as close to the truth as possible, but let's not tell him who your mother is. She's pretty famous for her views about returning archaeological discoveries, even those from many decades ago, to their countries of origin."

I was surprised he knew this about my mother. She wasn't *that* well-known, although I suppose one could say they worked in the same field. "Okay, I won't mention her." I paused. "You're nervous, aren't you? The big, bad, wanted-in-nine-countries thief is afraid of his grandfather?"

He scoffed.

Half an hour later, we climbed into the rowboat and went ashore. Nick rowed the small boat into a narrow, deserted inlet. When we landed, thumping roughly against the rocky shoreline, I would have sworn we were alone. But by the time we scrambled out of the boat, this illusion had been dispelled. We were surrounded by four nasty-looking men, all armed, all dark, all sporting mustaches like Metin's.

"Hosh geldiniz, Nicholas *bey,"* the biggest, meanest-looking thug said in response to Nick's cheerful grin. "Welcome."

"*Hosh bulduk,* Aslan," he responded, kissing the man on both cheeks in the Turkish manner. He tugged me forward with an unbreakable grip on my wrist. I leaned against him slightly, letting my hair brush his chin. I glanced shyly at the thugs, and then directed my gaze down. They were leering at me.

"This is my girl Ellie," Nick said. He was speaking Turkish. "She's a photographer."

"She works for you?" the man asked, looking at me suspiciously.

"She's a slave," he said casually, as if there were nothing unusual in the notion. "I own her."

Aslan, the ferocious-looking Turk, grinned. He studied me with interest, paying particular attention to the woven rope collar around my neck. He did not greet me as I meekly followed my "master" into the compound.

Chapter 13

ELLIE

Nick's grandfather turned out to be a delightful elderly man. He was charming, courteous and not at all intimidating. The notion that my life might be in danger from him seemed absurd.

Sir Avery Lindstrom had mischievous blue eyes, a lined and weathered face and thick, iron-gray hair. I noted a family resemblance between him and Nick in the bones of his face. He was in a wheelchair when we met in the smugglers' compound. The rambling, two-story building was divided into numerous small rooms and built in the lee of a massive cliff a few hundred yards from the bay where Nick had anchored the yacht. I remembered that Nick had told me it had once been a wealthy man's villa, but that must have been decades ago. It looked old and weather-beaten now.

"Nick has never brought a woman to meet me before," was the first thing Sir Avery said after we were introduced. "You must be special to him."

"I don't know about that, sir," I said meekly, bestowing my best sheep's eyes on the pale-haired man who stood tensely beside me. I spoke clearly because I noticed the old gentleman was wearing a hearing aid.

"How did you meet?"

An imp took my tongue: "It was one of those sudden things. No sooner did he touch me than I fell at his feet. The next thing I knew, he'd carried me off on his yacht like a thief in the night."

Nick got, if possible, stiffer, and Sir Avery shot him a quick, suspicious glance as I added, "It was *very* romantic."

"Ellie's a photographer." Nick's green eyes were glaring repressively at me. "She came to Turkey to photograph touristic sites for a travel piece. Unfortunately she ran into some minor trouble with the authorities." His hand had slipped into mine and tightened until he was all but crushing my fingers. I got the message: play along with me. "I paid a few bribes and extricated her from her difficulties."

"I see," said his grandfather. I didn't. I wondered what Sir Avery thought he meant by that vague explanation. The only difficulties I had were with Nick himself.

"Nicholas has always been chivalrous to ladies in distress," his grandfather commented.

This nearly made me burst into hysterical laughter. Clearly, Sir Avery was not as well acquainted with his grandson as he thought.

"Do you have an interest in archaeology?" Sir Avery asked me.

I shrugged. "It's really not my thing."

"Her primary interest is keeping me happy," Nick said.

In Turkish, Sir Avery asked Nick if I understood that language. Nick shook his head laconically, looking bored. "Pardon my rudeness," Sir Avery said to me. "You must get Nick to teach you some Turkish. He was a schoolteacher once, you know."

"Really?" I arched a glance in Nick's direction. "He never told me that."

Nick hooked his fingers around my upper arm. "I presume my usual room is ready for us, Granddad? I prefer to conduct lessons in private."

"Certainly," the old man said. "Show your friend to your room and let her freshen up. But return to me so we can have a little chat. Alone, if you don't mind."

"I think you're going to get raked over the coals when he gets you alone," I said to him a few minutes later.

"Looks like it," Nick agreed.

"How'd I do?" We were in the middle of a small, whitewashed room, furnished only with a metal folding chair, a card table, a large packing crate and a bare mattress on the floor. The afternoon sun was pouring in through the square window, making the room seem more cheerful than it really was.

"I could have done without that remark about you falling at my feet."

I shrugged. "Your grandfather was charming."

"He's always charming." He had dumped my things and his own on the card table and now began fishing a couple of blankets out of the packing crate. "Doesn't mean a thing." He threw the blankets on the bed.

His voice was weary, abstracted, and I ordered myself to stop picking at him. But his self-command annoyed me. I'd met few people so disciplined, so untouchable. If I hadn't seen his control briefly dissolve last night in the throes of lust, I'd have thought him beautiful but empty, with all the emotional depth of a robot. Because of those few minutes in his arms, I knew better. And, pathetically, given the circumstances, I was all the more intrigued.

"Were you really a schoolteacher?"

"When I was a grad student, sure."

"What did you teach?"

"You're full of questions, aren't you? Classics."

"Latin and Greek?" That explained the books in his cabin. "I took Latin, but I never did Greek, although I would have loved to be able to read the *Iliad* in the original."

"Yeah, well, it was a while ago."

"How the hell did a lover of classical literature turn into an antiquities smuggler?"

"Is the study of classical literature supposed to improve one's morals?"

"No, I suppose not, but—"

"Rather the contrary, I'd say. The Trojan War would never have been fought if Helen hadn't been carted off to Troy to be Paris's mistress. And as for piracy and looting, those guys were pros."

Before I could think up a retort, there was a rap on the door. Nick strolled over and opened it. "Well, well. I figured it was you. Eager to check us out? Ellie, my cousin Nigel. Nigel, my submissive, Ellie."

I glanced curiously at the man on the threshold for just a moment before dropping my eyes in approved submissive fashion. Nick's cousin Nigel was not what I had expected. Unlike most field archaeologists whom I'd encountered on my mother's digs, he was dressed in casual but elegant clothing. No T-shirt and ragged shorts or jeans for Nigel. No work boots or rough-terrain shoes. He wore a pure white button-down shirt and perfectly pressed gray slacks. His shoes looked like expensive Italian loafers. His hair was smartly cut and his grooming was immaculate. He looked more like an international banker than a smuggler.

I could see the family resemblance. Nigel looked a little like Nick, and even more like their grandfather. He had the same strong features and thick, straight hair as the old man. Like Nick's, his hair was blond, but it was a muddier hue, less bright, less golden. He was taller than Nick by two or three inches. And he was brawny—wide shouldered and heavyset, although not overweight.

He greeted me with a broad smile that softened his eyes. He took one of my hands in his and pressed it, touching my arm with the other hand in affable-politician style. Everything about him conveyed kindliness and good will.

"Your submissive? I am astonished." To me he said warmly, "I'm so pleased to meet you. Welcome to our island."

I bowed my head as submissively as I could. "Thank you, sir." *It's not your fucking island.*

"I hope our grandfather has made you feel at home. Are your accommodations adequate? We're roughing it here, of course, but I think you'll find it comfortable."

He sounded friendly, and I thanked him again. I felt confused. From the little that Nick had told me, these guys were villainous thieves. But now that I had met both Sir Avery and Cousin Nigel, I was wondering if Nick had lied to me. Who was the real villain here?

It didn't take long, though, for the man behind the mask to peek out. "You may call me Master when we are alone, pet," he said, smiling as if he was joking. But I sensed he wasn't.

"Fuck off, Nigel. You're not going to be alone with my slave. And that title is reserved for me."

Nigel laughed, a deep-toned, boisterous sound. "Our Nick is possessive."

"Right." Nick's tone was dry.

"When we were in college I snaked away his girlfriend. He has never forgiven me. It *was* rather mean of me. Dear Elizabeth."

I saw something ferocious flash in Nick's eyes. Elizabeth. That was the name of the girl who'd written the inscription in the poetry book.

"Ancient history. I'm sure Ellie isn't interested."

I was, actually. But I didn't say so. There was something deeply unpleasant beating between these two men. I didn't want to provide an atmosphere in which their animosity could grow.

I moved closer to Nick and slid my fingers through his.

"Is he a kind master?" Nigel was still addressing me, but I could now feel nasty vibes underneath the courtesy. It was creepy. It made me want to step back. Get far away from him. Hide.

"You do your best to please him, I trust? It would be unfortunate if he should be forced to sell you to one of his sex trafficking friends."

Because I was pressed against him, I felt Nick suck in his breath. He probably felt the catch in mine, too. Points to Nigel. Nick had led me to believe it was Nigel who was interested in human trafficking, not him.

Nick slipped one arm around me and brought me tight against his hip. "She needn't worry about something that's never going to happen. Stop looking for weaknesses. Ellie is devoted to me."

"No outsiders—we agreed on that, remember?" Nigel's voice was neither charming nor indulgent now.

"You can think of her as an extension of me." He pressed hard on my shoulders, and I understood what he wanted me to do. Although my spirit rose in rebellion, I checked it sharply. Dropping to my knees in front of him, I lowered my head in submission. His fingers caressed the back of my neck, not gently.

He moved slightly, so my face was against his groin. As if he expected me to pull out his dick and suck him off right here and now. For a frozen moment, I wondered if that's what he did expect. That would certainly demonstrate submission.

I was half-tempted to do it. That would probably shock the hell out of him.

"We have an arrangement," he went on, stroking my hair. "She attends to all my various needs, and I allow her to live."

The silence was fraught. Although I couldn't see either of their faces, I could sense Nigel's surprise. I could also feel Nick's cock rising underneath my cheek.

Nigel switched to Turkish. "Are you crazy bringing her here? Does she speak Turkish?"

Nick answered in the same language. "Of course not. She has no clue about what's really going on here."

"I don't trust you. After years of walking the straight and narrow, suddenly you're engaged in human trafficking and keeping slaves?"

"You know nothing about my life. I got sick of watching you lord about with all your wealth and all your women while I scraped in the dirt for a living. Art trafficking might pay nicely, but the business I'm in now pays even better."

"How about I take your little friend away from you and give her to my lads?

"Do that and you'll lower her value."

"Are you claiming she's special merchandise?"

"Exactly."

They were speaking rapidly and using slang, so I was a little behind on my internal translation. Shit. Had I misheard? I didn't think so. He had used the word for merchandise—a product, goods for sale.

My heart was pounding. *Was he serious?* I could feel Nigel's interest in me sharpen. "Please don't try to tell me she's a virgin. She looks young, but not that young."

"Of course not. Except for her anal virginity, which has its own value."

Thank god I was staring at the floor because I could feel my face turning red. How the hell did he know anything about my fucking anal virginity? Was *that* what he wanted to do to me? I couldn't believe they were discussing such a thing. I wanted to melt into the floor and disappear.

"Do you have any idea," Nick went on, "the price I can command for a young white female? American too, which many potential buyers will enjoy because of the rarity and humiliation factor?"

"How well-trained is she?"

"I'm working on it."

"Would you like some help on that? Or perhaps I should buy her myself? I'd expect a family discount, of course."

"Stay the fuck away from her. She doesn't know what I'm planning. I intend to sell her as minimally trained. That commands a high price these days among those who are into the harsher training protocols."

What the *fuck*?

"I must admit I'm surprised," Nigel drawled. "When I first heard about this trafficking venture you were involved in, I was skeptical. I didn't think you were so enterprising. Or so hard-assed, for that matter."

"It's been a long time since we've socialized, Nigel."

"True." Nigel sounded speculative.

"Wasn't it you who always claimed I wasn't indulging my true inclinations? Maybe you were right. Besides, the money involved is huge."

"If you think I'm going to trust you because of this one girl you're mistaken."

"I don't give a damn how you feel about me. Just stay out of my way."

The malevolence between them was even more palpable now. "I'm surprised that you would bring a woman into a situation fraught with danger."

Nick's hand in my hair tightened. "Is that a threat?"

"A warning."

"Lay one finger on her and I'll kill you," said Nick. His cool, casual tone seemed to make a mockery of his words.

"Do you really think you could? You, the precise and orderly excavator? You, the good boy from our youth?"

"Yes, I think I could."

So did I. I couldn't credit it, but Nigel seemed unimpressed by the deadly sense of purpose I could feel emanating from Nick. Didn't he know what Nick was capable of with those lethal hands of his?

Apparently not. "Sure, coz," he said, and, humming cheerfully to himself, strolled to the door. "Anytime you want to take me on, do let me know. Oh, and by the way," Nigel switched back to English. I guess he wanted to make sure I understood him. "The old man's waiting to see you. It seems he's finally found his precious treasures of Troy."

"What do you mean, he's finally found them?"

"He didn't tell you? I guess he doesn't trust your little slave here. For the past couple of days, he's talked of little else. See you at dinner, pet," he added with markedly less courtesy than he had displayed at first. "Do forgive Nick and me our squabbles. Just a little cousinly conflict."

He left, banging the door behind him.

I was trying not to panic. The trafficking thing freaked me out. Nick was planning to sell me? *I don't speak Turkish, I don't fucking speak Turkish.* Dammit, I almost wished I didn't.

I hoped this was all part of my captor's psyching out of his cousin, but he was so hard to read. I'd always thought I was good at reading people. But I'd made mistakes before.

"You okay?" he asked. I had been kneeling the whole time. He now raised me to my feet.

Was I okay? Not really. I was trying to figure out how I'd be expected to react to the part of the conversation that had been in English. "I don't know what you were saying to each other, but it sounded hostile," I managed.

"We can't stand each other."

"Your cousin has a bit of a Jekyll and Hyde thing going on, doesn't he?"

Nick raised his eyebrows quizzically.

"He was very polite initially, but that changed. Even though I couldn't understand what he was saying, his whole manner shifted when he was speaking to you. It was chilling."

"Kudos to you for seeing through him. Most people don't."

This didn't make me feel better, since Nick had just revealed something equally chilling about himself.

He fondled my hair with the palm of his hand. *Don't touch me,* I wanted to scream, but I bit it back.

"Stay here while I go check in with my grandfather. I'll be back soon."

Don't hurry back on my account. "You don't think he's really found any treasures from Troy, do you?"

Nick ran a hand through his hair and frowned. "Highly unlikely," he muttered as he followed Nigel out of the room.

Alone in the small room, I paced back and forth and brooded. The encounter with Nigel had freaked me out, and not just because of the leashed violence seething between the two cousins. I kept going over everything that Nick had told me about his own involvement in this madness. If he hated his cousin so much, why was he working with him? Why was he sailing around the Aegean instead of being on site at the dig? *Was* he involved in human trafficking? And—I had trouble even formulating this thought—did he really intend to sell me into some horrible human trafficking network?

I knew that my chance of surviving for long in such a situation was low. From what I'd heard about the lives of modern sex slaves, I'd rather be dead.

I had another attack of "this can't be happening to me." How had I ended up with such a threat hanging over me? I was realizing what an easy, sheltered life I'd led so far. My mom and I had never been wealthy, but we hadn't lived in poverty or misery, either. I'd been parked with relatives a lot while Mom was on digs, but I'd also traveled with her to many exotic locations. I'd watched her work. I'd met her friends. My first ever crush had been on a wicked handsome Egyptian boy who had earned a little extra cash by running errands for archaeologists working in an unexplored corner near the Valley of the Kings.

I remembered that golden moment on the shore when I'd conjured up Nick's sailboat like a sorceress bringing forth something from an imagined world. Somehow I'd entered that world, stepping, like Alice through the looking glass, into my own fantasy.

Nick was real, though. He had held me in his arms; I felt his hands explore me, his tongue caress me. I'd known the sweet, erotic pull of his mouth against my breasts. The flash of memory softened my flesh and liquefied my bones. Oh, Nick. Fallen angel, devil, cold stone god. I know you're dangerous. I know you're cruel. I know you're bad for me. Why do you fascinate me so?

Gazing out the square windows at the stark landscape, all rocks and scrub and harsh lines and angles against a cold blue sea, I thought about the twenty-three years that had somehow brought me to this strange point in space and time. My job at the photography studio in Boston, my apartment, Mark...they all seemed so far behind me now.

You wanted adventure, I reminded myself wryly. The gods have answered your prayers, with their usual irony.

Chapter 14

NICK

I had sworn to stay cool around Nigel, but that was impossible.

I wanted to get my hands on his throat. Squeeze the life out the bastard. Carve him up with my knife. Shoot the brains out of his fucking skull.

So much for distracting him with the temptation of joining a human trafficking cabal that traded merchandise like the lovely Ellie. I was ready to murder him just for the crime of imagining how it would be to have her.

Cool it, Gabriel. Don't fuck this up by starting to have emotions.

The plan was in its final stages, the trap was nearly in place. Tension leached into me like a heavy morning fog. One week. That's all the time I had left. By the fifteenth of the month, one week from today, I had to turn Nigel over to the professional agents who were breathing down my neck. If I failed, my aging, crippled grandfather would go to prison for the rest of his life. No matter what the old fool had done, I couldn't let that happen.

"Well, Nick?" said my grandfather when I joined him in his command center. I'd brought him the object that had resulted in Ellie's capture. A Roman statue of a woman, circa second century, C.E., not particularly well-executed but in relatively good condition. If I'd known the trouble the thing would cause, I'd never have sought it out.

"Well, what?"

"You've been gone for over a fortnight. Is this all you have to show for it?"

I ignored this. "What have you found? Nigel thinks it's important."

Granddad leaned forward in his chair. "Are you mad to bring that girl here? I've never known you to do anything so reckless before."

"I know what I'm doing."

"She might be a spy. Or a cop. Someone here to destroy us."

I laughed dryly to cover my guilt. "The only thing she's destroying is my sleep cycle."

"Never before have you allowed your amorous adventures to interfere with our plans. I don't like it."

"She's a superb photographer. She could be useful to us."

"How so?"

"The photographs we've taken so far are terrible." I handed over my camera. I'm good at many things, but photography isn't one of them. "See for yourself. They're poorly lighted. We're not going to make any sales from these."

Granddad flipped through the pictures, which included shots of a number of coins, busts and frescoes. "There are dark shadows on everything."

"I don't know how to light the exhibits. We need a professional to figure out things like that, and now that Mehmet's gone..." Mehmet had been our previous photographer. Unfortunately, he'd also been a drunk, and Nigel had gotten rid of him. I wasn't sure what had happened to the guy, but knowing Nigel, Mehmet was probably deep underwater someplace.

"It's true we could probably get more for the artifacts if we had better photographs," Granddad admitted. "Have you mentioned this to the girl?"

"I wanted to check it out with you first."

"Are you sure she can be trusted?"

"Yes. I've given her reason to fear me. She'll stay in line."

"Is the rumor I'm hearing about her true? She's some sort of sex worker?"

The fuck? "Of course not. Who told you that? My charming cousin?"

"He said you had acquired her as a result of some unsavory dealings you're involved in. I must say, Nick, I never expected such a thing from you."

I felt an absurd desire to defend Ellie's reputation. I suppressed it. "She's my girl. Let's just leave it at that."

"Nigel says—"

I cut him off. "Fuck Nigel."

"He doesn't trust you."

"He hates me. You know that. But because it distorts your old-fashioned ideas about blood being thicker than water, you don't want to admit it."

My grandfather sighed. He did that a lot around me. I'd been exasperating him for years. "I've never understood what happened between you. You were inseparable as boys. It wasn't until you were teenagers that things began to go wrong."

True enough. I had a flash of a happier time, back when I'd looked up to my older cousin. I'd loved him blindly, young fool that I was. Idolized him and tried to copy him. I don't remember exactly when I realized that Nigel was a bully. I'd learned at a young age never to show fear of him, but he specialized in terrorizing other kids. He was subtle about it, though. He liked to win people's trust and admiration before he screwed them to the wall. It amused him, I guess.

When I grew old enough to develop some values of my own, I began to realize my cousin was corrupt. He lied, he stole, he cheated his way through school, doing it all with such charming, open-faced hypocrisy that he never got caught. He wreaked havoc on some of my geekier friends. With each attack or deception, Nigel grew more arrogant. He loved the power he had over people. By the time we were teenagers, I knew he was one sick fuck.

In high school, he raped the girlfriend of my best friend Max, and did it in such a way that Max got all the blame. In college he targeted my girlfriend Elizabeth, lured her away from me and abused her. She never recovered from what he did to her.

"Nigel chose one path, I chose another," I said to my grandfather.

"And yet here you are with a girl you're calling a slave in tow. I guess you've both ended up in the same place, haven't you?"

Well, that pissed me off.

On the other hand, maybe he was right.

I forced myself to focus on Granddad. He looked weary. And old. He was seventy-eight and up to his neck in intrigue. The man had no fucking sense at all. Hadn't it occurred to him that his participation in Nigel's scheme could ruin him? Nigel must have charmed him into believing that together they were invincible. He was good at that kind of shit.

"Tell me what's been happening at the dig. Have you found anything or not?"

The gleam in Granddad's eyes grew brighter. "Look." He rolled his wheelchair over to a metal cabinet and unlocked the door. Carefully he removed a well-wrapped packet and began unfolding the plastic that encased it. Inside was a gold looped earring of ancient design and workmanship.

I must have muttered something under my breath.

"Does it look familiar to you?" Granddad asked.

"It's similar to the stuff Schliemann pulled out of the ruins of Troy."

"Exactly. It's evidence. Strong evidence. Even I didn't expect to find anything as provocative as this."

"Where was it?"

"In the south quadrant of the excavations. At a depth of about fourteen feet. We haven't found anything else there yet, not even potsherds, but we're concentrating all our energy on that spot. I expect we'll turn up something more soon."

Holy shit. If he was right, we could be on the verge of a major find. Dammit. A week from now the island was going to be overrun with Turkish federal agents.

"How soon? I want you out of here."

Granddad noticed my tension. "Why? Have you heard something?"

"No, but I have a bad feeling about this place. Every day we prolong our stay increases the chances of detection. If the Turkish government had any idea what we were up to, they'd be down on us like vultures. Do you still intend to leave before the middle of the month?"

"I hope so. If we're going to find anything more, we should find it soon. The excavations are already quite extensive. If not—well, I don't want to jeopardize our security here on the island." He grimaced. "If nothing else turns up I suppose we'll have to wait until fall and try again. The Aegean is far too busy with tourists wandering about on their yachts now that spring has arrived."

"And Nigel? How much longer will he be staying on?"

"A week to ten days. You and he will have to work together to seal the place up. Is it possible for the two of you to cooperate, or would that be asking too much?"

"I'm sure we'll muddle through somehow."

"Unless you go at each other's throats over the beautiful Ellie."

Fuck that. "I wouldn't worry."

"No? Seems to me it's happened in the past."

He meant Elizabeth.

"Not since university," I said coldly. "And it's damn well never going to happen again."

Chapter 15

ELLIE

Nick was away for a while, and I began to feel uneasy as the sun slid into the water and night stalked the land. I reached for the switch of the overhead light, a naked bulb that hung from a wire in the ceiling of the stark little room. With a flash the bulb blew. Shit. I hoped I wouldn't have another claustrophobia attack. I'd been doing so well lately. Especially considering the circumstances. Never before had I had anything that was *actually* dangerous to worry about.

I dug my hairbrush out of my pack and began to brush my hair vigorously. I'd never really figured out the cause of my panic attacks. This was common, I knew. Most people had no basis in reality for their anxiety, but I suspected mine had come from puttering around in my mother's archeological digs as a child. Once she had taken me inside a small pyramid in Egypt. We'd had to crawl through a hot passageway that smelled of bat guano. This hadn't bothered Mom at all, but it had freaked me out, and I'd finally balked.

To get me out, she'd had to turn around, which is hard to do inside a pyramid. She'd dislodged some dirt and some stone, and part of the passageway had crumbled, briefly separating us. I hadn't been able to see her, and I thought I was trapped, abandoned, left alone. I'd had nightmares about it for weeks, and sometimes even now, I dreamed of being stuck forever in a dark narrow passageway.

The panic attacks had erupted badly towards the end of my college romance with Mark, my only long-term boyfriend. I'd liked Mark, but we had little in common. He was too tidy, too well-organized, too careful to have everything planned out in advance. There was no spontaneity. But he was kind and affectionate toward me, and I'd thought I was in love. He'd never really excited me sexually, though. The things I imagined doing in bed didn't strike a resonant chord with him.

It wasn't until I'd had a couple of sessions with a counselor—at Mark's insistence—that I began to wonder if the attacks might be a warning, a sign from my subconscious that in sticking with Mark, I'd be flying in the face of my own free-spirited nature.

It hadn't been easy to break off with him. He'd been so disbelieving and hurt. And for the first couple of weeks I'd felt so guilty that my attacks had increased. But after a few weeks, my relief had been impossible to deny. I'd flown off on my trip to Europe with freedom singing in my heart. And the claustrophobia retreated into the depths.

Until now.

Maybe it hadn't been Mark at all. Maybe it was men, period. Maybe it was sex. Maybe it had nothing to do with any of these, and was simply a slight imbalance in my brain chemistry.

With nervous fingers, I put down the hairbrush and struggled to light the kerosene lamp I found perched upon the table. I was breaking matches and cursing over the task when Nick returned, entering the room silently and coming up so stealthily behind me that I yelped and nearly dropped the lamp.

"Sorry," he said.

"You scared me. I didn't hear you."

"Let me do that." In seconds, he had the lamp burning. The pungent smell of kerosene filled the air.

"It was getting dark and the overhead light burned out." My voice sounded jumpy, even to myself. "You've been gone for a while. Where were you?"

His eyebrows lifted. "You can't be questioning my fidelity. You're the only woman within 20 miles."

I caught my breath. "Don't taunt me."

Something in his face altered. His hand fell upon my shoulder. It was heavy, hard. "I was joking, slave. You should be naked and kneeling, not questioning where I've been."

"Sorry, I'm edgy." My fists were clenched in tight little balls, but I knelt since he seemed to expect it. I didn't actually mind it too much. It might be perverse as all hell, but I'd grown to like the feeling of his looming over me. I looked up, following his long legs to his crotch, where I could see the fabric tightening as he turned hard. He liked me on my knees, too. The Perversion Twins meet each other and sparks fly.

Do you have any idea the price I can command for a young white female?

"Will you tell me the truth about something?"

He stroked the top of my head, but he looked wary. "The truth about what?"

"You told me Nigel is involved in human trafficking."

"So?"

"He implied today that you were involved in it, too. Something about selling me to one of your sex trafficking friends?"

"He was trying to scare you. That's one of the things he does. He's a bully. He always has been."

"I want to know what you're planning to do with me when this is over."

"If we both get out alive, you'll be free to go."

I knew I was pushing it, but I couldn't stop myself. "You and he were talking about me, weren't you? In Turkish. I could tell by the creepy way he was looking at me. Assessing me. I felt as if I was in an auction and he was bidding."

There was a short silence. Then Nick said slowly, "I told him I was planning to sell you."

I didn't know whether to panic or to be happy that he had just leveled with me. He must have seen the expression on my face, because he added, "But don't worry." His big hands were caressing my hair. "That's not gonna happen."

I didn't know whether or not to believe him. "Why did you say it if it's not true?"

"I want him distracted."

"Distracted." I was the one who was distracted. I couldn't question him further about the things they'd said without betraying my understanding of Turkish.

"Obsessing about things that have nothing to do with what he ought to be thinking about."

"You're using me as bait?"

That cold look had come down over his features again. I hated it when he did that. I'd seen it often enough to know that it meant I wouldn't get any more answers out of him right now. "I'm sure this is difficult, but you're going to have to trust me. Believe it or not, there is a plan."

"It better be a good plan," I growled.

He shrugged. "It's not a great plan, but it's the only one I've got."

"Can't you tell me the plan? So I don't go blundering about, maybe ruining it by accident?"

"Turning you into a docile and obedient slave was supposed to prevent your blundering about."

In that quick, unexpected way of his, his hands shot out and fastened on my upper arms. He pulled me to my feet and backed me toward the nearest wall. He pressed me against it. One of his hands fisted my hair. My scalp burned as he tilted my head back, and, gods forgive me, that burn sent a shaft of excitement shooting right down to my sex. Intimate little muscles clenched in pleasure. I was starting to get off on his rough treatment. I was starting to want it.

In the dusky light from the hurricane lamp, his face was shadowed, accentuating the harsh lines of his cheekbones, the blatant sensuality of his mouth. I liked his fluid grace; I was drawn by the sight of him, the scent of him, the hard male strength of his muscles, even the rough texture of his work shirt and jeans.

It swept through me again—that same powerful yearning I'd experienced last night. Without thinking, I lifted my fingers to his face and touched his cheek. It was sand-papery with his evening growth of beard.

Something blazed in those green eyes, and he reached up and caught my wrist in a grip that bordered on pain. "Don't do that. If you touch me again, that'll be it. I'll take you right here against the wall."

I could feel my cheeks growing hot.

"I'm trying to keep my promise, but I don't need the provocation of you stroking my body."

I twisted against him, hating that it was so hard to prevent myself from just melting into goo. "You're the one who keeps grabbing me."

He released me and I fled to the open window, letting the evening breezes soothe my burning cheeks. But the room was small, and I could sense the heat of his flesh just inches away. I knew that if I so much as hinted that I was willing, he would carry out his threat. I was willing. I wanted him. I wanted this lean, lovely man to lie down with me and fuck me until I screamed for mercy.

"Ellie." His tone was low and hoarse, but even his voice drew me. "I'm not myself around you."

I felt compelled by the raw feeling in him, the emotional force he was usually so successful at concealing. "Who are you, then?"

"I don't fucking know. Someone dark. Someone I hardly recognize."

I turned back to the window, squeezing my eyes shut. I heard his step behind me. I felt his warm hands slide once again over my shoulders. He pulled me back against his body; his arms moved down and encircled my waist.

His hands slipped down and clamped onto my hipbones, pulling my ass more firmly against his pelvis. Oh shit. He surged against me, hard as iron, his arousal blatant and so damn tempting. I thought about dropping down, as he so frequently ordered, and taking him out. Rolling my tongue over the head. Sliding my lips along the length. Sucking him hard. My pussy muscles tightened and pulsed and I had to swallow a moan.

He turned me on so much. Damn, I hated the way he turned me on.

"It *is* going to happen," he said. "You know that, don't you? We can postpone it, maybe, but that will only make the obsession grow. It'll build and build until we can't control it anymore."

I shivered, lost in my desire for the man who had kidnapped me. I wasn't even asking myself anymore what was wrong with me for wanting him. I just wanted. Needed. It was becoming unendurable.

"It's time for dinner," he said, breaking the spell. "They'll all be there, drinking raki and getting rowdy, but we've got to face them." He paused, taking my chin in his hand. "Don't let me down. Do you have a dress you can wear?"

"Wow, you mean you're going to let me wear clothes? I have a dress, yes."

"Put it on." He brushed back the hair that was framing my face. To my surprise, he ran a long lock of it through his fingers, brought it to his lips, and kissed it. "I love your hair. And I want to show you off."

I swallowed. He loved my hair? That made me all feel all melty. "What about this thing?" I indicated the rope collar around my neck.

"That always stays on, slave."

Chapter 16

ELLIE

A little later, dressed in a silky dress made of synthetic fabric that traveled well in my backpack and a pair of sandals, I accompanied Nick downstairs to dinner. As we walked, he kept his hand locked around my wrist like a manacle.

Sir Avery and his henchmen ate in a large central room that was smoky, windowless and dark. It reminded me of the great hall of some medieval keep.

There must have been a generator somewhere on the grounds to produce electricity for cooking and lights, but the wattage in the room was low. I noticed that the dark encouraged the men's stares. My dress was flattering, revealing my slim legs and nipping in about the waist to lend my hips a flare that wasn't entirely natural. It didn't do much for my small breasts, but the neckline was flattering, and sweeping my hair up into a knot had given me a little extra height. It also revealed the rope collar circling my throat, which the males in the gathering eyed with dark interest.

I felt uncomfortable. I was content to stay close to Nick. His warnings about my being the only female among a group of men had just been words on the yacht, but now I sensed the testosterone simmering as they stared at me. There must have been close to twenty guys in the room. The only friendly face I saw was Metin, who sent me an encouraging grin. He was seated near the other end of the long table, though, so I couldn't talk to him. The rest of the men lounged around, smoking cigarettes and drinking raki, the powerful, anisette-flavored liquor favored all over the Mediterranean region. The more they drank the noisier they became. They also got braver about gawking at me. I kept my eyes down. No one actually touched me, and I kept pretending to understand no Turkish, although some of the muttered comments made me flush.

At least the food was good. "Who's the cook?" I asked Nick's grandfather, who was seated near me in his wheelchair. The broiled fish, served with its head and tail intact, one dead eye staring opaquely, was tender and fresh. I tried the grape-leaf dolmas, filled with a succulent mixture of rice, currants, pine nuts and mint, and the *barbunya* beans in olive oil. These, too, were delicious.

"Mustafa," Sir Avery answered, nodding to a burly, grinning man who was sitting on the other side of the table. "In the beginning everyone took turns, but that was a disaster. Mustafa lost his wife years ago and has been making do for himself ever since. He enjoyed his food, so he was forced to learn to cook."

"Now that your girl is here, *she* can cook," someone else suggested.

"I don't think so," Nick said easily. "I doubt she can equal Mustafa's culinary skills."

"What's the matter, doesn't she fill your belly with tasty deli-
cacies, Nicholas *bey*?" someone else shouted. "Or are you and
she too busy tasting life's other pleasures in bed?"

"None of your business, Ahmet," Nick retorted to the skinny
young man who'd produced the taunt. He went on to joke with
them, while I strove to maintain the quizzical expression of one
who doesn't understand what is being said. Nick translated none
of this, showing no special consideration to his "slave." At least
he didn't make me kneel at his feet, which I had half-expected.
He drank raki with the rest of them and laughed at their increasingly coarse and suggestive remarks.

I was introduced to several of the other men who were sitting
around Sir Avery and seemed to be particular friends of his.
Erdal, a strong but scholarly-looking man who had apparently
worked with Nick's grandfather for years; Aslan, whose name
meant lion, which seemed appropriate, since he had long hair
and a thick reddish beard that made him resemble one; and
Engin, a pleasant-faced young man in his twenties who knew
some English and seemed eager to practice it with me.

I avoided engaging the six men at the far end of the table.
"They're Nigel's crew," Nick told me under his breath. They
gave me sinister stares and did not speak to me.

I could tell Sir Avery's men were fond of Nick. My captor was
not as expansive and charming as the always smiling, always
hearty Nigel, but he was warm to the men, and he took their
teasing with good grace. Why not? He was one of them. A
smuggler, a crook. I wondered if they knew he'd once been a
teacher of Latin and ancient Greek. I tried in vain to mesh that
image with the sight of him, slouched and whiskery, downing

milky-white raki while he sucked on a pungent-smelling Turk-ish cigarette.

The more Nick joked with his friends, the more Nigel tried to single me out. As the meal finished and fruit was served, people stood up, moved around, changed places at the table, and Nigel had moved closer to me. Keeping my eyes down so I didn't have to see the lust blazing in his, I pretended to be awed and tongue-tied so I could duck most of his questions.

The raki had the most noticeable effect on Sir Avery, who became more talkative. "Did my grandson explain to you about my difficulties with the government of Turkey?" Sir Avery asked me, sounding peevish.

"No, sir, he didn't."

"Some years ago they accused me of removing objects from a site near Izmir. It was not true. I had never dreamed of doing such a thing—then." He paused and I noted the ripples of un-ease that crossed his face. "I didn't need to. I had an adequate income and the means to pursue my research. I also had the use of my legs. But now, as a result of my unfortunate accident, I can no longer be much use at my own excavations." He glared down at the blanket that covered his legs. His wheelchair had been brought to the table, but it didn't look too comfortable. "The good Lord played a rare trick on me when he didn't allow me to die in that cave-in."

I shuddered. I couldn't think of anything more horrible than dying in a cave-in.

Except being alive in a cave-in and waiting to die.

Sir Avery adjusted the hearing aid as he continued, "Despite my misfortunes, my enemies continued to hound me. They threatened my reputation. They told lies about me. Soon the grant money began to dry up." He sounded bitter. "Despite my decades of scholarship, I had no income. I have given much to the science of archaeology over the years, but what have I received in return besides criticism and neglect? Why should the work I have supported all these years not support me in return?"

This was his justification for his current activities. I didn't dare argue. Again, I found it convenient to stare submissively at the floor.

"It gives me no pleasure that I won't be able to report my find if the treasures of Troy *do* turn up here on the island. If I were to claim the fame that should be my due, I would be detained for excavating in Turkey without the necessary permits. I'm far too old and unwell to spend my twilight years in a Turkish prison."

"That would be horrible," I agreed.

"Be careful what you say," Nigel said to his grandfather in Turkish. "You talk too much."

"Nonsense," said Sir Avery in the same language. "Have some raki, my dear," he invited. Over my protests, he poured me a glass, adding three ice cubes, which made the clear liquid turn white. "And forgive my lapses into a foreign tongue. I've spent so many years here. My second wife was a Turk—did you know that? Our daughter—Nick's mother, that is—spoke Turkish as her mother tongue and learned no English until she was in school. She taught Turkish to Nick when he was a child."

With that, he wandered off onto the subject of the family history. I wasn't averse to hearing it. With Nigel riding shotgun on Sir Avery, I didn't dare offer any opinions about the treasures of Troy.

Sir Avery had been married twice, first to an Englishwoman, who had divorced him after bearing one son, and then to his Turkish wife, who had lived with him until her death a number of years ago. Nigel was the child of Sir Avery's British son, Nick the child of Sir Avery's half-Turkish daughter. Nick and Nigel were only half-cousins, I realized. But they'd been raised as brothers, shuttling back and forth between archaeological digs in the Mediterranean and private schools in England and the States after the deaths of all four of their parents in a plane crash in Brazil.

"Poor orphan lads, I didn't know what to do with them," said Sir Avery. "Nigel was twelve, Nick only ten. I'm afraid I didn't do a very good job bringing them up."

I refrained from commenting. Nick had switched seats to chat with Metin and some other guys. Maybe he figured his grandfather would watch over me.

"Nick was clever. He managed to acquire a fine education," Sir Avery went on. "As for Nigel, he doesn't have all the fancy academic credentials, but that's never prevented him from getting ahead in life, has it, my boy?"

"I have my business. I don't need degrees," Nigel agreed.

"What is your business, sir?" I asked.

"I'm an international art broker."

How convenient.

"Nick wanted to be an archaeologist like me," his grandfather continued. "As a child that's all he ever talked about. He had talent, too, and far more patience than Nigel. That's what it requires, you know, endless patience and persistence. Good instincts, too, of course."

"What happened to make him change his mind?"

Sir Avery looked puzzled. "He didn't change his mind. He's quite well known in his field." I must have looked surprised, because Sir Avery smiled and nodded. "He hasn't told you? He's never been one to toot his own horn. He's a highly skilled translator of ancient texts. That's his specialty. It would be difficult to find an ancient script that Nick is unfamiliar with. I was never good at that sort of thing myself."

I tried to factor this information in with what I already knew about Nick. His scholarly resume kept getting longer.

"Ellie."

Maybe his "training" had worked, because the sound of Nick's voice in my ear caused my entire body to leap to attention. He was standing behind my chair. When he placed his warm hands on my shoulders, his touch set off a riot of sparkles along my nerves. I tried to counter it with a large sip of raki, but I could still feel desire burning me all the way down to my bones.

Nick raised a glass to me. *"Sherefe, hayatim,"* he said, Turkish for cheers.

"Sherefe," I repeated, mangling the accent. *Hayatim*? That was an endearment. He must be drunk.

The rest of the evening passed in a haze. I gulped raki, which helped to push away my fear and confusion. When the fruit was eaten, the men moved the table aside. Out of the shadows appeared a tabor, then someone produced an oud, and a third man came out with an ancient violin. They began to play, not well or tunefully, but with great enthusiasm. As the music swelled, several of the workers got up and began to dance.

"Come, Nicholas *bey,* join us," someone shouted.

Nick rose. Someone handed him a battered wooden instrument—a crude flute. He played upon it while weaving in and out of the line of dancers, moving to the music of Turkish folk dances he'd probably been taught in his youth. The instrument was a poor one, but he seemed to take pride in making it sing. I watched, transfixed. There was a kind of magic in him.

He danced, whirling, one with the music, one with the night. As I watched him, my mind also whirled. His beauty assaulted me, spearing me like jagged lightning. With that nimbus of gold around his head and those long, tan supple limbs, there was none to touch him for pure masculine grace.

Like Pan now, not Apollo, his piping summoned me to join the revels, share the dance. My raki was finished, my head was light and my blood throbbing in my veins. I put down my glass and was moving toward the charmed circle when I felt the weight of Nigel's hand on my shoulder. He was not gentle. I shuddered as I felt his fingertips dig into the flesh of my shoulder. "He neglects you," his suave voice murmured near my ear. "Leave him and come with me."

He probably believed his voice was seductive, but to me it sounded sinister. He was probably thinking about my anal virginity! "You hate your cousin, don't you?"

"How I feel about him has nothing to do with this," he assured me, smiling in that weird-ass kindly manner of his. I noticed that he, too, had dressed for dinner. He was wearing different clothes, including a different white shirt and even a dinner jacket. Different shoes, too—even more stylish than the ones he'd been wearing a few hours before. There was a thick gold ring on one of his fingers and an expensive watch on his wrist. "But I might be able to offer you a pleasanter and more opulent life than he can."

"How extraordinarily kind of you," I said, not even trying to disguise my sarcasm. "But I have zero interest in ever becoming your fuck toy."

His handsome face darkened. I'd made a mistake. I'd just broken the docile submissive code of behavior. Damn my wayward tongue! And damn the raki—I'd drunk too much of the stuff.

"I see." His strong, tan face was thoughtful, predatory. The hand on my shoulder moved to my hair. With a jerk, he grabbed the knot of hair at the back of my neck and pulled on it until my scalp stung. Most of my hair slipped free of the knot and tumbled to my shoulders, where he caressed it as if he had a right to do so. I wanted to pull away, or maybe slap him, but Nick's warnings restrained me. I was playing the role of a slave, and slaves didn't stand up to assholes like Nigel.

"Maybe Nicholas will tire of you. I hope I'm around when he does. You need to be taught some manners."

Burn in hell, asswipe.

Avoiding his gaze, I turned my head just in time to catch Nick's eye across the smoky room. He must have noticed that Nigel had his hand on me. He laid aside his flute and left the dance, moving swiftly to my side. I watched him come, exulting in his easy stride, which was unimpaired by all the raki he'd consumed.

He stopped beside me, not yet touching me, but claiming me so obviously that Nigel's features dissolved into a scowl. "Trying to move in, are you?" Nick's words came out in a drawl, but there was a biting undertone.

"Your redheaded slave is disrespectful," Nigel said. "Either devote more time to her training, or turn her over to someone with a firmer hand."

Nick smiled an indulgent smile at his cousin, but I saw something flash in his eyes that warned me. "On your knees, slave," he ordered, and the reflex he had painstakingly planted in me kicked in. I dropped to the floor, not even thinking how ridiculous I must look. Nick's hand moved into my hair, which was falling down my back now that Nigel had pulled it loose. "Were you disrespectful to my cousin, girl?"

"I was rude, Master."

"Prostrate yourself before him and apologize."

What? No way. If he thought....The fingers in my hair wound a little tighter. From the hush that had fallen over the room, I knew everybody was watching. And listening, no doubt.

Swallow your protests even if I tell you to do something you hate. This will be tested, you can count on it.

Okay. I could do this. I swiveled in the direction of Nigel, who was facing off against Nick. I leaned forward. I could see his beautiful and no doubt expensive shoes under his perfectly-pressed trousers. I bowed my head toward the freaking shoes. When I didn't bow low enough, I was mortified to feel Nick's much less elegant work boot settle on my back and press me down to the floor. "My humble apologies, sir," I said, trying hard not to sound sarcastic. Let's face it, I didn't do humble well, but, on the other hand, it was hard to sound anything else but humble when your face is pressed to the floor.

"Very pretty," said Nigel. "But I'm afraid that's not good enough. I want more than an apology. Order her to give me a blowjob."

My stomach rose at the thought. There was a moment of silence, and I felt even sicker. Nick wouldn't give such an order, would he? I hadn't even given *him* a blowjob yet.

But I didn't know the rules for this master/slave shit. Could one guy demand that another deal out a punishment of that sort? Dammit, I'd been a fool. Nick had told me I had to stay submissive, but I'd snarled at Nigel the first chance I'd got.

It struck me as I crouched on the floor that I actually wanted to practice my cock-sucking techniques on Nick. I hadn't yet seen his cock, but I was sure it would be nice. *He* was my master, not the odious Nigel....

"The only person who touches my slave sexually is me," Nick said in his usual cold voice.

"Whip her, then. She needs discipline. I'll even provide my belt for the purpose. What an amusing spectacle it will be for our workers."

Nigel was enjoying this. I suspected he cared a lot less about disciplining me than embarrassing Nick. But Nick kept his cool. He removed his foot from my back and fisted a hunk of my loose hair. "If I punish her, it'll be in private. You may rise, slave."

It probably looked as if he was dragging me to my feet, but it didn't feel that way. He helped me. The room was swaying a bit, which was probably the result of my drinking too much raki. I'd never been much of a drinker. His arm went around my waist and he pulled me close.

"I didn't agree to a private punishment," Nigel said nastily.

"Tough," Nick retorted. "Get your own slave if you want to have a say in such matters." He smiled benevolently at the group of avid spectators, then seized my wrist and pulled me back into the area where the men had been dancing. "Come, my girl. I'm going to teach you to dance with all the joy of a Turkish nomad who has wandered for centuries on the steppes of Asia."

Chapter 17

ELLIE

As he led me to the dance area, Nick bent his head and whispered, "I will punish you, too, for being such an idiot."

"Sorry," I whispered back. "Thanks for not letting him hurt me."

He gave me one of the first genuinely warm smiles I'd ever seen from him. "I'll never let him hurt you."

That helped a lot. I still didn't know what game he was playing with his revolting cousin, but I guess I would take his word for it that there was a point to this masquerade. Oh, he had me under his spell, that much was true. I didn't have much choice but to play along. But his smile and the dance helped temper my humiliation at having been forced to scrape the floor and apologize to the detestable Nigel.

Nick taught me the ancient rhythmic steps and movements. They were lazy and sensual, the beat of the music a quiet throbbing that escalated as we whirled around and around. It was hypnotic, relaxing. In a chain we danced, linking hands, a group of bandits, a golden god and a woman, all charmed into an acceptance of one another. The dance made us equal, the dance made partners of us all. In and out of the smoke and the shadows we glided, repeating the steps over and over while the tabor pounded, the oud twanged and the violin crooned.

I felt a slow sweat flower on my skin. My heart beat thickly; my red hair, now loose, swirled around my shoulders. The music intensified. The line broke and the dancers performed singly, not touching, but side by side. The steps no longer mattered as the drum sounds rose and quickened. I knew only that I had to keep my body moving in rhythm with the music, that it was a joy to do so. In the dance I forgot my doubts, my fears, my very self.

Then Nick held me and my spirit took flight. In the ecstasy of the dance, he and I were one. I was gone from my body, gone from the room, lost in a place of unearthly splendor. I whirled there joyously, but it wasn't until Nick's hands cupped my cheeks that I knew.

I had danced with him before, time out of mind.

He was my fantasy lover, my mate.

He was beautiful.

And he was perfect. Like an ancient alchemist, I knew the gold from the dross. He was gold, pure as fire. Together nothing could stop us; we completed each other; we were one flesh, one soul.

Total bullshit, I know. I was in a raki-inspired wonderland.

"Nick?"

His sculpted face leaned closer; he brushed his mouth across mine. I gasped and parted my lips. I felt the erotic invasion of his tongue.

I heard voices laughing, and shouting encouragement as Nick's hands slid around my waist and drew me against his sweat-damp body. I felt his hard chest, his lithe and supple thighs, and the contact was sweet-sharp pleasure. Still moving to the music, he swayed his hips in sinuous half circles against mine while I slid my fingers into his gilt waves, holding his head still for my kiss.

The shouting, the laughter grew louder, closer. Others had stopped their own dancing to watch us. Nick murmured as he accepted the kiss, "My girl, I believe you're drunk."

I blinked and smiled at him, drunk on desire. Or raki. Or both. "Am I?"

"Assuredly. Hang on." Shifting his weight, he scooped me up in his arms. There came more laughter, more shouts, all unintelligible sounding—my ability to translate from Turkish to English seemed to have disappeared. Someone, I thought, was having a very good time.

"What are you doing?" I asked as Nick strode through the smoky room, hardly seeming bothered by my weight in his arms. One of my shoes fell off and I wriggled my bare toes at Metin as we passed. He smiled to me and waved.

"Taking you to bed."

The shouts and laughter faded as he carried me down a low, dark corridor, up a flight of stairs and into our room. He slammed the door and turned the key. The room was dark and silent, lighted only by the silvery gleam of a half-moon. Nick moved directly to the mattress on the floor and, dropping to his knees, lowered me upon it.

Keeping my arms around his neck, I pressed my face against his throat and inhaled the musky scent of him. "Are you coming, too?"

His chest heaved with a tight laugh. "Yes, I'm coming."

"Okay," I whispered. I released him, letting my body sink into the mattress. "I was afraid you were going to leave me alone in the dark."

"No," he said.

"Nick? Don't ever leave me alone in the dark."

Nick bent over and kissed my forehead. "I won't, *hayatim.* I promise."

Content, I closed my eyes. I felt him sliding my dress up my thighs to my waist, his hands warm and knowledgeable against my bare belly. I arched to help him pull the dress over my head. I felt no embarrassment or shame. I wanted him to look at me.

He didn't touch my bikini panties or my bra. He left me for a moment, then returned. I opened my eyes a crack.

"I want you," I whispered. I pushed myself back up to a sitting position and pressed my head against his thighs. I felt a little dizzy, but it wasn't too bad. I knew what I needed to do. I think I'd needed it since the day we'd met.

I reached for his zipper and pulled it down. It wasn't easy, because his cock was hugely swollen beneath my fingers, making his jeans tighter than they were meant to be. When I pried apart the snap at the top, his beautiful penis lunged out at me, and I giggled. He was going commando—no underwear.

I slid my fist around it and pumped a couple times, then sucked the head into my mouth. He sighed and grabbed my hair, pulling a little. I didn't mind. I guess I just like it rough.

Which was good, because he surged into me, driving his hips into my face until I gasped for breath. It took me a few moments to catch his rhythm, but I'd always liked giving head and he tasted delicious to me. I made my lips as round and smooth as I could and sucked on him hard. When he withdrew, I used my tongue on the rim and the underside, and then opened wider for him as he pushed into me repeatedly. I dug my nails into his butt with one hand, and sought his balls with the other.

God, I was thirsty for him. I don't know why I wanted it so much, but I did. The more I sucked his penis, the more I wanted it in my pussy, which was now drenched and aching for him. He sped up, and I was afraid he'd come and that would be the end of it, the way it always had been with Mark.

But he groaned and pulled out. I tried to take him again, but he laughed and forced me flat on the mattress. He made short work of my underwear. Pressing my legs apart with his hips, he slid down and spread them even wider with his hands on my inner thighs. "Keep your legs apart for me, slave," he ordered. "I want to fuck you with my tongue."

I almost came. He made it sound so deliciously sexy. As his mouth moved over my sex, my hips arched up invitingly. I was burning down there. Lost in the ache of passion, wet and ready for him. He nuzzled gently at first, exploring my labia and delving in between. "God, you're so wet for me," he murmured as his tongue stabbed into me.

I gasped and arched even higher. I'd never had a boyfriend who really enjoyed giving oral, but Nick clearly did. Nothing had ever felt as good as what he was doing to me now. My head buzzed, my muscles flexed, crooning sounds emerged from my throat. When he moved the tip of his tongue to my clit, I think I screamed his name. A finger slid into my pussy and fucked me hard while his tongue kept rubbing and sucking at my clit, and pleasure boiled over, gushing from my core and melting my limbs right down to my fingers and toes.

I was still in the throes of my climax when he left me for a second. He was back quickly, tearing something apart, and I realized it was a condom. I watched, still writhing with the final pulses of climax as he rolled it on his beautiful cock. That was going inside me. I reached for him, wanting it. I was lost in the dreamy feeling that this was right and that everything was just as it should be.

NICK

The floor rolled a little as I struggled with the condom, and I thought, damn this boat before I remembered we weren't on the fucking boat. Too much raki. Ellie was flying on the stuff, and I was none too sober either. Which probably meant I shouldn't be doing what I was about to do.

I hadn't intended it. The gods knew I'd been trying my best not to force myself on Ellie. She was so damn vulnerable, so brave, so alone. She was turning to me tonight only because she was besieged and desperate and there wasn't anybody else.

But her body was sweet and slender, and I needed her so much. She'd danced like a Gypsy princess, all proud and loose and limber, her wild fiery hair whipping the air around her as she twirled. She was passionate, a wavering flame that could easily ignite into brilliant, fervent fire. And she'd just exploded, keening out her pleasure in a voice that had just about melted my heart. It delighted me that I could show her that not all our interactions had to be crude or rough.

Images of the crude and rough things I yearned to do to her surfaced. Bind her, spread her wide, tease her until she begged for release. Spank her. Whip her. Force her to gratify every dark desire I had ever fantasized about. I clenched my fingers into fists, resisting those shadowy impulses. I'd never had trouble controlling myself before, but for some reason Ellie turned me into a hound yanking at an ever-tightening chain.

Her eyes were closed once again, accepting, trusting. She must be amazingly sweet-natured or she'd never have accepted me after all the shit I'd put her through. I gathered myself, all my discipline, all my self-control, trying to resist the urge to fall on her and bury my cock just as deep as it would go. Deeper. I wanted to plow her, ravage her, fuck her insensible. Her soft lips curved in a tantalizing smile, and fuck, I was so lost. I was going to take her despite my qualms. She'd probably hate me in the morning when the raki had cleared her system. I might even hate myself, but right now I didn't care. Let me have the night, then let the morning come and do its worst.

I slid naked into bed beside her. As I threw my thigh over her legs, I reveled in the smooth, silky feel of her bare skin against mine. Oh, God, she was sweet. Small, slim, light boned and lovely. She smelled like summer. Her fragrant hair was like wine.

Impatient, I stroked her breasts. Beneath my fingers, her skin felt warm and smooth, but she didn't stir as I caressed her.

"Ellie?"

No reply. Her chest moved slowly up and down with her breath.

"Ellie?" I groaned, realizing that her climax and the alcohol combined had sent her plunging into sleep.

Fuck! I could probably wake her, but damn, look at me. Condom on and ready to go. It was fucking hilarious. What the hell was happening to me? I knew myself for a worshiper of mind, of intellect, yet here I was, just as much as any other man, held in thrall to the demands of my unruly flesh. With Ellie, especially. She drove me nuts.

What *was* it about her? I couldn't recall ever having felt like this.

Oh, Ellie. Asleep. Why did I let her drink so much raki? Why had I swallowed so much myself? And why the fuck had I stopped her when she was giving me one helluva great blowjob? I should have just let myself come in her mouth.

I rolled off her, ripped off the condom and tossed it on the floor. Then I stroked myself with my trusty right hand, because there was no way I was falling asleep beside her with a hard-on this fierce. She didn't wake as I desperately got myself off. Not even my loud groan as I came made her stir. Damn. It was better than nothing, but it wasn't what I wanted. Even after I was empty, the feel of her beside me started stoking me right back up again.

Curling myself around her, I began conjugating Latin verbs—the least erotic pastime I could imagine. *Amo, amas, amat,* I muttered over and over until sleep came at last to end my torment.

Chapter 18

ELLIE

I awoke with a start, vaguely aware that something was wrong. I felt cold. Rolling more snugly into the blanket, I opened my eyes and gazed around the bare room. I could tell from the amount of light coming through the window that it was early morning. Nick, with his back to me, was just stepping into his jeans. I got a yummy flash of naked limbs before the blasted clothing covered his legs and ass.

Evidently, he had just left the bed. The sheets were still warm from his body. I was cold because he was no longer there beside me.

Nick zipped his jeans and snapped them, then, still shirtless, he dropped to the floor and did a series of push-ups. I blinked at the sight of the powerful muscles in his arms flexing as they absorbed his weight. He obviously had no idea I was awake. He worked out hard and fast, doing press after press, until droplets of sweat shone on his back.

He rolled over and did a bunch of sit-ups, hands behind his head. Then he raised his legs and bicycled. I was leaning on my elbow, watching and enjoying as he sprang to his feet and began punching the air and moving in a silent martial arts drill. His face had grown intent, his dancelike movements clean and graceful, his concentration complete.

I tried to recall the feel of that strong, lithe body covering me, separating my thighs, holding me still and thrusting inside. Had it happened? Surely not. I remembered drinking; I remembered dancing; I remembered his carrying me back to this room. I remembered the thrill of his cock filling my mouth, and the intense pleasure of his fingers and tongue on my sex. I remembered a powerful, mind-spinning orgasm. But after that? Shit, I didn't know what had happened next.

"Nick?"

He broke off in the middle of a stylized lunge and turned to face me. He was breathing rapidly from the exercise, but he had no difficulty talking. "You're awake? After last night, I figured you'd sleep till noon."

I groaned and massaged my aching head with my palm. "What happened last night?"

"You mean you don't know?"

"Um, not entirely. Did we, you know..."

"Did we fuck?" Nick pushed a floppy lock of sweat-drenched hair out of his eyes and hunkered down beside me. He bent over and kissed me lightly on the side of one cheek. "For shame. I exert myself all night on your behalf, going page by page through the *Kama Sutra*, and it makes no impression upon you at all?"

I laughed. "I'm sure I'd have remembered *that.*" A vague image of him wearing a condom came back to me, and I winced because that was as far as my memories seemed to stretch.

"But you don't? Ha. I'm insulted."

I noted the merriment in his sea-green eyes. It was so unusual to see such a thing in him that I wondered if I had wandered into Bizarro World. I reached under the sheets to feel myself down there. If we'd fucked all night, I'd have been a bit sore, surely. "Did I fall asleep on you?"

He sighed, his gold-dusted chest fascinating me. "You had a massive orgasm and fell unconscious. We slept together as chastely as if we'd taken holy vows. Just imagine how pissed you'd be if our roles had been reversed."

"Oops. Sorry. And you didn't..." My question trailed off as his merriment was replaced with a look of irritation.

"No. Unconscious is not willing."

I didn't know how to respond to that. For an amoral criminal, he was surprisingly faithful to the promise he had made to me.

"It's pouring rain," he said, opening the shutter on the window. "I was going to take you to the excavation site, but it's a bit of a hike. I'm going to go myself, though. I want to see exactly what the crew has discovered in the way of 'Trojan treasures,' and where they're finding the stuff."

I did my best to cope with the change in mood and subject. If he'd wanted it, I would have let him join me in bed now. But it didn't sound as if he cared much about the pleasure he'd missed. What a contradictory man he was! "You sound more skeptical today, as if you're in doubt about the find."

"One gold earring doesn't prove much. It may have come here through other means entirely." After a moment, he added,

"I'll leave you with my grandfather, if you think you can handle that."

I wasn't thrilled with the prospect. After discovering Nigel's two-faced nature, I wasn't sure how I felt about Sir Avery. His attempt last night to justify himself hadn't succeeded. I felt sorry for his straitened circumstances, yes, but surely that was no excuse for thievery. "I thought I wasn't safe without you nearby to protect me."

"My claim on you has been clearly established, I think, after last night. No one'll dare molest you."

"Not even Nigel?"

"Nigel will be with me," he said grimly. "Do you play chess? My grandfather loves to play."

"I'm not that good, but, sure, I can probably give him a game."

He smiled the sweet and sunny smile that was so rare—and thus so devastating. "O, thou fair Helen, that can tempt me with thy beauty and thy wit."

I flushed. "What's that from, professor?"

"I made it up," he said, pulling on his shirt.

"So you're a poet, too, as well as a crook?"

He snorted.

Tilting my head to one side, I said, "You're a puzzle. You translate ancient texts, you steal, you read Homer, and you knock people unconscious with a flick of your wrists. You're a versatile dude. Will you play your flute for me sometime?"

He raised his eyes from his buttons to stare at me. "How do you know about that?"

"You played upon Pan's pipes last night, remember?"

"Yeah, and you must have found my flute when you searched my drawers. Looking to understand me."

"But I still don't understand you at all."

He grimaced. "Why don't we keep it that way?"

He finished dressing and left me alone in the room.

Chapter 19

ELLIE

I played three games of chess with Sir Avery and beat him once, which seemed to gratify the old man. "It's rare that I find a woman who can defeat me at chess, my dear," he told me, grinning as he turned over his king. "No wonder Nick's fond of you. Do you beat him too?"

"We've never played."

"He's good. Taught the lad myself. He's patient, you see, and able to plot his moves out well in advance. Nigel was too reckless to play well, especially against careful, plodding Nicholas-of-the-poker-face. When it was obvious he was losing, Nigel would upset the board and stalk away. He could never stand to be bested by Nick."

"Did Nick best him often?"

"At some things—studies, mostly, or music."

"Does he play other instruments besides the flute?"

"Yes, several. Damn well, too. Nigel always made fun of his playing the flute."

More reasons to despise Nigel. "Did that bother Nick?"

"Hard to tell. You never know with Nick, do you?" He stared at me for a moment in silence, and then continued, "Nigel was better at sports. He was bigger and brawnier. He could batter Nick if he wanted to, and did. Nigel has a temper. So does Nick, when he's pushed. But whenever they'd descend to physical blows, Nigel would emerge the victor."

I doubted that would still be the case. Was being battered by Nigel the reason Nick had taken up hand-to-hand combat? I envisioned the grace of his practice session this morning. Was Nigel aware of his cousin's finely honed skill? I fiercely hoped not.

"Tell me more about Nick's childhood," I urged him. "It's not easy prying information out of him."

Sir Avery was not averse. The picture he painted was of a bright and perhaps too-sensitive boy who had grown up in the shadow of his more outgoing older cousin. "Nick's always been a bit of a mystery, my dear. Self-contained and intense. You never really know what he's thinking, do you?" Here a shadow seemed to pass over the old man's face. "You never really know how he feels."

It struck me that Sir Avery loved his younger grandson, but wasn't confident that the feeling was returned. I reached out and touched his hand. He smiled and patted my wrist. "No doubt he's the same with you, eh? Not overly affectionate, that's our Nick. Yet he's very taken with you, Ellie. That was evident when you danced. Maybe you didn't notice how everything in the room came to a standstill. Watching you, we were all transfixed.

It was as if you and he were the axis upon which the whole world spun."

"Whoa!" I interrupted, embarrassed.

"I know, I know, I'm being silly. But it was remarkable. Nobody's ever seen Nick behave like that."

It hadn't been normal behavior for me, either. Nothing in my life had been normal since he and I met.

"Oh, to be young and in love," said Sir Avery.

Ha! As if I would ever fall in love with a criminal.

Sex, on the other hand...he was smokin' hot and my hormones, at least, were in love.

Later in the day, Sir Avery asked me about my photography. I was taken aback when his questions grew technical, asking how I would light an archaeological exhibit to get the sharpest and most colorful close-ups.

"Why?" I asked. "Were you thinking of offering me a job?"

To my dismay, he nodded. "Our photographer had to leave the island. We could use a replacement. Do you have your equipment with you?"

"Not exactly. That is, it's on Nick's boat."

"Excellent. Let me tell you what we need."

Shit. The last thing I wished to do was take photographs for a bunch of crooks. I didn't want to help them in any way. But I had to listen and pretend to be enthusiastic while Sir Avery explained his plan for disposing of the stolen objects that they'd had been scavenging from the Aegean coast of Turkey.

"We'll be removing them, slowly, one by one, over the next year or two," he explained. "Most items are small—coins and potsherds and such—but there are also some larger pieces. These will be more difficult to export."

"I see." Nobody wanted to get caught with the loot.

"The objects must be properly photographed. It will make it easier for us to sell them. The pictures should be of the highest quality."

"So you can command the highest price."

"We did try to take some shots, but they didn't come out well. Nick says it's something to do with the lighting. Does that make sense to you?"

"Well, yes. Lighting is important."

"Here, have a look." He handed me several prints.

I flipped through them. "Who took these?"

"Nick."

Well, well. Versatile though he was, I'd finally found an area where his talent was lacking. The pictures were atrocious.

"Do you think you can do any better?" Sir Avery asked me.

"I don't know," I said noncommittally. *If I can't, I'll swallow my camera.* "I'd have to see what you have to work with."

"Nick can take you to the site tomorrow if the rain stops. *Inshallah* it will clear up. The damp is bad for my bones and muscles."

I didn't want to do it. Playing a role to save my own life was one thing. Becoming an accessory to a crime was something else. At this rate, Nick and I would be doing time together. I'd have to tell him that this was where I drew the line.

But Nick didn't return to the compound all day, nor did he show up for dinner. When he did come in late that night, just as I was preparing for bed, he was wet and filthy and in a foul mood. Ordering me to sleep, he disappeared down the hallway into the shower, where he remained for a long time.

I lay stiffly under the blanket on our mattress, armored in my clothes, half fearing, half desiring his presence beside me. I'd opened the curtains on the window to let in some light, and I wondered if this would annoy him. When he finally returned to the room, I didn't stir, pretending to be asleep, even though I expected him to come check me and find me faking.

But he didn't check me. He didn't come anywhere near me. He got himself another blanket and rolled up on the floor as far away from me as possible. He left the curtains open.

This sucks, I thought, as I huddled, shadowed by moonlight, in my cold and lonely bed.

Chapter 20

NICK

I was feeling edgy the next morning as we hiked toward the excavation site in the company of Metin and half a dozen workers. It wasn't far, but the mountainous track was more suitable for goats than humans. The sun was shining brightly, but the ground was still a little wet from yesterday's rain. Ellie and I were lagging behind the others because I had to compensate for her shorter stride. Although she was fit, she wasn't accustomed to steep hikes over rough terrain.

I'd asked her to check out the site so she could determine how to take the photographs we needed. She'd promptly objected, insisting she wasn't going to become an accessory to antiquity theft. I told her to have some faith in me and follow orders, which was not exactly warmly received.

She was curious about the site, though—that much was evident. "So, if there really is something there, it might testify to the historical accuracy of Homer's writings about the storm that drove the Greek ships to disaster after the sacking of Troy, right?" she'd asked me.

"That might be one interpretation, yeah," I'd admitted.

"If it was a shipwreck, why is the site so far inland?"

"It's not far inland. You'll see when we get over this rise. The coastline curves sharply, and the site is close to the bay where we left *Voyager.* The excavations are located on a small plain nestled between two promontories, and the island's only fresh-water source is nearby. If their ship was destroyed and the sur-vivors faced with the necessity of setting up an encampment, the valley's a likely spot."

"Is that why your grandfather decided to dig there?"

"Partly. He uses common sense as well as pure gut feelings. He trusts his instincts. That's why he's always been so good at this. I've seen him sniff out a find that many a more scientific archaeologist has missed."

"It must upset him that he can't work on the actual site."

"It's hell. There's nothing in life he loved more than putter-ing around in the excavations."

"I can see why he can't cross this mountain in his wheelchair, but couldn't he have some of his men carry him here?"

"He does that occasionally, but he's proud, and it's hard for him to admit that he needs to be carried."

"Is that why you're helping him with the illegal excavations? Because you feel sorry for an old man whose career has been de-stroyed?"

And she was off again. I gave her a scowl. "Do we need an-other session with my belt around your neck?"

"So why *do* you steal things?" she retorted. I was obviously losing my ability to scare the shit out of her. "I can't figure it out. How do you justify it?"

"Have I ever attempted to justify it?"

"Not to me, but—"

"Maybe I'm an amoral bastard who's in it for the rush of adrenaline it produces."

"And maybe you're a liar. Maybe you have reasons—and plans—that you're keeping secret."

I reached for her, stopping us near the edge of a fifty-foot drop. "Maybe you'd be wiser to keep your speculations to yourself, slave. Before I begin to regret that I didn't shoot you the other morning."

She smirked. Fuck. Look at her—those violet eyes flashing with confidence. In the beginning she'd stood up to me in spite of her fear. Now she had no fear. I must have revealed more to her about myself than I'd intended.

She was starting to trust me. Even though she believed I was a thief, she liked me. Well, I don't know about *liking* me, but she wanted to fuck me. She'd fuck me right now if I pulled her behind a boulder and laid her down in the sun.

I pushed her ahead of me along the track with a little more roughness than the situation called for. I couldn't let up on her. If she saw through me, so might everyone else. "Don't press your luck, sweetheart. There are limits to my good humor."

I meant it. The pressure was getting to me. Grandfather was showing no signs of being ready to leave the island, and Nigel had dogged my footsteps yesterday, asking too many fucking questions. I'd done my best to allay his suspicions, but I didn't feel safe. Late last night Metin had heard a noise on *Voyager* and awakened to see somebody—Nigel or one of his men—swimming away from the boat. He'd been snooping, obviously, and had managed to do some minor damage to the electrical system, damn him.

Remembering this conversation put me into such a foul mood that when we reached the excavations and Ellie did push her luck, I lost my fucking temper.

"I'm not going in there," she said.

After touring the open dig area, we got to the section that was under the cliff side. Most of the stolen art objects were stored in a cavern beneath the cliff. It was a natural museum, a good place to keep artifacts. The environment was naturally dry, providing an excellent protection against the ravages of climate. But Ellie balked at entering the cave, which was invisible from the outside. We'd found the entrance serendipitously when Erdal, one of the workers, had been puttering around on the cliff side, looking for mineral fragments.

"It's quite safe," I assured her.

She shook her head. Her body was rigid, her eyes dark with determination. "No."

"Most of the artifacts are in there. If you're going to take the pictures we need, this is where you'll have to do it. We'll have to light the cave artificially, and you're the only person who knows how to do that."

"Taking photographs for your little gang of thieves wasn't part of our agreement."

I felt my nerves start to fray. We'd already had this debate. "Our agreement, *slave*, was that you would obey my orders and I would allow you to live."

"I refuse to participate in your sleazy crime."

"Keep your voice down. Sinan understands English. A couple of the others might, too."

"I don't care. Look, Nick, this—all of it—is incredible." She waved her hand at our surroundings, the trenches and mounds, carefully grid marked and separated, level-by-level, in the manner that confirmed the presence of professional archaeologists. "It's even more impressive than I'd imagined. If the earring is authenticated and other objects found, it could be one of the great discoveries of this century. But it's Schliemann all over again, isn't it? He cheated the Turks, too. He absconded with the treasure trove of ancient Troy. I won't be a party to it."

Fuck. She had to choose this moment to rebel? Already her raised voice was attracting the workers' attention. "You'll do what I tell you."

"I won't." Her gaze didn't flinch from mine. "This is my line in the sand."

Well, I wasn't about to have any fucking lines drawn by her. Not here, not today. I clamped both hands on her shoulders and forced her toward the cave. I let my fingers slide up on her neck where some critical nerve bundles were...just to remind her. "If you want to argue with me, do it later, in private. In front of the others, you'll play your role, and do it convincingly."

But at the mouth of the gloomy, black cavern, she dug in her heels. I could feel her body start to tremble. "I won't. I can't. I'm not going in there."

The "I can't" didn't register with me. It wasn't until afterward that I understood. All I knew was that despite my absurd efforts to "train" this girl, she was defying me. And that Sinan, Nigel's right-hand man, was watching our altercation avidly.

Most of the workers with us today were Nigel's crew—men whose primary loyalty was not to my grandfather, but to my twisted cousin. I could not risk making them any more suspicious than they already were.

I twisted one of Ellie's arms up behind her in a position I knew would hurt. "Let's go, move it." I forced her down, through the black slit in the rock face that marked the entrance to the cave.

She cried out, surprising me because I hadn't hurt her that much. I already knew quite a bit about her pain tolerance levels. Had I miscalculated? The men were staring and muttering, and Metin jumped down to our side.

"What's the matter?" he asked, looking from her face to mine.

Ellie was struggling. Her head turned wildly to Metin. "Help me," she implored.

Fuck! Metin glared at me, his lips pressed tight. "What are you doing to her?" he asked in Turkish. He sounded harder and a lot less deferent than usual. "You said you weren't going to hurt her—"

"Shut up or I'll strangle the two of you," I said softly, also in Turkish. "You want to rebel, fine, but you can do it when we're alone. Loyalty and obedience in public. Without it we're blown."

"I'm sorry, Nick, I—"

"Save it." Trying to figure an explanation the others would believe, I added, "I'm going to bend down as if to examine her ankle. We'll say she yelped because she twisted it. You, Metin, pretend to look concerned, and as for you, Ellie..."

I switched rapidly to English, getting as far as, "You can just—" when she interrupted, saying in clear, idiomatic Turkish, "Don't do it. If you touch my foot, I'll kick you in the face. Enough. I'm not going into the cave and I'm not taking any photographs."

Shit! She spoke Turkish. I felt sick. All I could think of was that she must be law enforcement, after all. An agent, maybe for Interpol.

Fucking hell! She'd lied to me from the start; she'd made a fool out of me. I'd worried myself into a frazzle trying to figure out how to protect her. But she must be capable of protecting herself. I wondered who her backup was, and how long it would be before they struck. If they came in early, they'd destroy everything I'd planned, everything I'd worked my ass off to arrange. I wouldn't be able to save my grandfather, after all.

I lost it. I hissed in English, "We'll pretend I didn't hear that. We'll *hope* that none of Nigel's men did. Sinan!" I called the hefty, ugly man over at the same moment as I lifted Ellie into my arms. She fought me, but I was stronger and I used my strength. "The lady has tripped and sprained her ankle. I'm going to take her out to my boat, ice it, and bandage it up. Oversee things here for me, will you? Metin will help you, and I'll be back later."

"There's an electrical problem with the boat," Metin reminded me. "Someone slipped on board last night—I told you—"

"I won't need the lights for this." Still fuming, I hauled Ellie, who had gone curiously quiet, back up the track toward the sea, not setting her down until we were well out of sight of Sinan and his cohorts.

"You deceiving bitch." I dumped her in the shelter of the rock-studded mountains. "Who the hell are you working for?"

"Just because I speak Turkish—"

"You're some kind of fucking law enforcement agent, aren't you?"

She shook her head vigorously.

"Why are you even denying it?" I felt like strangling the bitch. For real, this time.

"I speak Turkish because I lived here as a child. I didn't tell you because it seemed safer to play dumb. I didn't mean to reveal it back there, but I was scared and angry, and you—"

"I'm fed up with your lies." Seizing her by the wrist, I hauled her along with me. "You'll talk, damn you. You'll tell me the truth."

"You're hurting me."

"Tough. I'm sick to death of all you sneaky government types. You're going to find out that it was real unprofessional to put yourself at my mercy."

"Nick, please. You're making a mistake."

"Be quiet, or I'll touch your neck the way I did that first morning. Only this time you won't wake up. Now walk."

For once, she obeyed me.

I rowed us out to the sailboat, which was anchored nearby in the quiet bay where we'd landed two days before. It was windy and the sea was rough. Spray doused us as I wrestled with the oars. I was glad of it—I had to expend the violent energy somehow. I was so fucking furious my vision seemed red around the edges. I don't often blow my temper, but god help the people around me when I do.

Who the fuck was she? Why was she here?

Chapter 21

ELLIE

I was cursing myself for my stupidity. It had been a bad time to defy my captor—when there were so many other people around. The real reason was that I hadn't been able to enter that cavern. My claustrophobic anxiety about dark, tight places had risen up and engulfed me. My heart had started pounding and I hadn't been able to catch my breath. My legs had gone weak and if Nick hadn't lifted me off my feet, I think I would have collapsed.

I hated it. I felt so goddamn weak and useless when the panic struck me. My thoughts and emotions would start to spiral down in an obsessive manner and I couldn't seem to stop it no matter how hard I tried.

Now that I was safely away from the cavern, my panic had receded.

Now I had something real to fret about.

He marched me down to the master stateroom. He seemed tense, as if he were expecting me to launch an attack on him. Did he think I was capable of fighting him? What was I, some federal agent who knew judo or kickboxing? I tried my best to seem innocent and non-threatening. But then I thought, screw it. I wasn't going to cower. I threw back my shoulders and straightened my spine.

He was wearing jeans and a white T-shirt today. His shirt was damp from the spray. I could see his hard muscles flexing under the cotton. I wanted to touch him, find his nipples, graze them with my teeth. Shit, what was wrong with me? I had made him furious, and god only knew what he was going to do to me now, but still I wanted him. I'd been pumping his grandfather for information about his childhood. Was I falling for the guy? Was there no end to my folly where he was concerned?

As soon as we got into the stateroom, he slammed the door and crowded me against the wall where the sink was, his tall body hovering over me in a pissed-off, threatening manner. "Hepburn sent you, didn't he?"

"Who the fuck is Hepburn?"

"Who the fuck are you?"

"I'm the same person I've always been. I have the same reason for being in Turkey. I just know Turkish. That's the only difference."

He grabbed my shoulders and shook me, as if he expected my secret identity card to tumble out of my clothes. "You're a professional. You're with Interpol, or maybe even the CIA. Or the Turkish authorities, I suppose."

"That's ridiculous."

"Is it?"

"Yes!" I clutched his forearms and tried to pry his hands off me, but he was too strong. "Look, you douche, I lived in Turkey from the time I was seven to the time I was fourteen. My mother was working on a dig in Central Anatolia. I went to school in Ankara. All my friends spoke Turkish, so I learned it without even trying, the way children do."

"If that's true, why didn't you say so?"

"Because I was terrified. I figured you'd never believe that an American tourist could speak Turkish. It's not exactly taught in U.S. high schools."

"Why didn't you admit it later, when you were no longer in fear for your life?"

I hesitated, and he answered for me: "Because it allowed you to learn things you otherwise wouldn't have known. Right?"

He pushed down on my shoulders. Again, as so often before, he forced me to my knees. He loved doing that. I didn't even resist. I knew how to sink down gracefully now. He pressed me down in front of him so my head was about at the level of his crotch. As he jerked me against him, I felt him harden, same as always. He might be furious, but he still wanted me.

When he hardened, I softened and grew damp. That always happened, too, dammit. Why, why did it keep happening? What was this blazing monster of need and desire that roared between us? Why wouldn't it leave me alone?

Nick grabbed a piece of rope from one of the shelves and bound my wrists behind my back. He wasn't gentle. He wrapped the rope up, almost as high as my elbows, and pulled it tight. It strained the muscles in my arms and shoulders. It fucking hurt. I yelled in protest. "You sadistic bastard!"

"Did I ever pretend to be anything else?" He grabbed a big hunk of my hair and wrenched my head back so I was looking up at him. "Tell me the truth."

"Fine—knowing Turkish did allow me to learn things. This in particular—you're the one who's involved in human trafficking. You told Nigel you were going to sell me. You said I was special merchandise, and you were going to sell me to someone who likes to brutalize and humiliate American girls. Which is what you like to do yourself, isn't it?"

He didn't reply. He had gone still. He was probably trying to remember what else he had said in front of me, thinking I didn't understand.

"What your grandfather and your cousin are doing is bad, but it pales beside your crimes. Do you know what happens to girls who are sold into sexual slavery? Do you even care? Do you stroke yourself while thinking about it? Does the idea of raping and dominating females get you off?"

"As a matter of fact, it does." His voice had turned icy. He came around in front of me, where I could see him. He reached out and tore open my shirt, leaving my breasts bare except for my bra. Then he opened his jeans and grabbed his erect cock in one hand and started doing exactly that—stroking himself. "Dominating you, in particular, Helen of Troy. It gets me off like nothing I've ever felt before." And while I knelt there watching because for some reason I couldn't take my eyes off him, he stroked faster and faster, while staring at me kneeling, my arms painfully trussed up behind my back, until groaning, he came, directing his cum at my face and neck and breasts.

"Fuck you," I said, because otherwise I was going to break down and cry. I hated him in that moment. I hated him because even as he humiliated me, I wanted to touch him, kiss him, feel him pounding between my thighs.

He got a towel from the head and wiped his seed off my skin. Then he untied me and dragged me over to the bed. I thought he was going to rape me...if he could get it up again, which he probably could if he mistreated me some more.

But he left me there and stomped to the door. "I'll deal with you later." At the door, he paused, his back to me, his body stiff. "I used to think I could never sink to Nigel's depths," he said in a hollow tone. "Obviously, I was wrong."

He went out and slammed the door.

Chapter 22

ELLIE

It was getting dark. I had been alone all day in Nick's cabin on the boat, and now night was falling. I was curled up on the bunk, staring at the blackening sky through the porthole and wondering when he would return. The lights didn't work. I had flicked switches and checked bulbs to no avail. Then I remembered Metin's words, "There's an electrical problem with the boat."

How long was he going to leave me alone? All day I'd been expecting his return. And dreading it. I kept reliving every nasty thing he had done to me, of which there had been many. We'd had exactly one sweet sexual exchange, but we'd both been drunk out of our heads at the time. Everything else we'd done together had been twisted and dark.

Hours passed, but there was no footfall, no sound except the creak of boards and the lapping of waves against the hull.

What if he left me here all night?

Does the idea of raping and dominating females get you off?
As a matter of fact, it does.

Was that true, or had we just been taunting each other? It was clear that he liked the rough stuff, but that wasn't the whole story. He could have fucked me many times over, but he hadn't. When I'd tried to get him off with a blowjob the other night, he'd interrupted me and given me an orgasm instead.

He'd noted his grandfather had been so successful because Sir Avery trusted his instincts. My instincts kept telling me that there was something more to Nicholas Gabriel than he had permitted me to see. Was I an idiot to have such feelings? He was years older than I was, and I'd only had one serious relationship with a guy before. What the hell did I know? Compared to him I was a beginner at the whole kink, yearning and obsession thing.

My so-called instincts were probably born of the need to survive in a dangerous situation. From the morning we'd met, the bright-haired god had been the only thing standing between me and endless night. I'd tolerate anything he did to me—I'd even eroticize it—as long as I could keep breathing.

I didn't know what to believe anymore. And, as it continued to get darker, I stopped caring, because with the dark came my fear.

I was mentally exhausted and more than a little confused. Weak, in other words. Prey to the terrors that came by night. More so than usual, I guess.

Because Nick had been so pissed over the revelation that I knew Turkish, I'd never gotten the chance to explain why I hadn't been able to bring myself to enter that cave. I'd never told him I was claustrophobic because I'd been afraid he might use it against me. Revealing a weakness to an adversary would be foolish.

I sat up and peered out the porthole. There was no moon. The sky was slightly overcast; it seemed too cloudy for stars. Out in the Aegean, so far from city lights and inhabited land, the darkness was absolute. Impenetrable. Before long, I couldn't see my body, not even the ghostly outline of my fingers held up in front of my face. But I could feel my body. My harsh breathing, my skittering heartbeat.

Soon my heart was flapping as if it meant to take wing and fly away. My belly cramped and my face was as hot as my hands and feet were cold. I was breathing too fast, using up too much air. I tried to tell myself that I would not run out of air, that it was impossible to run out of air. But my sensible, rational mind held no sway over the childish part of me that feared the blackness and dreaded suffocation.

Control yourself, you dumbass.

But I could not.

Sweating, I flung away the blanket. The beating of my heart was so strong and painful that I expected each hammer stroke to be the last. It was so ironic. I'd rebelled against Nick at the dig this morning because I couldn't face entering a dark, subterranean cavern. I'd been afraid the place would bring on a crippling anxiety attack. I'd avoided it, incurring Nick's fury in the process, only to suffer the full effects of the attack here, instead.

What a stupid fool I'd been. Surely the cave wouldn't have been as dark as this tiny cabin. In there, at least, I wouldn't have been alone. Nick would have been with me. Nick, who protected me, Nick who had promised never to leave me alone in the dark.

I began to cry silently. I curled up in a fetal position on the bed. Unreality was settling over me. I began to wonder if I really existed, if anything existed around me besides endless night.

It was so dark. And I was afraid to be alone. I sobbed until my throat was raw; I dug at the dirt until my fingers were bleeding and numb. The air around me had been dank and musty, but soon it was thin and dry. Soon I felt dizzy and my lungs protested as they gasped for air. I was a child, but old enough to know I was facing death. I was already in my grave...locked up in airless darkness, writhing, scraping, and screaming to get out.

I jolted upright in bed, where I must have fallen asleep. Was I dreaming? Fuck. I wasn't sure exactly where I was. All I knew was that I had to escape. I rolled off the bed and crawled across the floor, pressing my fingers wildly along the wall until I felt the vertical crack that marked the door. I knew it was locked. I'd pounded on it earlier, attempted to spring the lock with a nail file, all to no avail. I located the handle and clung to it. But it was locked, locked. I pressed my face to the cold metal of the door and wept.

Chapter 23

NICK

I was drinking raki with Metin and staring belligerently at the sea. "Fuck all women," I ranted. "Do you have a woman, my friend?"

"Not at present. And you shouldn't use that language about Ellie."

"You've defended her from the start, haven't you?" I swilled the milky white liquid in my glass, and then gulped a swallow that burned all the way down. "I should have let you take her. You're closer to her own age, at least."

"I'm older than I look. And I would have been happy to take her, had she had eyes for anyone besides you."

I scowled at him over the raki glass. Metin flushed slightly and looked away. He played with his own glass for several moments before adding, "I don't think you should have left her alone tonight."

"She's better off alone," I said, tormented by violent images of all the things I wanted to do to her. I yearned to punish her for lying to me. I could think of all sorts of delicious ways to torment my disobedient slave.

"I don't think she's safe," Metin said.

"None of the men would dare bother her."

"One would."

I stared at him over the rim of my glass.

"He boarded the yacht and messed with the electronics. He tried to sabotage the radio," Metin reminded me. "He hates you. I think he would dare anything. I'm not saying anything will happen. Just that you shouldn't give him the opportunity."

I sipped again, staring over the water toward the boat. Max's boat. A memory came to me, vivid and shattering: my best friend Max pale and shaking with a combination of grief and anger as he told me what Nigel had cruelly admitted about his rape of Max's girlfriend. Max had been accused of that crime because he and the girl had been together. He'd left her alone for a short time, and Nigel, vengeful because the girl had dumped him for Max, had followed them and raped her. He had blindfolded her first so she wasn't sure who he was.

A few years later, it had been my girl Elizabeth whom Nigel had pursued. He'd eventually succeeded in snaking Elizabeth away. They'd been together for a while, but he had abused her. I'd never learned exactly what Nigel had done, but it had ruined her. And cost her her life.

Elizabeth had hanged herself a few years later. She'd left a note blaming Nigel for the trauma she couldn't seem to escape.

Nigel was going to pay for that. Soon, very soon.

If I didn't fuck things up.

I only had a few days left before Hepburn moved in.

Hepburn, the dude who had married Elizabeth after Nigel had broken her.

Hepburn, the man who had vowed vengeance for the death of his wife.

Who the fuck is Hepburn? Ellie had asked. I'd assumed she knew, but now I wasn't so sure. Maybe she was exactly who she had always claimed to be—Ellie Heath, innocent bystander with a camera who had gone camping on the Aegean coast of Turkey and walked straight into my own special hell.

Rob Hepburn was the spook behind this whole scam. He worked for some cloak and dagger federal agency. He was determined to get Nigel and he didn't give a fuck who else he took down in the process.

I'd been fine with that in the beginning. I wanted to destroy Nigel just as much as Rob did. The dirtbag had tormented me for most of my life.

I didn't know Rob too well. I'd met him once or twice when he'd been married to Elizabeth, but it wasn't as if we were friends. After she'd left me for Nigel, Elizabeth hadn't had much to say to me, and I'd had less to say to her. But when I'd heard she was dead...fuck. I'd been amazed how much that hurt.

He'd come to me last fall, as a courtesy, he'd said. That was when I'd first found out about my grandfather's slide into thievery. I hadn't even believed it until Hepburn had shown me his proof—stolen artifacts, an astonishing number of them. And my foolish Granddad in it up to his scrawny neck.

"Nigel's dirty," Rob Hepburn had told me. "We believe he's involved in all sorts of things—drug smuggling, illegal weapons trading, maybe even terrorism along with the art theft."

"So arrest him."

"I want more than an arrest. I want to put him away in a Turkish prison. And you're going to help me do it."

"I love the thought of Nigel rotting in a Turkish prison, but why the fuck do you need my help?"

"I don't. But Sir Avery does. If we take Nigel down for this, your grandfather will be implicated too. I shouldn't care about that, but I met the old guy a couple of times. Beth loved him, as I'm sure you know."

I'd heard that Hepburn had gone a little crazy since Elizabeth's death; or at least, that he'd been fucked up enough by losing her that he'd been putting the screws to everybody he knew. I got the impression that the guy was hanging on by his fingertips. It made me edgy, but I could empathize. I'd been like that too, when I'd lost her.

"I need someone on the inside. But your cousin is shrewd, which is how he has stayed out of reach of the authorities for so many years. He trusts nobody who hasn't been working with him for years."

"However much he might distrust one of your guys, he distrusts me even more."

"We can set you up with a cover story that will fool Nigel."

"Nigel will never believe I'm involved in antiquities theft."

"So maybe it's not your true calling. Maybe you're just helping your grandfather out while pursuing other goals."

"What other goals?"

When he'd suggested the human trafficking angle, I'd wondered whether Hepburn and his intelligence agency friends had been spying on me. Probably. Not that I knew a damn thing about human trafficking. But I did know about master/slave relationships of the kinky, consensual type. Hell, I'd been a deviant for years.

Nigel was aware of this. We'd been boys reading porn together. Adolescents fantasizing about all the chicks we were going to fuck. Since I'd always been fond of a woman on her knees in the bedroom, preferably with her hands bound and her mouth ready to service me, it would be no great leap for Nigel to believe that I'd progressed to human trafficking, like a weed smoker to heroin or crack cocaine.

Not only would he believe it, he would be intrigued. And he'd probably want to get in on the action.

So the plan took root. My old friend Max, who had suffered at Nigel's hands years ago in high school, had provided the funding. Max had started a software company and become a billionaire in his 20s. *Voyager* was Max's own private yacht.

I was the fool on the ground. Taking point. Most likely to be screwed. Metin was my loyal Sancho Panza, the amateur whom I hoped wouldn't get screwed. And Ellie? Who was Ellie? I wish I knew.

I remembered something Hepburn had said at the start: "Don't even think about crossing me. I might put a man on you to make sure that you don't."

A man. Or a woman?

"What's the matter?" Metin asked. He had been watching me, I guess, while I reminisced.

I put down my glass. "I think I'll take your advice and go back to *Voyager*."

"Good. I have some other advice for you, if you will listen."

"Well?" I glared at him, wondering what he'd meant by "I'm older than I look." The kid did look older than the twenty-one he'd admitted to when I'd hired him. It struck me that I didn't really know much about Metin. He came from a family of fishermen in the town of Kusadasi, near Izmir; he had a better education than many of his friends and he was interested in antiquities. That was all I knew about his background. Metin was frank and friendly, but he didn't talk much about himself.

"I think we should get Ellie and your grandfather out of here tomorrow. I know you said the fifteenth, and it's a bit early, but things are getting out of hand."

"I intend to get them out as soon as possible."

"By force, if necessary."

"You're prepared to use force?"

"Of course," Metin said with a shrug. "Why not? He is old and she is a woman. It is our responsibility as men to take what actions we must to preserve their lives."

Life is simple in Turkey, I thought a few minutes later as I rowed back to the yacht. No confusion of values, of identity, of sex roles. Protect your woman. Use force if necessary.

I'd already used force against Ellie. Several times. Not rape, not yet. But, damn, I had never been so tempted to ravage a woman as I was when I was around her. Maybe it would never be rape with her, though. Every time I touched her, she was hot for me. I could scarcely believe it, but it seemed that fate had thrown a girl into my path who was not appalled by the things I wanted to do to her. She was strong and she fought me, but she had that gleam in her eye. And that wetness between her legs.

It made me hard just thinking about her. Part of me didn't care who she was or how she had come into my hands. She made my blood boil every time I was near her. My heart was pounding now because the boat was right there and she was on it, and soon I would have her at my mercy again.

Except I didn't. Because when I got on board and made my way down to the cabin where I'd left her, I was shocked to find her crouched on the floor in the darkness, whimpering and shaking all over. Holy fuck. I dropped to my knees beside her, terrified that she was ill or injured. Had I freaked her out with that little jerking off performance? That had been so fucking crude.

She flinched from the beam of my flashlight and covered her face with both her arms.

"Ellie? Good God, Ellie, what's wrong?"

"You promised." Her voice was so faint I could barely hear her. "You promised never to leave me alone in the dark."

Understanding flashed through me. The lights left burning at night, the open curtains that let the moonlight enter, her absolute refusal to enter the cave. I also remembered the drunken promise to which I'd paid so little attention.

I understood, and felt once again the bitter guilt from which there was no hiding place.

I was one sick fuck, all right. Nigel had nothing on me.

Chapter 24

ELLIE

He grabbed a blanket and wrapped it around me, then lifted me into his arms and carried me out on deck. Overhead the clouds were clearing and a light dusting of stars was visible. The moon was also rising low over the horizon, dissipating the blackness. And with it, my terror.

"Ellie?" He sank down on the bench seat in the stern and cradled me across his lap. "I've got you. You're gonna be okay."

My limbs were vibrating fiercely, a reaction to the havoc wreaked upon my body by the panic. The shaking was annoying, but I didn't try to fight it. I welcomed it, knowing from experience that it signaled the end of the attack. I pressed my face against his warm chest, absorbing his calm, his strength, his comfort. His arms were firm around me; his thighs beneath my own trembling legs supported me wholly, bearing my weight without stress or strain. He felt good. Strong. He would protect me.

"Ellie, I'm so sorry." He bent his face down toward mine. Not to kiss or caress me, but to soothe me. "You're claustrophobic? I should have realized." He was stroking my hair gently. "I'm an idiot. Fuck me—I should have known."

I was beginning to feel better already. Just being close to him helped so much. I don't know what it was about him—it didn't even make sense. But there was a part of me that trusted him. Even though he'd treated me roughly from the start, it had never seemed as if that was the whole story. Every now and then, a gleam of light would shine from him, like the flash from a distant lighthouse through the fog.

That gleam was there now. Steady, bright.

"How could you know? I was trying to hide it from you. I'm terrified of small rooms and of the dark."

"I forgot about the power being out on the boat. Damn. I shouldn't have left you alone for so long anyway."

"It's stupid. A weakness. It's not even rational."

"That's why you refused to enter the cavern. I should have guessed—you'd given me enough hints."

"I'm okay now that I'm out of there." I reached up and feathered the gold hair around his ears. "If you hadn't come back when you did, though, I think I might have died of fright right there on your floor."

He caught my fingers in one hand and kissed them. Each finger separately, and then my thumb. I felt a tingle deep inside. I guess my hormones were getting back to normal.

"How long have you suffered from this? All your life?"

"Only for the past few years. I started having anxiety attacks when I was in college."

"Have you tried to figure out what they stem from?"

"I think I was in a cave-in when I was little. In a small pyramid with my Mom. It freaked me out. My memories are vague, but I have nightmares about it sometimes."

"I'm sorry," he said again.

I turned my face against his throat, breathing in the subtle, masculine scent of him. "It wasn't your fault. I hate feeling like such a coward. It's embarrassing to have an attack like that. There wasn't even a good reason to panic. It's not as if I haven't spent a lot of time in that cabin. It's not as if anything bad has ever happened to me there."

He stiffened. Oops. Wrong thing to blurt out. I tried to cover it by plunging on: "How could you dream I might be an undercover agent? Nerves of steel are required for that profession. I clearly don't have those."

He laughed shortly, but I could feel his tension. "I'm sorry for everything I've done to you in that cabin. I just—there *was* a reason for it. Well, not for all of it. Some of it was just me being a fucking animal." He shook his head. "I'd say I'm not really like that, but I'd be lying. There's a monster inside me that's decided you're its natural prey."

"What do you mean, there was a reason for it?"

He hesitated. "I still can't tell you that. Anyway, it's not as though there's a bad guy on one side and a good guy on the other. It's a fucking snake pit you tumbled into that morning."

"But you're not going to sell me?"

"No. God no. I'm kinky as fuck, but I agree with you that human trafficking is a despicable crime, worse than antiquities smuggling, worse than just about anything. I'm capable of a lot of nasty things, but I'm not capable of that."

"I just...you're so hard to read, Nick."

"Well, I try to be hard to read. But it's a lie, a trap for my cousin. I wanted him to believe it because, it's the sort of thing he *would* believe. But I could never... I don't blame you for doubting me, but sex trafficking—that's not something I could ever do."

"Okay," I said.

"Okay?"

"I believe you. Even though you told Nigel you were going to get more money for me because of my anal virginity."

He groaned. "Shit. You understood that."

"You nearly exceeded my Turkish vocabulary with that one, but yeah, I figured it out. Although where you were coming from on that, I can't imagine. How do you even know?"

He began to laugh. It was so unusual to see him laugh, that I started laughing too. "For all you know," I continued, a little punchy now, "I could be a regular virgin. Just think how much I'd be worth then."

"Please don't tell me you're a regular virgin or I'm going to feel even more perverted that I already do."

"Relax. I haven't been a regular virgin since the night of my senior prom."

He shook his head. "Why aren't you mad at me?"

"It comes and goes," I admitted. In the light of the rising moon, I could make out the bemused expression in his eyes. The shaking had stopped. I felt warm and safe. As we looked at each other, communicating with our eyes, something changed in the mood between us, and I felt a new and different kind of tension in my throat, in my breasts, my sex.

I hadn't died of fright. I was brimful with life.

I wanted to celebrate life with the man who, like Apollo, had brought light into my darkness. Here on Homer's wine-dark sea it seemed as if I could feel the breath of the god.

"Nick."

"Ellie." He bent his head and kissed my mouth. Sweet, sweet. Cuddling closer, I opened my lips to the invasive questing of his tongue, and then advanced my own. When our tongues touched, fire ran through me. I reached up and touched his cheek, which was rough with golden whiskers. I rubbed my palm there and imagined that roughness against my breasts, belly, and thighs.

I kissed him more aggressively, licking, biting, giving myself up to pleasure.

"You must be feeling better."

"Much."

I felt his hand on my body, molding my breasts. His fingers plucked my nipples through the cotton of my shirt. They hardened. My breasts seemed to swell; there was congestion in my belly, a liquid, fiery ache. He bared my breasts and plucked again and again. His hands were magical. He stroked my nipples with the pad of his thumb until they felt like berries about to burst.

"You're perfect," he whispered. "Silky and firm and just the right size. I bet not even the original Helen of Troy had prettier breasts, *hayatim.*"

"So I'm Helen now, am I? The most beautiful woman in the world?"

"The face that launched a thousand ships," he said solemnly.

"I need someone to compare you with—some hero of old, some glorious, golden-haired youth. Let's see—how about Achilles, the great invincible hero, the champion of the Greeks?"

"You'll have to do better than that. Achilles wasn't fond of women."

"Hector, then? He was noble and heroic. I always preferred him to Achilles, actually."

"Yeah, me, too. But I can't get that image out of my mind of his poor broken body being dragged around the walls of Troy." He rolled over, pressing me down beneath him. "Don't make me dead, please." He moved his hips against me. "I'm feeling very much alive."

I was finding it hard to continue this discussion, but I made a valiant effort nonetheless. "If I can't make you a hero, how about a god?" I reached up and stroked his burnished hair. "Apollo, the sun god. He liked women, at least some of the time, which is about as much as you can expect from the ancient Greeks. And he was the healer, the god of light, the patron of poetry and song."

"I'm not a god. A demon, maybe. Fucking black-hearted and dangerous to know."

"I kinda like the kinky," I confessed as he took one of my nipples between his thumb and forefinger, then bent his head and licked it. I gasped, then cried out when he tried his teeth against the areola—not too hard, just enough to drive me over the line into super-lust. "I mean, I'm not as horrified by that deviant stuff as you seem to think."

"Yeah?"

"In case the crashing orgasm I had the other night didn't make that clear."

"You were pretty drunk."

"Not so drunk that I didn't know what I was doing. It's sort of embarrassing to admit this, but when you're rough and, you know, with the orders and stuff, it gets me hot."

"Ah, Ellie, what am I going to do with you? Here I was making all these good resolutions about how I was never going to touch you again, and you're telling me it's okay?"

Thought, protest, denial—all melted away. I wanted him, all of him, his all-too-human weight upon me, the thrust of his cock inside me. "Yes. It's okay." I cupped his face between my palms. "I want you."

"Are you sure? Because if we start up again, this time I'm not going to stop. I've been longing to fuck you ever since the moment I first saw you."

"So what are we waiting for?"

He kissed me long, hard, and slow. When he raised his head, we were both gasping. His eyes, I noted, had gone all predatory and dark. "Come on, then." He stood up, taking my hand in his. My own legs felt so weak I could hardly walk.

"Where are we going?"

"Back to the cabin. To my bed."

"I don't think I can go back in there—"

"Yes, you can." His voice was firm, authoritative. "The moon is rising and the curtain will be open. There are candles in the galley that I can commandeer. You're not going to panic."

Hand in hand, we descended below-decks, guided by the beam of his flashlight. He found the candles and some matches. At the threshold of the master cabin, he lifted me into his arms. He carried me inside, slammed the door behind us and bore me over to his bed, where he laid me down. Then he lit the candles and opened the curtain to let moonlight pour into the room.

In the flickering candlelight, I smiled up at him. He smiled back, a big genuine smile that made him look so different from the cold bastard he often pretended to be. Holding my gaze, he began stripping off his clothes.

Staring at his lean, hard body, I thought him the most beautiful man on earth. The flat belly, muscled flanks, the tight curve of his buttocks were all I had imagined and more. I gazed happily at his cock, springing out of a golden mesh of hair.

"I've got condoms." He crossed to the top drawer to get some. Returning, he stretched out beside me, caressing me gently from shoulder to thigh. He lifted me enough to pull off my top, and then his hands drifted over me.

I laughed, then sighed as he grazed the tips of my breasts. He found the snap of my jeans and opened it. The zipper made a soft sound as he moved its tab down. "Raise your hips for a second," he ordered, stripping both jeans and panties off me as I obeyed. He tossed them on the floor, and then slid his hands along the insides of my thighs.

His hands and his mouth gave me such pleasure. Kneeling over me, he caressed my ankles and pressed kisses to my knees. He was gentle, giving. Yet he was subtle, too, for he knew ways to excite me, and he ruthlessly exploited them.

He moved higher, skirting my mound. Devil. He knew that was where I most wanted his touch. I lifted my hips in search of his hands, but he moved on to my belly and breasts. He suckled me, tenderly at first, then harder. I cried out as his teeth bore down. It was good pain, and he knew how to control it. The tension in my lower body deepened to an ache. His tongue soothed my breasts, but it was not enough.

Just when I thought I couldn't stand it anymore, he caressed my sex. His fingers, his thumb, the heel of his hand, pressing, invading, revolving in the most deliciously intimate way.

I moved against him, lost in sunshine, swimming in luminous realms of light. My body gathered itself and reached for its pleasure, but he drew it out, advancing and retreating as he teased and tormented my clit. He held me on the edge, thrashing.

I moaned as he slid a finger deep into my pussy and found a spot on the inner wall that positively glowed with pleasure when he stroked it. He had me gasping and moaning; any second I'd be begging. My hands were clawing at the sheets. He fingerfucked me, harder and harder, and just as I neared the peak, he tongued my clit.

I cried out, clutching at his shoulders as my climax hit. It thundered through me, sweet bliss. If it was possible to feel joy in every cell of my body, I felt it then.

Nick held me tightly while I rode the waves, sheltering my convulsing body. When I finally emerged on the other side, he kissed my hair and cheeks and eyes as he brought me safely down.

I opened my eyes to see his bright head silvered by moonlight. He smiled at me. "You're very sweet, *canim.*"

"So are you." And because I wanted him to feel the same intense pleasure I'd just experienced, I reached my hand between our bodies, going straight for his dick. He jumped as I touched him. I marveled at the feel of his smooth, warm flesh. I closed my fingers around him, stroking the tip with my thumb.

"Ellie—" His voice was hoarse, breathless.

"Don't you like it?"

"Yes. *Yes.* But if you keep doing that, I'll explode."

"That's the plan. I'm not going to sleep on you this time. I want you inside me, Nick. Deep inside."

Chapter 25

NICK

"It's where I want to be," I told her. I was feeling good. At ease with her, as if we were old lovers who'd been together many times before. And because I felt comfortable, I showed her how to touch me to give me the most pleasure. She was so sensual. A sexy woman who enjoyed the arts of love. She might be antsy about the dark, but when it came to sex, she had no inhibitions. I loved the sound of her laughter, the desperation of her sighs.

There was something else I wanted, though. I reached into the cubby at the head end of the bed where I kept the rope. I could be gentle, but I didn't want her to forget that kinky was the way I liked it.

She presented her wrists willingly. I bound them together and raised her arms over her head. "Keep them like that," I ordered, not actually tying her down. Shipboard berths really didn't make the best locations for elaborate bondage games.

"But I want to touch you," she said, writhing a bit. "I guess this means I should call you Master? I keep forgetting that."

I chuckled. My sweet red-haired slave still had a way to go before she'd be winning any submissive of the year prizes. But that was okay with me. I liked her fine the way she was. She looked amazing lying there—her hair wildly strewn on the pillow, her skin still flushed from her orgasm, her nipples hard little peaks, her hands bound.

When I moved to cover her, she parted her legs eagerly. I could tell she was aroused again. She was moist, warm, and willing. So soft. Fragrant and delicate, like rose petals. I caught my breath as I eased inside her.

I wanted to take it slow, but I was hard-pressed by my body's demands to thrust fast and furiously. I wanted to string it out so she'd feel and remember every moment of this.

She lifted her hips and rotated them against me. It was too much. I couldn't stop myself from plunging deep and wild.

She gasped; we both did. "You're finally in me. At last."

"Does it feel okay?"

She giggled. "It feels awesome. May I lower my arms? I want to grab your ass."

"You may not. I like you helpless, even though you're about the least helpless female I've ever encountered. And stop talking." I kissed her long and hard, swallowing any of her random words. "I'm gonna fuck you hard."

"Do," she gasped. "Please do."

I slid my palms under her buttocks, raising her slightly as I drove into her. She felt magnificent around me—silken, hot and tight. Almost as delicious were her breasts pressing against my chest, the nipples hard and pointed, the rest of her so soft. I pressed random kisses to her mouth, her throat, her eyelids; I buried my face in the wild profusion of her hair.

I was already so hot from tonguing her and seeing her come that it wasn't going to take much to send me over the edge. Still, I tried to drag it out for as long as I could. I'd wanted her so much, and I was finally claiming her. I needed to savor that.

She was mine in every way, and it thrilled me to know it. I wanted her to know it, too, so I kissed her hard and rough and allowed my hips to slam into hers. Her warm, slick tissues gripped mine tightly, sending sweet pleasure roaring through my cock and balls, winding me higher, making my rhythms frantic.

"Ohmigod!" There was a catch in her voice as her body coiled beneath me. I could feel her thighs go rigid and knew she'd reached another peak. The knowledge filled me with exultation. I felt good, strong. I could go all night; I was potent as a god. But when she started pulsating around me, I lost all control.

She was kissing me passionately. She must have lowered her arms, because I felt her nails digging into my buttocks as if to pull me deeper inside her, and I went crazy. I was helpless as a torrent of intense pleasure swept through me. I shot through space, an arrow exploding from a bow. The entire world seemed to shudder as I released.

Fuck. Amazing.

Several minutes later, when I'd stopped panting and my heartbeat had settled back into its normal rhythms, I leaned up and grinned at her. I untied her wrists, wishing I had a pair of comfy cuffs to keep her in, but BDSM toys had not been among the gear I'd packed for this escapade. "I think I'm going to keep you prisoner forever."

Her violet eyes opened and looked playfully into mine. "That good, huh?"

"Mmm. Yeah. My naked captive and sex slave."

"I could get into that."

"I thought so."

The lighthearted aftermath of love lasted while we prepared for sleep. We were tender with each other, touching and kissing and sighing like lovesick idiots.

Instead of falling asleep, we ended up fucking again. The second time was just as good as the first. "*Canim, hayatim,*" I muttered in the spasm of orgasm. With her I tended to revert to my mother tongue.

When she laughed and climaxed joyously, my world seemed luminously bright.

* * *

I woke up before Ellie, and eased out of her embrace. She'd been sleeping curled to my side, her head nestled against my shoulder. I kissed her fiery hair, surprised at the protective feelings that shot through me. Still sleeping, she rolled over, making a faint melancholy sound as if she knew she was once again alone.

I shaved and washed, wishing the damn boat had a shower. Physically I felt great, but my mental state got increasingly edgy as I recalled the details of our night. I'd done the thing I'd tried not to do. Okay, it hadn't been rape, but the circumstances were not exactly normal, either. Would she have fucked me if she weren't dependent upon me for protection in a hostile environment? I'd snatched her forcibly and brought her to this place, so anything she did with me, no matter how pleasurable, was done under some sort of coercion.

Plus, I'd been using terms like "my life, my soul" for her, and she understood Turkish. What was *that* all about? I'd never been accused of saying things I didn't mean in bed. Rather the contrary. Women tended to get pissed because I displayed so little affection when I fucked them.

Deep inside, I was aware of some weird atavistic fear of giving myself up to anything that resembled romantic love. It wasn't something I cared to examine too closely. It made me edgy, uncertain, maybe even a little scared.

Why, then, hadn't I been more cautious with Ellie? With her my self-discipline failed. She was uncovering feelings in me that I usually kept hidden.

The sexual passion she inspired truly did go beyond anything I'd experienced before. It was freaking me out. I'd been in an altered state of consciousness while making love with her. It was as if we were coming together in another place, another time, not here on a sailboat in the Aegean Sea on a moonlit spring night. The same thing had happened on the night we'd danced. There was something unreal about both interludes.

I shook my head, trying to clear it. *You're not falling for Ellie. You're hot for her, that's all.*

What a mess. I remembered her huge eyes, the joyful flush on her face as we'd played together, exulting in passion, again and again. She was going to be hurt by this. I'd already hurt her. She was a sweet, warm, giving woman—far more generous in spirit than I would ever fucking be. I prided myself on being a cold-hearted bastard. The kindest thing I could do for her now would be to stay away.

Anyway, how could I think about romantic entanglements when I had so many other things to worry about? If I had any scruples at all, I'd leave the girl alone.

I groaned at the thought. No more sex, no more kink, no more sweet hot passion? Shit. I wasn't sure I could give that up. I'd never been good at self-denial.

I flashed back to an image of her sweet body twisting beneath mine, her lovely eyes dilated with passion, her hips arched, her breasts glistening with my sweat and her own, and I turned rigid with a twitching, aching hard-on.

Fuck! I needed a cold shower.

Chapter 26

ELLIE

When I woke, I wasn't surprised to find myself alone. Nick always seemed to be up and about while I was still asleep. I would have liked to snuggle with him a little longer, kissing him and admiring his lean body by the light of the sun, but there would be time for that later.

I opened one of the portholes and inhaled the fresh ocean air. It was a beautiful day—sunny and sparkling. In the thick glass of the porthole, I caught a glimpse of my reflection, and hammed a smile.

I found Nick leaning over the instrument panel with a pair of pliers in one hand and a screwdriver in the other. Metin was with him, offering advice. I was abashed to see Metin. I wondered if he'd slept on board last night, if he'd heard some of my more impassioned cries. Then I remembered that Metin believed I'd been having sex with Nick since the day we met. It was a little late to be embarrassed in front of him.

"*Gunaydin,* Metin," I said, the Turkish for good morning. "*Gunaydin,* Nick."

Nick merely grunted.

"*Gunaydin,* lovely lady," Metin said, sending me a wide grin. "Your man is in a bad mood, trying to fix the radio."

"The electrical system's been sabotaged," Nick snarled. "Fortunately they didn't do an expert job. The lights are already working and we'll have communications again soon."

"Is that why the lights wouldn't work? Sabotaged by whom?"

"Three guesses," said Nick.

"Nigel."

"Bingo. Nigel or one of his thugs. It happened night before last. Metin heard a noise and saw someone swimming away. The creep escaped before he could stop him. We can't take the chance of its happening again. From now on one of us is going to have to keep watch on board."

I gazed at his golden-blond hair and longed to run my fingers through it once again. "Why should Nigel want to sabotage your radio?"

"I told you he doesn't trust me."

"So what does he think you're going to do—call in the customs patrol?" I spoke lightly. "If you did, you'd be arrested, too."

Nick said nothing. Metin was looking idly out to sea. No one offered an explanation.

It took a while for Nick's coldness to make an impression on my lovesick brain. He never had been overly demonstrative. If he didn't wish to pull me close and kiss me in front of Metin, I could understand that. After all, we'd supposedly been lovers for several days. We were adults, not teenagers; there was no reason for us to be all over each other every minute.

But I would have liked to hold his hand or perhaps to sit beside him, shoulders touching. At breakfast he sat across from me, farther away than Metin. He didn't seem to notice my frequent attempts to catch his eye.

Never mind. Maybe we'd be alone together after breakfast. Maybe we could go back to the stateroom and fuck.

But after breakfast he announced we were returning to the compound. "My grandfather's finally consented to leave. He'll be packing up his things, Ellie, and I thought you could give him a hand. He can't get around too well in that wheelchair. I know he'd appreciate some help, even though he's too stubborn to ask for it."

"Of course I'll help him. Is he giving up on the search for the Trojan artifacts?"

"For this season, yes. Nothing else has turned up. It's beginning to look as if we haven't got an ancient settlement at all, just some random pieces left by some temporary visitor to the island."

"He must be discouraged," I said, feeling sorry for the old man.

"A little. But he hasn't given up—he's vowing to return next fall and finish the job."

"You never told me what happened yesterday after I made that scene at the cavern. Do they know I speak Turkish? Did they hear what I said?"

"No," said Nick.

"They concluded you and Nick were having a personal argument," Metin said. "The men gossiped about your tempestuous spirit, saying, leave it to Nick to choose such a one." He grinned at Nick and added, "One thing they don't believe, though, was that you were taking Ellie away to bind up her ankle. It was more likely, they said, that you intended to beat her."

I felt myself blush. He hadn't beaten me, but he had spanked me a few times during the night. I'd loved it. "I suppose I'd better act chastened today," I said dryly.

"Be thankful you've still got your cover," said Nick. "Don't blow it again."

"What about the photographs?" I asked in a small voice. "What are we going to tell your grandfather about them? The truth—that I have claustrophobia?"

Nick hesitated. "I don't know. Let me think it over. Nigel's hot now on getting those pictures taken. For your own safety, it's probably better that he doesn't start thinking of you as less useful than I promised you'd be."

I shivered a little at the underlying threat.

"Don't say anything yet," Nick added. "I'll stall them for another day or so."

Nick didn't join me in the cabin, where I dawdled for a few minutes before we left to go ashore. He didn't sit next to me in the rowboat. By the time I was installed with his grandfather in the compound, I had some serious misgivings. Nick had made sweet, fervent, almost desperate love to me all night long, but not once in the hours since the dawn had he kissed me, or touched me, or smiled.

Something was wrong.

* * *

"Is something the matter, Ellie?" Nick's grandfather asked later that afternoon.

"No. Everything's fine."

"Are you having trouble with Nick?"

Some actress, I chided myself. I'd have to do better than this. I paused in the painstaking task of wrapping small clay potsherds in plastic and packing them in a box. "Why do you think that?"

The elderly man's blue eyes seemed to twinkle. "Everybody knows you two had a disagreement yesterday. Hauled you off to his boat so he could yell at you in private, I understand. Nigel was talking of organizing a rescue party."

"I doubt Nigel had my welfare at heart."

"No, probably not. He'd have been glad to embarrass Nick, though. I stopped him. I figured you could handle the matter yourself." He waited. When I didn't speak, he added, "I hope I wasn't wrong."

I could feel myself color slightly. "I handled it. Everything's fine."

"Nick can be moody," he observed after a slight pause.

I made a noncommittal sound.

"Are you in love with him?"

I gave a careless laugh. "Oh, yes. For now."

"No doubt he knows it, and that'll be what's scaring him."

"Scaring him?"

"You think he can't be scared? Cool-under-the-collar, unflappable Nicholas?"

"He's not likely to be scared by me." Rather the contrary, I thought.

"A woman's affection might scare him. Especially if he felt drawn to her, too."

"Why?" My voice was no higher than a whisper.

"Because the women he's loved have either died or left him. The young Nick was different from the cool customer we see now. He was sunny and affectionate, full of life and joy. He adored his mother. She died. He transferred his affections to my wife, his grandmother, but before too many years had passed she, also, died. Finally, he loved a young woman he went to college with. Elizabeth was her name, a lovely girl, if somewhat fickle."

"I've heard about her," I interrupted. "Nigel lured her away, apparently."

"That's right. A most unfortunate situation."

"What happened to her?"

"She also died."

My mouth dropped open. "I didn't know that. How?"

"I'm not certain. But the point is, Nick's had woman problems ever since. That can happen when you lose too often. He's not the most forgiving person in the world. Oh, yes, Nick's been getting back at the fair sex for a while now."

I considered the implications of this. Was that why he could sometimes be so hard-assed and cruel?

"I'd like to see him settled," Sir Avery went on, sounding wistful. "With a woman he loves, and maybe a family."

I blinked. A family? A woman he loved? What did those things have to do with me? "Why are you telling me this? I haven't known your grandson long, and soon we'll probably go our separate ways."

"If so, I'll be sorry for it. You strike me as the sort of woman who'd be good for Nick."

"Forgive me, but you hardly know me, Sir Avery. How do you know what sort of woman I am?"

"I'm an old man who has seen much, my dear." After a moment or two of silence, he added, "I know, for example, that you're secretly appalled by the task your fingers are performing now. Wrapping those potsherds for illegal sale."

My fingers faltered.

"Nick never should have told you the truth. It offends your sense of values, perhaps even your sense of history, to know what we are doing here." He paused while I raised troubled eyes to his face. "You don't criticize, yet you make me feel ashamed."

"I—I'm sorry. I never meant to..."

"I know. You're uncomfortable here, but you're loyal to Nick. You won't betray us, however much you might despise the nature of our activities. Am I not correct?"

I slowly nodded.

He chuckled and patted my shoulder. "I'm fond of you, my dear. If my grandson gives you any more trouble, come to me and I'll set the rascal straight."

I didn't see Nick again until suppertime. His withdrawal was all the more obvious when the men tried to get us to dance again. Nick refused, and no amount of teasing could get him to change his mind.

He didn't avoid me. He was courteous, yet distant. Even when the meal was over and he rose and took my arm, saying, "It's late, Ellie. Let's go," there was no fire in him, no anticipation.

When we reached our room, I felt all the tensions of the day rising like mist to surround me. We were finally alone. Surely now he would catch me in his arms. Surely now he would hold me, kiss me, or, hell, even order me to kneel. Surely that cold expression on his face didn't mean that he didn't want me anymore.

Even as I had these feelings, I hated myself for them. Just because we'd had good sex last night, I seemed to have forgotten the way he'd been abusing me.

"I'm going to have to spend the rest of the night on the boat," he said, his voice expressionless as his face. "To prevent any further accidents to the yacht's electronics."

"And you want me to stay here."

He handed me the key. "You can lock the door. You should be safe."

I met his crystalline green eyes. They were fathomless as the sea. "Fine," I said, trying to sound as cold as he did.

"Good," he said, and turned to go.

The words came out without my volition: "Why are you treating me like this?"

"Like what?" he asked, but I saw the muscles jump around his tight-clenched jaw.

"As if last night didn't happen."

He hesitated, and my heart took a dive. "I've got a lot on my mind."

"Okay." That was hard to argue with, but I wanted a clearer answer. At the same time, though, I was asking myself what the hell I'd expected? Hearts and flowers? He had kidnapped me, and now he had fucked me. End of story.

"You're not going to make a big deal about this, are you?" he said.

"No. It's just..." I fumbled for words. "You were so sweet and affectionate last night."

"You mean after I tied you up and jerked off on you? Or after I fucked you?"

My breath left me in a rush. *Oh, yes, Nick's been getting back at the fair sex for a while now.* Jerk. My stomach felt hollow. I should have known better than to let myself start crushing on the man who had put a rope around my neck and whipped me with a belt.

"Get out." He'd seen me panic; he'd seen me in a state of sexual bliss. But I was damned if the asshole was going to see me cry.

Chapter 27

NICK

I made for the door, feeling every bit like the jerk I was trying to be. I couldn't let her get too attached to me. It would hurt her even more if she started harboring any doomed romantic feelings. She deserved someone better than me. Someone kinder. Someone less fucked-up.

But at the door, I fumbled with the handle, palms slippery with sweat. A great sense of misgiving came over me. I felt dizzy and had to lean my forehead against the door. Her violet eyes, dark with pain, haunted me. Shit. Not like this.

I turned. She was staring at me, frozen, her hands clenched into fists. "Just go," she said, her mouth forming the almost-silent words.

"Fucking hell." I went back and jerked her against me, cradling her for a moment, and then hauling her off her feet. Next thing I knew, I was whirling around and around with her in a confused, silent dance. "I'm sorry, I didn't mean it. It's just that

I'm no good for you, no damn good at all. I was only trying to free you. You don't need a man like me."

Her head came up, her eyes searching mine, her lips so damp and wet and open that I couldn't resist them. I wrapped my fingers in the hair and sought her mouth with all the hunger of a starving man. For an instant she was stiff, resistant...for an instant she fought me. Then she made that familiar crooning sound in the back of her throat and pressed against me, arching.

"Ellie, Ellie, Ellie..." Muttering the litany of her name, I carried her over to the mattress and laid her down, falling upon her, crushing her beneath my hard and ready body. I drove against her belly, cursing the clothing that divided our flesh. She whimpered and dragged her fingers down my spine; I could feel the imprint of her nails.

Tomorrow I'll stop, tomorrow I'll leave her fuck the alone, I promised myself as I rose to my knees and tore at her jeans. She helped me. She was as eager as I was. I could feel her thighs trembling as I bared them. They convulsed around me as, not even bothering to strip off my own jeans, I unzipped and freed my dick. She pulled me down on her, sliding her hands under the tight blue denim to clutch my ass as I arched and drove into her.

Christ! She was so soft, so silky smooth, so sweet. She fit my body perfectly. Glove-tight, she surged around me. Breathing hard, I thrust in long, slow strokes, rough cloth against silken skin, half-aware that I might be hurting her, yet hearing nothing but pleasure in the low, ecstatic cries she gave. Our rhythm increased. She writhed and wrapped her legs around me as if to draw my entire body inside her. "Please," she panted. "Please, Nick, please!"

Tomorrow I'll make her see that I'm bad for her. Tomorrow. God forgive me, but I can't stop it now.

I loved her. Harder, faster, deeper. Then suddenly I felt as if I were outside myself. We were both transported into a tunnel of light stretching ahead in time and back in time in an endless series of meetings and partings, unions and reunions, births and separations and deaths. I cried out her name, but it was not her name; it was a name I'd never heard before. And yet she answered, calling out to me in an unknown language.

Total freak-out.

As the convulsions of orgasm rocked us both, I knew the bodies that gave such pleasure were dust and ashes, reborn like the phoenix to live a short while, then die. But we were joined; we were mates. Our souls were eternal. I might deny it; I might dismiss the experience, laugh, or try my best to forget it—in fact, I was sure I'd dismiss it as soon as the weird-ass climax faded. But it would still be true.

Chapter 28

NICK

Having weird, mystical-shit sex with Ellie didn't exactly do good things for my peace of mind the next day while I worked my ass off dismantling the excavations. I suppose it was better than brutal sadistic sex, for her, anyway. For me, who knew? My head was a total mess.

It didn't help that I was afraid Nigel was about to bolt. That was always the risk—that he would spirit himself out of the way before the troops came in and arrested him. He had always been a slippery rat. He seemed to sense the traps that were laid for him. Gossip had reached Metin, who had a knack for getting along with everybody, that Nigel and his small group of loyalists were packing up their gear.

I needed to get Granddad away before Nigel left. I wanted him, not my grandfather, to be caught with the loot. If my cousin was planning to skip out on us, I had to follow through with my plan to distract him.

Which meant using Ellie.

When I returned to the compound after an afternoon keeping watch on *Voyager,* I hoped Ellie would be glad to see me. Even though it wasn't bedtime, I pictured her lying in bed, waiting up for me. Her silky-soft skin. Her lush, fragrant hair, her small breasts, so pale but for their crimson-brown peaks that jutted when I stroked them. Her slender thighs and the moist, dark triangle in between.

I wanted her naked this time. Making love almost fully clothed had been exciting, but tonight I wanted to see her. I wanted to watch her body arch in the moonlight. On her hands and knees, arching her spine in pain/pleasure as I spanked her ass and thrust into her from behind. I imagined plucking, twisting, pinching the crests of her breasts as I rode her. I knew now how much she liked that. I needed to watch her writhe and hear the little gasps she released as she made her pleasure sounds.

I'd buried all my qualms from the previous night. I couldn't stay away from her. No, this fire would burn until there was nothing left to feed it. Maybe I shouldn't have kindled the blaze in the beginning, but it was far too late now to damp down those flames.

She was sitting on the chair and brushing her lovely hair when I entered our room. For a moment I envisioned her tied to that chair, naked, her arms bound behind her and her legs spread apart. I couldn't seem to help it—every time I looked at her, I thought of sex.

Get it together, fool.

She smiled at me. "You look tired. Rough day?"

I crossed to her and kissed her, thinking how domestic this seemed...I came home from work and here was my beautiful partner waiting for me. We had come a strange distance in just a few days from me holding a gun on her and wrapping a belt around her throat.

"You should be naked and crawling to greet me, slave."

She laughed. "Stop trying to dom me all the time. I don't know what your game is, Nicholas, but I'm beginning to realize that about 80 percent of everything you say is a lie. I don't know who you are, exactly, but you're not who I thought you were."

Well, she had that right. I decided to go with it. "Do you trust me, Ellie?"

"Not really," she said, with a certain charming candor.

"Let me put it this way—how much do you trust me?"

Grinning, she held her finger and thumb about a quarter of an inch apart.

"Try this: how much do you trust me to keep a promise that I make to you?"

Her expression melted. "Fine. Maybe in some respects you're trustworthy."

"I am going to ask you to do something for me. Something dangerous. Something you will hate. But no harm will come to you if you do this thing for me." At least, I sure hoped it wouldn't. I was going to make damn sure she was protected. "It'll be unpleasant, but that part won't last long."

She blinked. "If you are going to ask me to go into that cave and take those photographs—"

"That's not it. More unpleasant even than that, I'm afraid."

I had her now. Silly brave girl.

"What could possibly be more unpleasant than that?"

I swallowed. This part was difficult even for me to say, much less expect her to do. "I want you to flirt with Nigel. Make him think you could be his submissive."

Her face went pale. "Are you crazy?"

"Nothing will happen to you. I promise. I won't let him hurt you. I just need access to his stuff, and for that, I need you to distract him for me."

"He creeps me out. And I don't want to submit to anyone except you."

I rounded the chair and draped my arms around her from behind. She resisted for a couple of moments, then let her body go partially limp. I stroked her back, fondled her hair, and instantly had a hard-on. So what else is new?

"If you do this for me, I'll explain everything. You're right that I'm not who you think I am, but I need you to go on playing the part you've been playing so well for the past few days. My not very submissive slave, who has caused me one headache after another. Who is not very trainable and might be better off with another master."

"How about with no master?"

I leaned forward to kiss the top of her head. "I need to get you and my grandfather safely away from here. The price for that is Nigel on a silver platter. That's as much as I can tell you right now. Please trust me and, for once, follow my orders."

She twisted around in the chair to stare at me, her violet eyes wide. "You're working undercover?"

I gave the slightest of nods.

"Oh my god." Her face lit up. "Okay. I'll help you if I can."

Fuck. She did trust me.

I told her what I wanted her to do. She was skeptical. I really couldn't blame her.

"You'll be safe. Metin will be looking out for you. Granddad will be there and he's already grown fond of you. He won't let anything happen. And I won't be gone for long."

"But what if..."

"It'll be okay. Just stay in the main hall where everyone else is. Don't go anywhere with the creep. The worst he can do is insult you. I don't think he'll even do that, but if he does, remember what I've told you about maintaining a submissive mindset. Just bow your head and let whatever he says float over you. Don't respond."

"What if he touches me?"

"He might. He's a touchy kind of guy. But as long as he doesn't touch you in a sexual manner—and I'll kill him if he tries that—it should be endurable, right? In public, what can he do? It's not considered polite to engage in public displays of affection in Turkey, particularly with a woman who belongs to someone else. He would incur disapproval, even from his own men."

"I'm not sure he'd care."

"He's not all-powerful. He has weaknesses, and I am going to use them. If it works, this'll all be over, and we'll be able to clear out of here."

"Okay," she said, still sounding uncertain.

I couldn't think of any way to reassure her that wouldn't be a lie, so I kissed her instead.

Chapter 29

NICK

I talked to Metin, and then I went after Nigel.

He was hanging out with his thugs in the main hall, drinking. His guys were drinking, anyway. Nigel rarely indulged in alcohol. He had always been contemptuous of people who gave in to their weaknesses.

From the delicious smells coming from the kitchen, dinner was being prepared. My stomach growled, but I ignored it. Dinner had become a ritual around here, and a dependable ritual was exactly what I needed.

I sat down among them and accepted a glass of raki. They didn't exactly make me welcome, but I ignored the vibe. "Can we talk?" I said to my cousin after knocking back the milky liquid. Fortunately, it took more than one raki to affect my mental acuity.

Nigel gestured to his men, who obediently rose and moved away. I suspected some of them could still hear, so I spoke English. Several of them would understand, but I didn't really care about that.

"I don't know how sincere your interest was," I drawled, "but I've decided to get rid of my slave. She's not as tractable as I hoped she'd be. I'm going to auction her off via an intermediary I know. Just in case you want to get in on that action."

His eyes narrowed. "Why would I care about your leavings?"

I was tempted to remind him that he'd cared in the past, but I resisted. I was having a tough enough time keeping myself from smashing his face in. "No reason. Except that I've seen you following her with your eyes. She's easy on the eyes, isn't she? Too bad she's so difficult to train."

He smiled in his lazy, superior manner. "Maybe your methods are faulty. I heard she caused some trouble at the dig yesterday. Refused to take the photographs?"

"She had a problem with her equipment."

Nigel cocked a disbelieving eyebrow. "That's not the way I heard it."

"Whatever. I don't care whether you're interested in her or not. The arrangements will be made through an agent of mine." I slammed my empty glass on the table and stood. "If you want the guy's contact info, let me know. Otherwise forget I mentioned it."

"Does she know?"

"Of course not. I want to keep it that way. She's enough of a headache as it is."

He was about to say something else, but I cut him off with a gesture and stalked away.

I called up to Granddad that I was going to spend the night on my boat and left the compound.

I met Metin, as previously arranged, in the shelter of a dark cliff. He had brought the items I'd been keeping locked up on the boat: several small but valuable Hittite coins and a couple of gold earrings. They were hot and precious. I hadn't stolen them; they were plants donated by Hepburn. Where the fuck he had gotten them, I didn't know and I didn't ask.

Nigel had always been careful. It was one of the main reasons that he had so far escaped prison. He made sure never to implicate himself. He had lackeys to cart around his stolen items. He never carried anything suspicious on his person, not even a fake passport. Even though he was working closely with our grandfather, he'd made sure that if anybody got nailed for this, it would be Granddad, not him.

Yeah, nice guy.

He had my number, but I also had his. I'd known him all my life and I knew stuff about him that few others knew.

He wouldn't be able to resist going after Ellie tonight. I didn't think he would try to rape her, given the number of people in the building, but he was sick enough to want to taunt her. He would gloat over her, taking pleasure in her ignorance of my supposed plans to sell her.

Stuff like that got him off.

She would be alone and vulnerable. He wouldn't be able to resist. And while he was stalking her, I was going to hammer the last fucking nail in and make sure that when Hepburn moved in a couple of days from now, Nigel would be caught with the goods on him.

Assuming, of course, that everything went as planned.

It usually didn't.

I waited in the dark outside the room where Nigel slept. It was, of course, the best room in the place—the largest, the one closest to the bathroom, the one with the best view of the ocean. I'd have given that room to Granddad, but Nigel's mind didn't work that way. He wanted the best of everything, and if it didn't come naturally to him, he found a way to take it.

Fine. I planned to use those tendencies against him.

He left the room, as I'd expected he would, striding past the corner where I was concealing myself. Better still, his hound, Sinan, shadowed him. Sinan served as a sort of bodyguard for Nigel, although I doubted that was his actual role. But he seemed to be loyal to my cousin, and he stuck to him and proba-bly shared most of his confidences. Nigel trusted him more than he trusted anyone else, but Nigel didn't fully trust a soul. Nor would he hesitate to stab a comrade in the back if it suited him.

I was afraid they might go to Ellie's room, but they descend-ed the stairs to the ground floor. I'd set Metin to keep watch on Ellie tonight. I was pretty sure Nigel was going to hassle her, but I hoped I'd be able to finish my own task before things got ugly.

Nigel's room was empty. I was careful as I slipped inside it, though. I wouldn't put it past him to leave some sort of booby trap in place. He had a damnably suspicious mind.

And, sure enough, he wasn't going to make things easy for me. There was nothing of interest in his room. Metin had been right. Nigel had already packed up. His personal possessions must have been taken to his boat. Fuck. I'd figured as much, but it made my task more difficult.

I slipped back out of the room and out of the compound. I had planned for this eventuality too. I got what I needed from the cache I'd left under some rocks on the beach, donned my wet suit and mask, and swam silently out to Nigel's moored motor-boat.

Chapter 30

ELLIE

I was nervous during dinner so I felt thirstier than usual. I drank water and a little fruit juice. Not the raki, though. After an hour or so, when Nick didn't return, the combination of liquids and nervousness made it imperative for me to find the bathroom. I put it off for as long as I could, since the only toilet on this floor was down a corridor toward the back of the compound. There was one on the upper floor, but Nick had told me not to go up there this evening.

So far, Nigel had left me alone. He was at the other end of the table, talking to his men. Unlike Nick, he never danced or joined in the musical activities. I wondered if this was because of what Sir Avery had told me about Nick always being better at music and the arts. How ironic that something the young Nick had been teased about was valued among the males here in Turkey.

I set off down the corridor toward the toilet. The weird thing was that I realized as soon as I stood up that I felt a little drunk.

But I'd taken no alcohol. Maybe I was just tired from staying up all night fucking? The thought of curling up somewhere and going to sleep was appealing. A cold thought came to me: had I been drugged? Where the hell was Nick? I hoped he'd hurry up and come back.

I made it into the toilet, which was one of those traditional Turkish toilet holes in the floor. I didn't like them, but I'd lived in some of the less developed parts of the country long enough to be accustomed to them. They were perfectly nice porcelain bowls...they were just set into the floor, with footrests carved into the porcelain on either side so you could swat down in relative security. I pulled down my panties and squatted to relieve myself, glad there was a latch on the inside toilet door. It was strange being the only female in the entire place.

There was a small tap and bowl inside where I could wash my hands, but no paper towel to dry them. Typical. I made do, tidied myself up, and unlatched the door.

When I stepped back out into the dimly lit corridor, Nigel was there. My heart clutched. I ordered myself not to be silly. He probably had to use the facilities, too.

"I'm sorry if I've made you wait," I said, stepping out and to the side. The hallway was narrow, and Nigel had planted himself smack in the middle of it. I could not get by without touching him, which was something I really didn't care to do.

Instead of entering the toilet, he folded his arms across his chest and said, "Where is your master tonight, little slave?"

His tone was not unpleasant, but something in the depths of his blue eyes was. I dropped my gaze and let my shoulders relax, trying to appear submissive. "I'm not sure," I said, which was true enough. "I think he had things to do on the yacht."

Nigel slid an arm around my shoulder and walked me farther along the corridor, which ended in a door. I didn't know where that door went, and I didn't want to find out. I glanced back over my shoulder. Where was Metin? He was supposed to be watching out for me.

I was still feeling dizzy. Had I been drugged? The corridor was dark and narrow and my claustrophobia began to kick in, too. This was not right. Nick had told me to flirt with Nigel, not to go off by myself with him.

I tried to detach his arm from my back, but he was solid muscle. "I want to go back to the dining room. I haven't finished my meal."

"Don't worry, pet. I'll make sure you're filled up."

My body shot into fight or flight mode, with the incipient claustrophobia kicking my adrenaline levels even higher. "Please let go of me, sir," I tried, with one last attempt at following orders to act submissive. When he didn't, I sucked in breath to scream. Maybe there weren't too many people in the compound who would help me, but Metin was there. And Nick's grandfather...although the latter had poor hearing.

"Shut the fuck up," snarled Nigel, jamming his big hand across my mouth before I could get out more than a squeak. He dragged my struggling body to the end of the corridor and flung open that last door.

It led outside. Away from safety. Away from witnesses. The fucking brute had me.

Chapter 31

NICK

Nigel's boat wasn't as nice a vessel as Max's yacht, but it looked fucking fast.

I assumed there would be a man on board, guarding the boat. I was right. He didn't see or hear me coming. I slipped in behind him and got him in a headlock before he knew what hit him. I knocked him out with a blow to the head, trying to do it hard enough to keep him unconscious for a while, but not hard enough to kill him. It was Selim, one of the younger and stupider members of my cousin's little band of outlaws. Although I didn't know him well, I was pretty sure he wasn't religious, which suited my purposes. The Islamic prohibition against alcohol wouldn't be in play. I pulled out the pint of raki I'd stashed in one of the wetsuit zipped pockets and sloshed some around in his mouth, poured a little down his neck and chest, and took a hit myself before emptying the bottle over the side and wedging it under the netting behind him. He would have his own story to tell Nigel tomorrow, but it would look as though he'd fallen asleep on the job.

Once that was taken care of, I went below to find the master cabin. Because I knew what I was going to do, this part went smoothly. All I needed now were Nigel's precious custom-made shoes. My cousin is obsessive about his appearance; always has been. Has to have the best of everything. But I swear the guy has a fucking shoe fetish. I hated to think about how much each pair must cost. On a dig, where most guys traveled light with old clothes rolled in to a backpack and the tools of their trade far more important to them than what they wore, Nigel stood out for having the best leather on his feet.

Too bad for him.

From my pocket I removed a special tool that Rob Hepburn had provided me with when we'd set this thing up. I wasn't sure if it was standard spy gear or if it had been specially engineered for this job.

What this item allowed me to do was slide either a fragile gold earring or an ancient coin into a thin sliding thing. I could then hold the device to the side of one of Nigel's Italian loafers, press a button, and presto, a blade slid out the side and inserted the contraband into the heel of the shoe, leaving hardly a trace behind to reveal that the shoe had been tampered with.

Hepburn had told me that the last time my cousin had been stopped at a border, he'd been impossible to detain because he'd been clean of any contraband. This time Hepburn was going to make sure it didn't happen. He'd provided me with six stolen objects, all small enough and slim enough to be hidden in the heel of different shoes of Nigel's. I found four pairs of shoes in his room, in addition to whatever he was currently wearing on his feet. That gave me eight individual shoes to work with. Nigel's expensive shoes had just become even more valuable.

It didn't bother me that Nigel hadn't stolen this stuff. I hoped he'd go down for the crimes he had actually committed, but if Hepburn wanted to ensure that he didn't twist out of the charges the way he always had before, that was fine with me.

I'd have liked to stay longer and really go through his stuff, but I was antsy about leaving Ellie. Even though I figured she'd be safe enough with Granddad there and Metin to watch out for her, I'd already been gone too long. Besides, I wasn't sure how long the guard dog would remain unconscious.

I went back to the dude and searched his pockets for a mobile phone. Cell coverage on the island was spotty, but sometimes it worked. I didn't want him to be able to send a text.

Phone found. No signal, but I tossed it in the sea anyhow. Then I slipped into the water and stroked back to shore.

Chapter 32

ELLIE

When Nigel closed the door and slammed me up against it, I realized that it wasn't submission he was looking for. For the first time I saw the man Nick had warned me about. He might be beautifully dressed and groomed, but Nigel was a beast.

"So...do you know what your lover told me today? Not that I fucking believe him for a moment, but you might want to think about it before you answer the other questions I have for you."

Uh oh. This wasn't what I had expected "flirting with Nigel" would consist of. "I'm not sure what you mean, sir," I mumbled, through his fingers which were still jamming my mouth closed and keeping me from screaming.

"He tells me he's decided to sell you to a new master. Someone rich and cruel, no doubt."

Even though I knew this was bullshit, it still jolted me to hear it again. Nigel wasted no time rubbing it in: "How does it feel to know that he values ancient objects of metal and stone more than flesh and blood people? What did you expect when he took you? That he would one day return you to your country of origin?"

Was this supposed to make me leave Nick and turn to him? I'd expected a more suave approach. Where was all his fake charm?

"He'll probably sell you to some wealthy Arab or perhaps farther East to someone in Thailand or Malaysia. Maybe for a while you'll have an easy life in some cozy harem, but when your master gets sick of you and your beauty begins to fade, it'll be the streets for you. Sex, drugs and booze, if you can get it. Dead before you're 30."

Does he actually expect me to believe that? "Why are you telling me this?"

He cupped my chin in his hand. I felt the strength in his fingers, and was afraid. He was not like Nick. There was no tenderness in Nigel.

"A woman alone in a rough place like this is a temptation for some of the men, you know. I wouldn't want anything to happen to you."

"How kind of you," I said, trying to restrain the sarcasm.

His other hand came up and anchored in my hair. I couldn't move. I felt nothing but disgust. "Does he please you in bed?"

There was something about this scene that amused him, I sensed. Something was going on that I didn't understand. "He's adequate. I've had better."

The irony intensified. "Is that so?" He jerked me closer. I hadn't seen the movement coming, and I flinched. Was there a way out of this? My rapid heartbeat told me that my body was getting desperate to think of one. "The thing is, I don't think this slave marketing thing is really gonna happen, do you?"

"I hope not," I said, having no clue what my answer should be.

"Because Nick's being involved in human trafficking is all bullshit, isn't it?"

I was beginning to get seriously alarmed. Nothing about this was happening the way I'd anticipated.

Nigel shook my body so hard my hair went flying. "Answer me, bitch."

"I'm not sure what you're asking."

"What I want to know, what you are going to tell me, is this: what are you and your precious choirboy planning? Who is Hepburn?"

I froze. *You're working with Hepburn, aren't you? Who the fuck is Hepburn? Who the fuck are you?*

Nick hadn't referred to Hepburn again last night, and in the rush of emotions that had followed since then, I'd forgotten all about that interchange.

Nigel's hand had slipped down to my throat. I shook my head, hoping I looked as clueless as I was. "I don't know. If he's planning something, he hasn't informed me."

Nigel hit me. Pain shuddered through my face and jaw, making me realize that Nick had never done anything truly violent to me. Nigel had just punched me in the face, knocking me sideways. I lost my balance and fell in a heap on the ground, my head ringing and my vision blurred. Nigel was strong. I felt as though someone had just slammed a two-by-four into the side of my head.

From somewhere high above me I heard his voice say, "That's a sample of what you'll get if you don't answer my questions." He seized me by the hair and jerked me to my feet. More pain burned in my scalp. I would have screamed if I'd been capable of making a sound, but the first blow had knocked the wind out of me. "Do you think I'm a fool to fall for your tricks?" He sounded furious. If I'd been able to see him through my dazed eyes, I'm sure he would have been foaming at the mouth.

I could taste my own blood on the inside of my cheek. I must have bitten myself when he'd struck me.

He dragged me a couple of yards away from the building. I'd never been out here at the back before. It was rocky, as most of the island was. The compound was close to one of the many overhanging cliffs. From somewhere not too far away I thought I could hear the waves of the Aegean crashing, but it might have been the ringing in my head.

He shoved me toward the almost-vertical cliff of earth and stone that loomed over the old villa. I stumbled on some loose rocks. I think one of my shoes came off, but Nigel didn't stop hauling me into the dark, out of sight of anyone who might have come to help me. Not that anyone would. Where the hell was Metin? He was supposed to be keeping watch on me while Nick was away.

I heard footsteps approaching fast, and thought, thank god, but my hopes were crushed when I heard a rough voice say, "Boss? I got word to meet you back here?"

It was Sinan, the only one of Nigel's crew whose name I knew. He seemed to be the leader of the workers whose loyalty was more to Nigel than to Sir Avery. He had never acknowledged my existence, and he continued to ignore my plight now.

"Any sign of my fucking cousin?"

"No," said Sinan. "The sidekick is out of action now, too. He's been drinking that cherry juice, unaware of what's in it."

Metin. Drugged. I'd had a bit of the cherry juice, too, but it had been too sweet for me, so I'd mostly drunk the water. I was probably supposed to be a good deal more disabled than I actually was, but I couldn't see what good this would do me against two strong and vicious thugs like these.

"Good. I have this under control. Go back and keep watch. I don't want to be interrupted."

Having nothing to lose, I said in Turkish, "Sinan, please help me. You know I am with Nick. Nigel has dragged me out here against my will, and—"

Nigel struck me again, cutting off my plea. Sinan continued to walk away, although I thought I saw his shoulders hunch a little at my cries, as if he were trying his best not to hear.

Nigel threw one arm around my neck while the other squeezed both my wrists together behind my back and twisted. I writhed in pain but couldn't dislodge him. Disgust filled me as I felt his dick turn hard in his pants. I think tears were coming by then, but I hardly noticed. I was trying to breathe, trying to resist and losing all hope.

"Here's the thing. Nick has been stealing artifacts for about half a year now. I just heard from one of my contacts that an object we removed from a dig near the Turkish border with Syria was returned to the Turkish government. Odd, don't you think? The buyers to whom we sell our wares are not likely to pay large sums of cash for something that they altruistically give back. How do you explain that?"

I was just as astonished to hear this as I was pretending to be. Items stolen by Nick were making their way back to Turkey? Why was he stealing antiquities if he was returning them? Was the whole story about contributing to his grandfather's thievery a ploy?

Hope soared in me. That would explain so much.

You mean you're working undercover?

"I can't explain it," I said. "I don't understand why you're even asking me. Before my master brought me here, I knew nothing about his business dealings."

"What did you and he fight about yesterday?"

"We had a silly argument. What does it matter?"

"You're a sex slave, supposedly. You don't get into silly arguments with your master."

Okay. I admit I didn't have a good quick answer to that one. After a pause, I tried, "I haven't proven to be quite as trainable as my master hoped."

"No, Ms. Helen Heath. I'm sure you haven't."

He hit me again. I don't think it was quite as hard this time. He probably wanted to be able to question someone who still had a few teeth in her mouth.

"You're no fucking sex slave. Haven't you ever heard of facial analysis software? You're not the only one around here with a camera. I had one of my guys take some pictures of you the first night you showed up, and guess what—it didn't take long to find your face on the internet. Next time you try to go undercover, you might want to purge Facebook and your blog of your profile picture."

"I'm not undercover," I gasped, sure he was going to smash my face in. I wasn't the freaking person who was undercover, dammit!

"You think I don't know who your mother is? She's well known for her views on the supposed evils of the illegal antiquities trade, in Turkey especially. She's associated with several organizations that try to stop such heinous activities. You're probably working for one of her groups."

"Why? Just because I'm her daughter? My mother and I don't see eye to eye on a lot of things. Haven't you ever heard about children who rebel against everything their parents represent? Folks, like, maybe you?" I paused, and then added viciously, "Weren't your own parents good, decent, respectable archaeologists before they died in that tragic plane crash over the Amazon River?"

He didn't like this. Not one bit. This time he jerked my head back, ripping out god only knew how much hair by the roots. "I'll ask you one more time. What are you and your boyfriend planning? Why are you here?" He grabbed me by the front of my shirt and slid his foul fingers beneath the rope collar on my neck. He twisted, wrenching it tight, cutting off my air. Then he whirled me around, and flung me against a small building—I think it was a tool shed—at the rear of the compound. The hand at my throat moved down to my breasts. At least I could breathe again. But he squeezed my breast as if he were juicing fruit. I gasped in agony, and he churned his hips against me, clearly aroused by my pain.

He'd struck me. He'd interrogated me.

Rape was next on the agenda, it seemed.

Followed, most likely, by murder.

"Nothing to say?" One of his fingers ran around my mouth, roughly exploring both my lips, and then forcing my mouth open. "If you won't talk, let's see if we can find another use for this mouth. Remember that blowjob I asked for?" He stuck two fingers in my mouth, making me gag. "I'll take it now. And then I'll fuck you." I felt him fumbling with his belt. "When I'm done with you, I'll turn you over to my men and make you blow them and fuck them too, until you're sticky and covered with cum."

I did the only thing I could to resist this guy, who was bigger and taller than Nick and much more brutal. I spit in his face. If anyone was going to be covered with body fluids, it would be him, not me.

Of course he hit me again, but I figured I'd rather be knocked unconscious than have to give the creep head.

"What the *fuck*," yelled a harsh male voice from somewhere nearby. Nick was coming at a run from the other side of the compound. His voice turned harsher still as he shouted, "Down, slave."

My response to his command was instant. I went limp, sinking away from Nigel until I hit the ground. Above my aching head I heard a strange sound, less a sound than a parting of the air where just a moment before my body had been. There was a thunk, and the shed wall seemed to shudder. Nigel bellowed and staggered backwards, away from me. He started screaming curses while I huddled, trembling in the dirt. I lifted my head only the tiniest amount. Nick was poised there, looking hard and tough in his too-tight jeans, his hair shining. His rough, unshaven face was cold, impassive. He might be totally uninvolved with me, for all the animation he displayed.

His knife, which I recognized, was sticking in the wall of the shed, gleaming darkly as the moon popped out from behind a cloud. Nigel staggered beside me, one hand clutching his bleeding shoulder. "If you were aiming for my heart, you fucking missed," he roared.

"I told you to stay away from her," Nick said in a deadly tone. "It's a good thing your dick is still in your pants, or my aim would have been six inches lower, and your fucking heart would be silent."

Chapter 33

NICK

Standing there confronting the monstrous sight of Ellie in Nigel's power, all my bitterness and resentment came surging up out of the dark place where I'd tried so hard to keep it hidden. I saw my handsome, hated cousin seducing Elizabeth, the woman I'd loved in college. I had never found out exactly what he had done to her that had destroyed her bright mind, but I knew it was foul. No one had been able to save her after Nigel got through with her. Not even Hepburn, who had also loved her.

Now Nigel was hurting another woman I cared about. Somehow he had gotten her alone. It couldn't have been for long, but from the dazed look on her face, it had been long enough.

Still, she'd obeyed me instantly when I'd given the order. He hadn't broken her.

"Nick, thank god," she said, sounding shaky.

"Are you all right?"

"He hit me. I think I'm spitting out teeth."

I felt my control start to go. Nigel was holding his shoulder, but there wasn't much gushing blood. Not enough to suit me. Too bad. I should have aimed lower.

I wanted to deal with Nigel and get Ellie the fuck away from here. "I warned you what would happen, asshole," I snarled at my cousin.

Nigel recovered, shook himself off, and came at me, arrogant, despite with the knife wound. "You should have stayed on your boat. But since you haven't—" He feinted with his right fist, then released the first real blow, an impressive left hook. I saw it, ducked, twisted, and laughed softly as Nigel's punch missed me altogether. I waited until the bastard realized the full magnitude of his error.

What a conceited idiot. Just because he'd beaten me to a pulp a few times when we were kids, he thought it would still be that easy? Fuck him. I exploded, attacking with feet and elbows, fists and knees. He went down. I fell on him. A black haze came over me. I wasn't even sure what I was doing. My limbs were flying. I was going to kill the fucker. He had poisoned the lives of the people I loved for too many years.

I felt his body recoil as I struck him. I felt muscles give and bones shudder. In a couple minutes I'd feel blood seeping until my fists were thick with it. You know what? That was fucking okay with me.

"Nick!" Ellie screamed. "Stop it. He's had enough."

Fuck that. I wanted to kill my blackhearted cousin. The rage was so strong in me that I couldn't think. I pounded him some more, and then caught one of Ellie's wrists. I wrenched her closer, dragged her to the ground, and pressed her down on her back. Next thing I knew I was straddling her body like a conqueror. Kill the man or fuck the woman? Tough choice. I guess this was what bloodlust felt like.

Nigel lay doubled up beside us, groaning.

"Nick. Please. Stop."

I fought for control. Her calm voice helped. She didn't sound afraid. I clung to the sound of her voice.

"It's okay," she said. "You can stop now."

Aggression still coiled in me, rolling around like a living thing, but I was beginning to be able to think. To reason. Was this what happened when you tried too hard to control all the details of your life, to figure out the angles, to analyze the possibilities, to intellectualize your feelings, to rise above the monster that dwelt deep within?

The monster lay in waiting for a moment like this. A chance to erupt and wreak havoc. To beat, to rape, to kill.

But Ellie's eyes were searching mine, and her clear gaze centered me. We stared at each other, taut with tension, neither of us certain what the next moment would bring.

"Nick?" she repeated, her voice no more than a whisper. Her face was red, I saw, even though the light back here was dim. Her hair was askew, and around her left eye, swelling was starting.

Shuddering, I lifted my hands away from her. I ran shaking fingers through my sweaty hair. "Ellie." He had hurt her. I'd almost hurt her, too. "I'm not myself. I could have hurt you."

"You could have killed Nigel. He's your cousin. Your flesh and blood."

"He'll live." I managed to vault to my feet. "Let's go. I'm taking you back to the boat."

"Yes, *please*," she said. Was that more of her damn sarcasm? No, of course not. She wanted to get away from here. She needed ice for that eye, that jaw. She needed caring, not violence. "Ellie?"

She came closer and touched me, nothing more than a light finger brushing against the side of my cheek. Reflexively I grabbed her hand and held it to my lips. "You warned me that around you things are not always what they seem."

She knew something. Okay. No time to discuss it now. A clatter in the hallway suggested that the men were coming out to investigate the racket. "We'll go to *Voyager*. Where the fuck is Metin?"

"They drugged him. They tried to drug me, too, but I didn't drink much."

I swore. Nigel had been one step ahead of me. That was always a danger when your adversary was not only black-hearted but also smart.

Chapter 34

ELLIE

We hardly spoke at all on the way to the yacht. Nick was clearly trying to come down after an explosion of bloodlust, and I was starting to notice the pain of being struck several times in the face by Nigel. I could feel my eyes and cheeks swelling. The left side was worse than the right. By the time we rowed out to *Voyager*, I could hardly see through my bleary, stinging eyes. Nick had to carry me up the steps and sling me over the side. I lay on the deck where he had put me, curling up against the pain and humiliation of what Nigel had done to me. Tried to do to me. That must be what it felt like to be a trafficked woman—helpless, aching, and miserable, with no possible hope of rescue.

Fifteen minutes later, I lay in bed in the master cabin on the *Voyager,* waiting for Nick to join me. He was in the head. He had washed my face and applied ice. He'd been gentle. He'd taken care of me. He'd come for me, at last.

And he wasn't a thief at all. That thought had kept making me smile as he'd rowed us out to *Voyager*. It had been a magical smile, apparently, because when he'd seen it, Nick's rage and aggression had melted like a snowball in the sun.

I couldn't deny that on some primitive level, the attack on his cousin had roused something similar in me. I understood how someone could attack a cruel, vicious man. Particularly if he was hurting someone who couldn't fight back. Did it mean Nick cared about me? Or was it just a stronger form of aggression than most females have inside us? Could I hurt—or even kill—in defense of someone I loved? I don't think I'd ever contemplated that before.

I yawned and looked at the clock beside the bed. Midnight. Was it last night that we'd lain together here, laughing, sighing, and giving each other pleasure? My heavy eyelids closed as I re-experienced those delicious moments. I was almost asleep, when the head door opened and my fierce lover burst back into the room.

I eyed him over the hem of the sheet, which I had pulled up to my chin. He was tall and strong, and his gilt hair was slightly darkened from the sweat of his exertion with Nigel. His finely molded cheekbones seemed more prominent than usual. His eyes blazed emerald bright.

He was dangerous, primitive. He'd beaten up a man on my account. Those hands could crush me if he chose. But in the impassioned moment when he might have done so, he hadn't hurt me. I sent him another beaming smile.

"Here we are in your cabin again," I said cheerfully. "Me, your captive, awaiting my master's pleasure. What are you going to do to me this time?"

He stared at me for a second or two, then jerked his shirt over his head, and dropped his hands to the snap of his jeans. A bolt of heat pierced my vitals, then radiated throughout my body. "Not a whole lot. I mean, I'd like to tie you down and fuck you in every hole, just to prove you're mine, but you're hurt."

"You can do that," I whispered, amazed at the way his word enflamed me. The ache in my face and jaw seemed to fade. "My libido still feels healthy."

He shook his head, grinning. He kicked off his shoes and stripped himself of his jeans. I squirmed at the sight of his thrusting cock. "Yours looks okay, too," I added.

He got into bed and reached for me under the sheet. I was naked. He caressed me gently.

"Even so," he said. "Gotta try to be gentle." He pulled the sheet down, I felt his gaze burning into my breasts. My nipples responded by buttoning into hard little nubs. He murmured his approval. He ran his fingers through my hair. Static electricity caused it to cling to his palm. He caressed my shoulder, rubbing the skin over my collarbone with his thumb. Then he trailed the tips of his fingers along my arm until he captured one of my wrists. I could feel my pulse beating intemperately. I reveled in his vitality, his strength.

"Ellie. You had a rough time tonight. I'm so sorry it took me so long to get to you. I knew he'd try something, but I never thought he'd have the chance to take it so far."

"Make me forget."

"Are you sure? Your face must be sore. You'll have a black eye tomorrow. Maybe two."

"He touched me. I need to replace that memory. I need to blot it out." I wasn't sure if I could explain it. As he drew me closer, my breasts pressed into his naked chest, and the tension in my nipples seemed unbearable. I needed him to take me, hard and fast.

Before I could say anything more, he jammed his mouth to my throat, below the point where I was hurting. Despite his intentions of gentleness, he was a little rough; I could feel the possessiveness that was still riding him. I needed to delete the fact that Nigel had touched me, and so, it seemed, did he.

But after a few seconds, his lips gentled, and his hands and body began to court me.

"I need you, Ellie." His voice was thick. "I want to kiss you, touch you, be inside you." His hands punctuated his words as they slipped over my buttocks and lifted me atop him, tight against his pelvis. I felt his penis leap as he writhed beneath me. "It totally messes with my mind to think of another man's hands on you. Damn, Ellie. You're mine."

His low, breathless words made me burn, as did his lean, magnetic body. I melted into him. My belly ached and my muscles convulsed as I absorbed the feel of him against me.

"You want me, don't you?" He pressed down with his palms and rotated my lower body against his.

"Me, want a bad-tempered, violent thief like you?" I pushed up and let my long waves of hair fall into his face. "A man who orders me about, locks me up and threatens to rape me?"

He caught the playful note in my voice. "I thought I promised *not* to rape you?"

I lowered my head and nipped his throat. "I never made any such promise regarding you."

He laughed a little, and then returned my gentle nip. His strong white teeth against my flesh felt like heaven to me. He drew back, eyes hard with satisfaction. "I was afraid Nigel might, though."

"Well, thank you for coming in time to prevent that. It wasn't all bad. I learned some interesting things from him."

"What things?"

I wriggled my hips, making him groan. "Must we discuss it now?"

"No. I wanted to kill him, though. Seeing you there, like that, with him.... I never should have asked you to take such a risk."

"Show me how you're going to make it up to me."

His hands ghosted over my flesh, touching me with every degree of pressure from insubstantial fingers on my breasts to a sharp slap on my buttocks. I responded in like manner, blowing on his nipples and moving sensuously against his hips. When we could wait no longer, he gave me one of those delicious orders of his: "Sit up and straddle me."

I obeyed. I felt his hands at my waist, rearranging me so my thighs were on either side of his hips. I took his cock in my hand, reveling in the hard smooth column of flesh. He let me stroke him, but the feel of his muscular body beneath mine and his arms around me was just too tempting. My face and jaw were still hurting, but beneath the pain my need was as deep as the ocean.

"Nick," I whispered gazing down in wonder on his strong body lying supine beneath me. His supple muscles were arched against me; his golden hair crinkled against my bare flesh. Together we were beautiful. With my artist's eyes I took in the sight of our two bodies so perfectly mated. I'd like to photograph us, I thought.

"Are you okay?"

"Oh, yes."

"Fuck me *hayatim*. Take what you need."

"I need everything."

"Slide yourself down on me, but go easy. I don't want to hurt you. You've been hurt enough."

"You can't hurt me," I insisted, grasping him firmly and stroking up and down until I could see the tiny drop of fluid escape the tip.

He laughed softly. "I can and I probably will. But I can make you suffer in other ways, you know, little slave."

I was beginning to like it when he called me his slave. It thrilled me in a dark place that I'd never even explored before I'd met him. "How?"

"I can restrict your orgasms. No climax for you until I give you permission."

"What if I can't stop myself?"

"Severe punishment," he said, but there was teasing in his voice. "Well, maybe not so severe tonight. Someday, though..."

With his hands underneath my buttocks, he shifted me so just the tip of his cock entered me. I arched against it and felt it slide a tiny bit deeper, but he held himself back from pushing in more. "That's about an inch. I think I'll make you beg for each inch. How much do you want the next one?"

"Oh my god, I'm begging, Master. Not just the next inch, please, but all of you."

He pressed a little further into me, then stopped again. "Not good enough, babe." Reaching around behind me, he grabbed a couple of pillows and shoved them behind my back, propping me up a bit. Then he slid his hand between us and rubbed my clit. It was so intense that I practically leapt off his cock...not because I wanted to, but my body spontaneously bucked at his touch. "If I had a feather, I would use it here." The tip of his finger tickled my oh-so-sensitive bud. "Have you ever tried that? Really maddening. Subtle, yet so intense. With a feather, I could keep you keening on the edge of orgasm for as long as I wanted. And, believe it, there will be times when I do want to. Why? Just because I can."

I was panting now. The fingertip he was using on me felt almost as maddening as a feather.

"Another inch?"

"Please," I gasped.

"Please what?"

"Please, Master," adding, under my breath, "sadist."

His fingers dug into my ass as he drove deeper. I don't know how he could contain himself, but he still didn't go in all the way. Looking down I could see his thick cock grasped by the outer lips of my pussy, both of us flushed and sweaty, both of us breathing hard, our muscles taut and trembling. He rocked against me, causing pressure inside, outside, all around my core.

"More." I tried to force myself to grasp him, engulf him, pull him inside me, but he kept resisting. God! I needed to feel him thrust. I needed to ride him. I needed the thrill as we slammed together. I needed the union, the mating, the obliteration of our separate parts...

The hand that wasn't rubbing my clit slid up and around one of my breasts. "Does your breast hurt? Did he touch you there?"

"He touched me, but it doesn't hurt."

"The only one who hurts your breasts is me." He pinched my nipple. Did it hurt? Only a little. I was too aroused to feel real pain in any area that was also erogenous.

"Why do you want to hurt me?" I whispered. "Does it excite you?"

"It arouses something dark in me, yeah. But it's not so much that I want to hurt you....it's more that I want you to feel the intensity. I want you to love it, whatever I do to you."

"I do love it."

"I'll never give you pain that isn't good pain. Do you believe me, Ellie?"

"Yes." I didn't totally understand it, but I knew what he meant. I think I had always yearned for it, too. But it wasn't something I'd been able to ask for, because it seemed so dark, strange, and twisted. "Am I twisted?"

He chuckled, looking down again at the place where we were partially joined. "Oh yeah. You and me both, love. We're so fucking twisted. You want more?"

"Please. I need more." I was squirming on him, arching and bowing my body, trying to get him closer, deeper.

"So eager," he taunted, stroking my clit in that elusive manner. "If you weren't hurt, I would tie you down so you couldn't move at all. You'd be forced to take what I give you and only what I give you, just as gradually as I want it to be." He stopped speaking—his voice was breathless, and I could tell he was on the knife-edge of his control. "I will do that. One of these days." He pushed a tiny bit deeper. He groaned, shaking his head. "Fuck. This is tough," he said, laughing a little. "It drives me wild to see you so desperate."

"Fuck me," I urged him, tilting my hips again. "I need you inside me. All the way."

He held my hips poised there, halfway in or maybe slightly more. I could feel my pulse pounding in my pussy and I thought

I could feel his heart beating in his cock. His gaze held mine with such a searingly intimate look that I could hardly bear it. "Please," I whispered again. I was repeating myself, but I couldn't think of any other word to say.

His control snapped. He seemed to gather himself for a moment, then he slammed into me, all the way—his pelvis grinding into mine. He was hot and fierce; it was like being taken by the sun. When he withdrew and filled me again, he hit some spot on my inner walls that was even more sensitive, and the pleasure unspooled within me, making me cry out in wonder. But it wasn't the climax, not yet. My pussy muscles clenched around his cock...thrusting now, driving, jackknifing into me. My entire body tightened into a ball of fevered delight.

"Look at me," he ordered.

In my delirium, my eyes must have closed. Opening them, I saw how intense his expression was. He looked ferocious, but I liked it. His mask was gone. Behind the wildness, I could glimpse tenderness. "You're mine, Ellie." With each word, he gave a furious thrust. "I. am. so. sorry. that. bastard. hurt. you. Never. Again. I. promise. Never. EVER. again."

I couldn't speak, so I just nodded.

"Come for me," he commanded, doing something to my clit again.

My eyes must have started to close again, because he said sharply, "Keep your eyes open and come."

And just like that it happened. As the explosion ripped through me, I forced my eyes to stay locked with his. He was the lifeline I clung to as the waves crashed around me.

"You're mine," he whispered. "Mine to plunder, mine to use, mine to take, mine to keep."

Just before his climax, his entire body turned hard as stone. A marble god—his cock marble hard, too. But then he shattered and cried out, and I knew the stone coldness was an illusion. He was warm and bright and full of life.

"*Seni seviyorum,*" he said, Turkish for "I love you."

"*Ben de seni seviyorum.*" I love you, too.

Chapter 35

ELLIE

Long minutes later, I said, "Don't go to sleep yet." I curled against Nick's warm chest, nuzzling the smooth skin at the base of his throat. "Can I ask you something? You weren't angry with me, were you? When you found me with Nigel?"

"With you? No. I was angry with him. And with myself, for putting you in that kind of danger."

I wasn't sure I believed him. There had been a moment when I hadn't been sure which of us he was going to attack next— Nigel or me.

He must have sensed my skepticism, because he added. "As I've told you, I'm not myself around you. Anger, passion, emotions flying all over the place. That's not the way I usually behave."

"I think I prefer your wild emotions to your cold, shut-down pose."

"Women have cheated on me—it enrages me. It's guaranteed to send me over the edge."

"But you knew I didn't want to be anywhere near Nigel."

"As so often around you, it's not my brain, but my dick that's in control."

I lifted my head to meet his eyes. "I know about Elizabeth and Nigel. Did you love her?"

He hesitated. Was he finally going to talk to me... share something of his past? He had just told me he loved me. Did it count if it was muttered at orgasm?

"I thought so at the time. We were young. When I caught her betraying me, it blew my mind. And with him, of all people." He shook his head as if the memories were a heavy burden. "She begged me to give her another chance. But I couldn't take her back, not after that. I never thought she'd stay with Nigel, but they ended up having one of those toxic relationships for a while. I found out later that he was abusing her. Bastard. He's charming and handsome—bright on the surface but rotten at the core."

I'd never even found him bright on the surface. I'd seen the rot quickly enough.

"I knew Nigel would come after you," Nick went on. "He's so fucking predictable."

"I thought you were going to kill him. That really scared me. After just finding out you weren't a thief, I didn't want to see you turn into a murderer."

The change of expression on Nick's face was almost comical. "What do you mean, you found out I wasn't a thief?"

"Nigel told me that some artifact you'd stolen had been returned. Real thieves don't give back the loot."

"Wait. What? How the fuck does he know that?"

"And you admitted you were working under cover, trying to save your grandfather. You also told me a few days ago that you had a plan. I'm still not sure what the plan is, but clearly there is more to you than I originally thought."

He was silent, so I prodded, "You told me you'd explain."

"I will. It's just—if Nigel knows the stuff is being returned, somebody has fucked up. Shit. That means he's on his guard. No wonder he's planning to abandon ship earlier than he'd intended."

"He mentioned he'd heard of one case where something had ended up back in the country instead of in private hands."

"There've been a lot more than one case, but it's been done in secrecy. He shouldn't have heard of any cases. Damn. Someone has been careless."

"Well, he's definitely suspicious. He tried to make me tell him what you were planning, but of course, I didn't know."

"People are onto my cousin. Serious people. They want to take him down. Not only for antiquities smuggling, but for other crimes as well. So yeah, I've been helping them achieve that goal."

"It's true, then." I was exultant. "From the beginning you've been playing a role with me. The big, bad antiquities smuggler."

"I had to. I couldn't risk you knowing. I've brought enough trouble down on your head as it is."

I listened while he explained that it had been Nigel who had gotten his grandfather involved in illegal antiquities trading. "I don't pretend that the old boy hasn't taken avidly to a life of crime, but it never would have happened if Nigel hadn't facilitated it. I didn't even know what was going on until an old acquaintance clued me in. The authorities were going to go after both Nigel and Granddad, but I managed to talk them into giving Granddad a break. But to make it work, all his thefts had to be undone by me."

"Undone?"

"Since I've been involved, everything he's stolen has been returned by my agents. Granddad and Nigel think the stuff has been sold to certain private art collectors—the sort of folks who aren't fussy about provenance."

I worked through the implications. "But it hasn't?"

"Not any longer. The private collectors are no longer in the loop."

"Someone must have had to fork over money in exchange for the artifacts. Right?"

"Fortunately, my friend Max, whom Nigel used to bully when we were in high school, is a billionaire. He's the one who lent me the yacht.

"For the scheme to work, it was essential to make Nigel believe that I had turned to the dark side. That's where the human trafficking thing came in. He and I grew up together, so we know each other's weaknesses. He knew that if anything tempted me—" He paused. "Just to be clear, slave trafficking could never tempt me, but kinky sex is a different story. Nigel doesn't draw much distinction between the two. The principle of consent is something that has never resonated with him."

"So you told him you were into human trafficking, and he believed it?"

"I didn't tell him outright. I made sure he heard it from other sources. And then you came along. I realized that it would all seem much more believable if I had a slave in my possession." He grinned at me. "A beautiful young woman who would act submissive around me and obey my every order."

I winced. "Okay, so I wasn't exactly perfect."

"You did fine."

We took a break from the story for some intense kissing. Which turned into intense yearning, desire and need. Soon the question of Nick's true character began to seem irrelevant. Whoever he was, I adored him.

Chapter 36

ELLIE

Early the next morning, Nick and I rowed back into the rocky inlet of Golden Dolphin Island. Metin remained on the yacht, and Nick had tried to get me to stay there, too. "I want you safe. There's no telling what might happen today."

"Well, you're not going back there without me. Besides, I'm scheduled to take the photographs today."

"There's no need for you to do so. I'll tell them you're too injured and upset by what Nigel did to you."

"I'm not going to hide from that bastard. I'm bringing my camera and coming to the excavations." I lifted my chin, which was swollen and aching. I had a black eye, too, but I was determined to wear it like a badge of honor. "It's something I have to do."

He stared at me for a long time, his green eyes seeming to see deep inside me. At last he nodded. "Okay, *canim*. I'll be there to lend my support."

We landed the boat and hiked over the rocks to the compound. There was a clattering of dishes from the kitchen. The men were up and eating breakfast. "Good, I could use a glass of tea," Nick said as we entered.

They were all seated around the table—Nigel, looking far from his usual suave self, with pale skin, a shitload of bruises, a bandage on his shoulder where Nick's knife had struck him, and a swollen-shut black eye; Sinan, narrow-eyed and more bandit-like than ever; and the workmen, all conversing animatedly until we walked into the room, when a heavy silence fell.

"Gunaydin," I said. I was conscious of a collective hostility as they stared at us. What? They didn't care for the evidence that Nigel had attacked a woman? Of course, Nigel's men were always hostile, but Sir Avery's crew usually had a smile for me.

Instinctively I reached out and grabbed Nick's hand.

"How're you feeling this morning, Nigel?" asked Nick.

Nigel's swollen face widened into his habitual charming smile. "Much better now that I see what a fool you are. I can't believe you've had the nerve to come back here."

"You're the one who should be hanging your head in shame for assaulting Ellie."

Nigel didn't even bother to deny the charge. "I underestimated you," he said to me. "But you've both underestimated me."

"Where's my grandfather?" Nick snapped.

I heard the swish of the wheelchair from the doorway to the corridor behind us. "Here I am."

Nick and I turned. Sir Avery was sitting stiffly in his chair, looking sad and frail. In his lap he was cradling a large-caliber handgun.

"Good morning." He raised the gun, holding it in both hands. "Yes, it's loaded. And yes, I'm aiming it at you."

There was a long, electric silence. I sensed Nick closing in upon himself. He didn't speak, and I was at a loss. Had Nigel convinced their grandfather that the rumor he'd heard about a stolen object returned to its rightful country was true?

Sir Avery looked only at Nick. "I trusted you. It breaks my heart to learn that you could do this to me."

Nick said, "Not sure what you think I've done, but I wouldn't hurt you for the world." Never dropping his gaze from his grandfather's, his voice cracking in a way that just about broke my heart, he added, "I love you, Granddad."

Sir Avery's face crumpled, but he held the pistol steady. After a moment he managed, "Don't insult my intelligence."

Nigel had risen from the table. He was gloating. He moved across the room to a table where he opened the lid of his laptop. "You didn't count on this, did you? Listen." He pushed a button and I heard my own voice saying, *It's true, then. From the beginning you've been playing a role with me. The big, bad antiquities smuggler.*

To which Nick's voice replied, *I had to.*

And as we listened, appalled, to part of the conversation Nick and I had had the previous night in our cabin on the yacht.

"You bugged my cabin." Nick's voice was totally devoid of expression.

"I'm afraid so."

"When? The night Metin saw someone swimming away from the boat?"

"That's right. When I realized I wasn't going to escape without being seen, I fiddled around a bit with your fuses and your radio. I didn't want you to guess the real reason I was there."

The cabin had been bugged for more than one night? That meant...

"It took you long enough to confess your real role in all this," Nigel taunted. "But listening to everything else you've been doing there has thoroughly entertained my men."

Nick's face darkened. I could feel his whole body tense. I squeezed his hand hard. Keep control, I told him silently. Now is the time to keep control. But my cheeks were hot with shame and anger at the thought that Nigel had been a silent, smirking witness to us having sex.

"What a shame you decided to clue her in at last. If you'd continued to lie, I'd have nothing, and our grandfather would continue to believe you trustworthy."

Tight-lipped, Nick turned from Nigel to Sir Avery. The old man's grip on the handgun had not wavered. "If you've listened to the entire conversation, Granddad, you know that it was my intention to save you from this mess you've landed yourself in. Nigel is the target, not you."

"Nigel is your cousin. Betray him, and you betray our entire family."

"Nigel's a criminal. He has been for years. He's corrupted you."

"Be that as it may, blood is thicker than water," Sir Avery said stiffly. "I hope they were paying you well for your betrayal."

"Nobody's paying him," I cried. I was angry for Nick's sake. I hadn't thought I could hate Nigel any more than I had last night, but the way he was twisting things turned me inside out.

"Nick was offered a chance to keep you out of prison and he took it. It was just a matter of time before you'd have been tried and imprisoned."

The stare Sir Avery gave me was different from anything I'd ever seen before in his eyes. There was hurt there, but even more, there was anger. Maybe his temper was like Nick's. It didn't often erupt, but when it did, he was implacable. Any regard he might briefly have had for me was gone.

I felt a spasm of grief. How had things gone so wrong? I'd begun to think of Sir Avery as my friend.

"I'm not interested in your opinion, young woman. There's only one thing I want from you. We're going to the excavations now to shoot those photographs. That much use, at least, you shall be to us."

We argued with him. But Sir Avery would not listen. He paid no attention to Nick's warnings that he'd better get the hell off the island today. "I'm not leaving until the site is secured and those photographs taken," he vowed. "I've sunk all my savings into this venture and I'm going to sell those pieces if I can. The dig will be closed and the cavern will be sealed. When this unpleasantness has blown over, I'll return to the island and continue my search for the treasures of Troy."

"You're a stubborn old fool," Nick was driven to proclaim. "You'll find no treasures of Troy from a Turkish prison."

Sir Avery ignored him.

"What are you going to do with us when you've finished sealing up the cavern?" Nick demanded of his grandfather as Nigel bound his hands behind his back, taking pleasure, it seemed to me, in jerking the cords so tight that Nick's face whitened.

"Nigel has suggested shooting you."

"I don't believe you're cruel enough to murder me." He paused, glancing at his cousin. "Or to permit anyone else to do so."

The cold in depths of my stomach seemed to be spreading throughout my body. I was certain he wouldn't hesitate to murder Nick if he ever got the chance.

"For myself I don't give a damn," Nick added. "But Ellie's been an innocent bystander, from beginning to end. It isn't right for your wrath to fall upon her head."

"How noble," Nigel cut in. "Do what you will with me, but spare the lady? Too bad you didn't think about her welfare before kidnapping the girl and forcing her to gratify your lusts."

I think Nick would have hit him again then, if he hadn't been bound. As it was, there was little he could do except seethe with emotions he was no longer making any effort to control.

It was Sir Avery who calmed things down by saying, "Neither of you will be harmed. We'll leave you on the island—you, Ellie and your friend Metin. Your yacht will be disabled. No doubt you'll have the wherewithal to survive here until your friends come to the rescue."

This seemed odd to me. Weren't they afraid that, once rescued, Nick would be able to provide the authorities with enough evidence to nail them? How long did they imagine they could keep this illegal operation running?

I was trying to remember exactly what we had said last night in the cabin. They wouldn't have learned much about Nick's real intentions from any prior recordings, since I hadn't known myself. And he had broached the idea of me pretending to submit to Nigel in our room here in the compound, not on the boat. I knew he hadn't told me everything last night. I'd brooded over how closed off he could be, but now I was glad he had spoken so little about his plans. Apparently the crooks didn't know that they were about to be rounded up by the Turkish authorities or Interpol or whoever Nick had been working with. That was something he hadn't fully disclosed to me.

I wondered how soon the reinforcements were going to get here. Maybe not soon enough.

Within the hour, surrounded by Nigel and half a dozen armed and hostile men, we were marched to the site of the excavations. Several of the laborers were already there, packing up. They were all Nigel's crew.

At the low entrance to the cavern, I hesitated. The dread in my belly seemed to be going round and around, up and down, like an out-of-control roller coaster car. Descending into a hole in the mountain was my nightmare. I was prodded forward by a jab in between my shoulders from Nigel's rifle. My hands had not been bound—I was carrying my camera equipment. But they were shaking.

"Easy," Nick whispered. "I'll be right beside you, and it'll be over soon."

The cave's entrance was hidden behind a thick slab of stone that melted seamlessly into the cliff face. It was just a small hole, and we had to crawl to enter, but once inside we could stand—or rather, stoop. A narrow passage led to a large inner chamber. The uneven rock floor of this passage sloped downward at a sharp angle, and not even the light of half a dozen powerful flashlights was sufficient to ensure safe footing. I stumbled once and felt Nick steady me with his body. But my stomach kept churning and my palms were damp.

"Hurry it up," Nigel growled, prodding us again from behind. The passage turned to the right and widened. The ceiling rose higher, until at last we were able to stand erect. We rounded a massive stalagmite and entered the central chamber.

I looked about me in awe. The roof of the cavern now vaulted over our heads, and the air smelled fresh, even sweet. The chamber was like a natural cathedral, and it was not as pitch-black here as it had been in the entry passage.

The ceiling, which must have been close to twenty feet high, was encrusted with stalactites that hung down like monster icicles. Somewhere in the highest part of the dome was a narrow fissure through which a sliver of sunlight poured. Relief flooded me. The light was not enough to aid in my photography, nor could one see into the corners of the chamber without the aid of a flashlight, but we could see objects and people's faces. The fissure lessened my feelings of being trapped. My muscles slowly began to untense. I'd been braced for a claustrophobia attack, but now I believed I could keep the panic at bay. At least for a little while.

I studied the cavern's contents. The first thing I noticed was the statue I'd seen Nick filch from the western coast of Turkey. It had been removed from its crate and posed erect near the center of the chamber, as if on exhibit.

Such was also the case with the other artifacts, which consisted of several large statues, some temple pillars and friezes, an early Christian stone altar and a baptismal font. These were too bulky to transport unless careful precautions had been taken in advance—costly precautions that Nigel wouldn't bother with until each item was sold.

"Okay, let's get started," Nigel ordered. "I don't want to kill the whole day."

At my direction, the workmen set up lights and reflectors. When Nigel expressed annoyance at the length of time it took me to get the lights into the correct position for each shot, I turned on him, saying, "Unless you want dark shadows distorting the artifact in each picture, you'll allow me to work at my own speed."

While I worked, Nick's hands were untied, and he was forced, at gunpoint, to help move some of the smaller items out of the cave, where Sir Avery's men transferred them to Nigel's boat.

It was well after noon by the time we were finished. I was tired, hungry and thirsty. The workmen had eaten lunch, but nothing had been offered to Nick and me except a can of warm beer, which we had shared. I'd done my best work, despite the adverse circumstances. I took pride in my art and could not bring myself to do anything less.

After taking my final shot, I informed Nigel that I was ready to leave.

"Fine," he said genially. "We are ready, too. Bring him over here, please," he said to Sinan, who, with the help of one or two other men, had once again bound Nick's arms behind his back.

"Now what?" said Nick, sounding bored. "We've done your dirty work. If you really expect to make good your escape, I suggest we close this place up and get the fuck out."

"That's precisely what I intend to do. Unfortunately for you and your girlfriend, you won't be joining us."

"Why not?" I asked. My stomach had turned to ice.

"You're going to kill us." Nick's voice was expressionless.

"You leave me no choice." Nigel relieved me of my camera with all the photos I'd shot. "I'm afraid I can't tolerate the idea of your spilling everything you know to the authorities."

"Granddad will never allow it. You'd best follow the original plan and make your escape while you still can."

"He won't even know," Nigel said coolly. He then nodded to one of his men, who was standing a few feet away from me. I realized that the guy was reaching for his rifle, which was leaning up against the cavern wall. He slowly moved it into firing position, bringing the barrel up in my direction.

I'd always wondered what I would do if I actually faced my death. Freeze? Shake? Cry?

Turned out I didn't even think about it. My body acted faster than I could process the threat. I ducked and ran, weaving to make myself a more difficult target. Not that I expected to escape. But I wasn't going to stand there numbly and take a bullet.

Behind me, Nick bellowed and exploded into action.

Chapter 37

NICK

Something detonated inside me. Ellie charged toward the exit, but she could not outrun a bullet. "Down, Ellie," I screamed, and she obeyed, flinging herself to the ground as I attacked, driven not by thought but by the reflexes I'd drilled into her.

They'd made a mistake in neglecting to bind my ankles. Moving onto the balls of my feet, I channeled my energy and leapt at the dude about to shoot my girl, knocking his weapon out of his hands and kicking it away. I kneed him in the groin, and then stepped back and kicked him in the head. He crumpled, went down hard and didn't get up. Ellie scuttled away from the action. Since no one else was immediately threatening her, I turned on Nigel, screaming like a banshee, and bull-charged him.

I was kicking him, too, feet flying, trying to get him in the same sore spots where I had struck him the previous night, but by then his thugs had started to move. Besides Nigel, there were two of them. I had already taken out the third. Not good odds, especially with my hands bound.

Fuck it. I was going to see how many of the bastards I could take down with me. I got one more, kicking him in the balls and putting him at least temporarily out of the action. But Nigel and Sinan, his chief lieutenant, jumped me and beat me to the ground. "Hold him," Nigel growled, and I saw the unholy light in his blue eyes as I was dragged to my knees. Sinan pulled my head back by the hair so the asshole could personally send his fist into my already-swollen jaw.

"You bastard," Nigel muttered between a series of coarser expletives. "I can't tell you how long I've waited for this day." He hit me in the ribs and belly, and then kicked me in the side as I sagged to the rough floor of the cave. The kicks kept coming, but I kept fighting. Fuck the pain. I had to stay alive to protect Ellie. That was all I could think of as I struggled. I refused to admit that I was going to lose this fight. Not until something struck me in the head and my vision dimmed did I realize I might not get up again.

"Stop hurting him or I'll shoot."

It was Ellie's voice, clear and high, speaking Turkish. It took a second for me—and everyone else—to process what must have happened. But the sound of a gun firing—it caused an echo to bounce around the walls of the cave—got their attention. The beating stopped.

I managed to prop myself up on one bruised elbow, and through blurry eyes I could see that she had grabbed the rifle dropped by the asshole who had been about to shoot her. She'd fired it once at the floor of the cave—dust was rising from the spot—and she was now pointing it in what looked like a competent grip at Nigel. She said, "What kind of a coward would kick a man when his hands are tied behind his back?"

"Are you okay, Ellie?" I gasped, trying to get my breath.

"I'm just peachy."

"Shoot him," I said, wishing I could do it myself. I doubted she would obey that order, though. And, unfortunately, Ellie wasn't the only one with a gun. Nigel jerked my wretchedly weak body against his legs and put his own pistol to the side of my head.

"The question is, can your bullet hit me before I pull the trigger?"

"Fucking shoot him," I said. If she didn't, Nigel would kill us both anyway.

"How good a shot are you?" Nigel said, still sounding calm. He was every kind of evil bastard, but he was not a coward. "Because I can't miss."

Ellie kept her cool, too—so much so that I was fucking proud of her. I'd known she was kick-ass almost from the first moment we'd met, but this was above and beyond. "Just take your men and get out of here," she said. "You go your way and we'll go ours."

I felt Nigel hesitate. He wanted to kill me. I think he'd probably wanted to kill me for years.

But he didn't want to die.

"Deal," he said. He snapped an order for his companions to leave the cavern. Muttering, the ones I hadn't managed to take down began to do so, dragging the unconscious asshole who had aimed his rifle at her with them. The screaming-testicles dude managed to stagger out by himself, one hand between his legs. Ellie kept her sights trained on Nigel even after he lifted his weapon away from my skull. I was barely conscious, and the pain of the beating was beginning to hit as my adrenaline ebbed. Nigel must have played the odds and figured that Ellie wouldn't shoot him now that he had agreed.

The thing was, I knew Nigel couldn't be trusted to keep a deal. I knew it, but I felt like a ragdoll, and there was nothing I could do.

But incredibly, Nigel seemed to be leaving. Ellie kept the rifle on him and stayed far enough away from him herself that he couldn't attack her and knock it out of her hand. She was so amazing and so brave that I wanted to seize her in my arms and hug her hard. Kiss her into oblivion. She had just saved my life.

When Nigel and the last of his men left the cave, their flashlights vanishing down the short passage that led to the exit, her legs collapsed. She sank to the floor of the cave.

"Ellie?" I croaked. I felt as if I'd been hit by a bus. My head was throbbing; my ribs were burning, and I hoped I wasn't going to throw up. It was, I decided, a distinct possibility.

I began to crawl toward her. Fuck me, there was no way I could walk.

"I'm okay. It's just reaction, or something." She lifted her head, squinting to try to see me. The cave was much darker now that they'd gone and taken the lights. "You're hurt, Nick, don't try to move." She rose and stumbled toward me, but I kept coming. I wanted to be near her. I needed to reassure myself that she was really all right.

She came to me and untied my hands. We slumped back to the cave floor together. I was still shocked, I think, both by the beating and by the ruthless way Nigel had been ready to murder us. I had no trouble understanding why he wanted me dead—he had hated me since childhood—but her? Even though I knew what he was and had been trying to months to bring him down, it still surprised me to discover he was a cold-blooded killer of innocents.

I reached for the rifle Ellie had commandeered. No one had expected it of her. Including me. "They might be back," I said, checking the gun to see how much ammunition it had. My fucking hands were shaking. My wrists were deeply scored where the ropes had cut into them. Safe, non-harmful bondage was not something these creeps practiced.

"I didn't know you could use firearms. That was awesome, what you did, Ellie."

"I was imitating what I've seen on TV."

"Seriously? It looked pretty damn authentic."

"Okay, I've been to the firing range a couple of times," she admitted. "In high school I dated a gun freak. But I might well have missed Nigel if I'd had to fire."

"I doubt it. He's a big target."

From just outside the cave came the muffled sounds of shouted directions, muttered curses and some hammering. Ellie and I looked at each other. Her eyes were wet and there were tears on her cheeks, but I don't think she even knew it. Her jaw stayed firm, strong, and her hands kept touching me gently, as if she couldn't believe I was still with her and that we were still together.

I felt the same way. By now, I'd expected one or both of us to be eating dirt.

I lifted the rifle. Fuck. My ribs were hurting. At least one of them was probably broken, given the pain I felt while taking a deep breath.

"I'd better take it. You don't look so good, Nick." When I hesitated, she added, "Don't worry. I will shoot if I have to. I will kill that goddamn freak if he tries to hurt you again."

I gave her the gun. We didn't stand much chance if they returned with a higher number of men and more weapons. Nigel had at least two more guys in his crew. They'd been occupied with carrying the loot down to his boat, but he could have called them back.

While we waited, Ellie scooped up some rocks to use as missiles. She also pulled out a rather pathetic Swiss Army knife from the pack where she had the camera equipment they hadn't taken with them. I wished I had the strength to hug her. She was determined to fight.

But they didn't come back into the cave. Instead we heard the ominous grating of rock upon rock. I think I realized before she did what they were doing out there.

More pounding, shouts and creaking. Then we heard Nigel's voice, muted, sounding farther away than it ought to sound:

"The men and I are leaving now. Not sure if you can hear me, coz. We've moved that boulder at the entrance into its original position, flush against the cliff wall. Now we're sealing it up from the outside in such a manner that it cannot be opened from within.

"So, unless you're discovered by your friends—which is unlikely, I'm afraid—you will die there. Of perfectly natural causes. No awkward bullet wounds to be explained if your bodies are ever found."

"Fuck you," I groaned. No bullet wounds was fine with me. I wasn't planning to die anytime soon, and being abandoned in a fairly large cavern with plenty of air to breathe didn't scare me.

But Ellie was different. "Oh no," she whispered, sounding scared for the first time since this nightmare had begun. "Please no."

Something twisted in me at the sight of her huge eyes widening in her pale, lovely face. She had been so brave. She had confronted her claustrophobia, entering the cave and taking the photographs without revealing to anybody how monumental a task this had been for her. She had faced Nigel down in a manner that I'd never expected...and beaten the asshole, too. Shit. It wasn't fair that her hard-won courage should be snatched from her at the last moment.

Damn. I couldn't think of any fucking way to forgive myself for bringing her into this mess. If only I'd set her free right at the start. If only I hadn't developed a crazy yearning for her. If I could find a way to save her life, I'd gladly give up my own.

As this thought shot through my mind, I realized that the impossible had happened. I'd fallen for her. Madly, deeply, truly. How sad and ironic that I should discover this now, when it was probably too late.

Chapter 38

ELLIE

I felt sick. It was as if a big hard hand had reached into my chest and squeezed all the blood out of my heart. Nick was hurt—beaten more badly than Nigel had been the previous night. As the realization set in that we were trapped here, I shrank against him, cradling his injured body, but also needing comfort myself. I could see my own tears gleaming amid the gold of his hair. Then silence gathered, pressing upon my eardrums until I wanted to scream to break its awful tyranny.

We were sealed inside the cave, and it seemed so freaking dark. It wasn't actually dark at all, but my mind was sliding into panic mode.

The brain doesn't always behave in the most sensible way. I'd almost been shot and Nigel had put a gun to Nick's head, but instead of obsessing about the narrowness of our escape, I was plunged into terror about something much more amorphous. All I could focus on was that I was trapped underground with someone I cared about lying injured beside me. Not my mother, this time, but Nick. I felt dislocated, as if we were not on an island off the coast of Turkey, but lost in time and space in the narrow passageway of a small, undistinguished pyramid, where my mom and I had been stuck when I'd been a child.

Nigel's crew had taken their flashlights with them, which made the cavern seem much darker, even though some light was entering through the fissure in the ceiling. I hated the dark. Fucking dark. I had to get out, out, *out*. I couldn't stand this—it was going to break me wide open and spill my pieces everywhere.

I wrestled with my terror. It flowed over me in waves: a riptide of fear that would leave me mindless, irrational, insane. I battled it just as I'd always done, until I finally remembered that fighting just made it worse. Why did it always take so long to remember that?

I reached deep inside for something to hold on to. For courage, dignity, strength. I had those things, didn't I? So what if I get scared sometimes? Who doesn't?

I dropped my face against Nick's shoulder and hugged him. *Don't fight it.* I let the darkness roll over me; let the terror come.

And it did come. The fast and furious what-ifs began, as always, but this time I countered each of them with a relentless answer: *What if I die of fright?* Then I'll be dead and none of this will matter. *What if Nick dies?* Then I'll be alone. *What if we survive, only to succumb slowly to a horrible death by thirst and hunger?* What will happen, will happen. Everybody dies.

"Hang on, Ellie. Don't be afraid. You're not alone in the dark."

Tears coursed down my cheeks. Nick had been severely beaten. He must be in terrible pain, yet he was thinking of me. "I'm doing fine," I lied. "I'm okay."

Nick shifted and groaned again. "You shouldn't be trying to move," I said. "Please try to rest, and save your strength."

"We'll be okay, babe." He squeezed my fingers. "The cave is huge and fresh air comes in through the fissure in the roof. Light comes in too—it's not that dark in here."

"We still have the lights I was using for the photography. I don't know how long the batteries will last, though. They were on all morning. They took my camera, with all the pictures."

"My pack is over there against the wall. Can you reach it? There's a flashlight in there and a bottle of water."

I did, and was relieved to find both items. There were actually two liters of water in the pack they'd allowed Nick to carry on his back to the cave. But how long would that much water last? I offered Nick some. He only took a couple of sips. I took a sip myself, then recapped the plastic bottle.

"Okay then," Nick said. "There's no immediate danger. By tomorrow this island will be crawling with law enforcement types. They'll get us out of here."

I rubbed his scored wrists gently to restore the circulation. "Will they be able to find us?"

"They will," he said in a firm voice. "Don't forget about Metin. He knows about the cave. He's a smart kid."

If he's still alive, I thought grimly. I suspected Nick was thinking the same thing. Nigel would surely have taken steps to eliminate Metin. I pictured the handsome young man with the dark, merry eyes. *Please be all right, Metin. Please look for us. Please find us.*

"Are you sure you're okay?" Nick reached up a finger to touch my cheek. "This must be scary for you. I'm so sorry." His hand fell back to his side and clenched into a fist. "I should never have dragged you into this mess."

"Ssh, Nick. Please lie down." I shifted our positions so he could lay his poor head in my lap. I was sure it must be throbbing. "If you hadn't carried me off, I wouldn't have fallen for you." I tried to joke around. "Or had so much amazing sex."

He chuckled. "We'll have more amazing sex, I promise you." There was a long pause, before he added, "Fallen for me?"

I smiled. That would have been so easy for him to ignore. "Don't pretend you didn't know. It was sorta love at first sight, but a little delayed because of harsh treatment and spankings and ropes around my neck."

"You were calling it Stockholm syndrome a few days ago."

"Yeah, well that was before I knew you loved dancing and music and ancient languages and poetry. Or that you persistently put other people's welfare before your own."

Nick seemed stunned; he met my eyes, but couldn't seem to get any words out. That was okay. Word were unnecessary between us now. "Close your eyes," I ordered. "Rest a bit."

When he was quiet, I found the flashlight and turned it on so I could estimate the extent of his injuries. His beautiful face was badly bruised. I poured a tiny amount of the water from the bottle onto a bit of cloth torn from my shirt and wiped his abrasions clean. Then I gently examined his body. The worst battering seemed to be around his face and his ribs, where the skin was already bruised. Asshole Nigel. Nick and I probably had some matching bruises now, although his injuries were much worse than mine.

Nick should be wrapped up warmly in a blanket, but we didn't have one. He needed a doctor, or at least some decent first aid. Once again tears pricked my eyes. I remembered the way Nigel had had the others hold Nick down so he could beat him. Hatred burned in my gut. For the first time I understood how truly evil Nigel was.

I hoped that guy named Hepburn got here before Nigel could escape. Somebody had to put the bastard down.

When I'd made Nick as comfortable as possible, I set out on a quick exploration of the cave. Gritting my teeth, I forced myself to venture through the narrow passage that led to the entrance. If there was any chance of getting out that way I wanted to know about it. But the boulder at the entrance had been firmly wedged against the inner wall.

I knew another upsurge of panic then, but this time I didn't even try to fight it. Of course you're terrified, I told myself. Who wouldn't be?

Returning to the central chamber, I ran my flashlight beam over the ceiling where the fissure was. I tried to estimate its height. Fifteen feet? Twenty? If I could hoist myself up there somehow, could I squeeze through the opening and escape? I examined the opening from several angles, and then slumped with dismay. It was too narrow. And without a rope, there was no way to reach it, anyway.

Afraid to use up the batteries of the flashlight, I switched it off and sank down next to Nick to think. Was there some way of levering that boulder away from the entrance? Human strength and ingenuity had moved that stone before. We ought to be able to find a method of moving it again.

When Nick stirred again and opened his eyes, I told him the results of my explorations. "You probably know more about engineering than I do. How can we shift that rock?"

"We can't. It's huge. They had tools and levers. We don't."

"A lever is a relatively simple tool. Can't we find something in here to use as one? A plank of wood, maybe?"

"Nigel wouldn't be stupid enough to leave anything like that in here."

"Don't be so pessimistic. There's all kinds of junk in here. How about the crate?"

"What crate?"

"On the day you carried me off, you were stealing a crated statue. I know the statue's in here since I photographed it a little while ago. What happened to its crate?"

"The wood in that crate, even if you could find it, wouldn't be strong enough to shift a stone that large."

"I'm going to look for it, anyway," I said. Switching on the flashlight, I started to do just that.

Chapter 39

NICK

I sat up again. I managed to contain my groans of pain this time, although I really didn't feel any better. In fact, I felt worse. My muscles were starting to stiffen up.

I was astonished at her composure. But maybe it wasn't so surprising. The things we fear the most often prove to be less daunting than we expect when they actually occur. Besides, Ellie had already confronted the worst of it when she'd decided to enter the cave and take the photographs.

She had been trying to comfort me, and I'd let her. Here we were, trapped in her worst nightmare, and it was her strength that was sustaining us both. Maybe that was okay. Maybe I had to let her strength sustain us now, in case we needed mine later. If I *had* any strength later, which was beginning to look doubtful.

I felt a fierce upsurge of affection for her. She was brave, determined and optimistic, which made me hopeful, too. If there was a way out of here, we'd find it. And if we did, if we survived, maybe I'd be able to make some kind of life with her. It amazed me to contemplate, but maybe I wouldn't have to go through the next fifty or sixty years a lonely vagabond, running away from women, from commitment, from love.

I didn't want to tell her that the odds were against us, though. This cavern had remained hidden for three thousand years. I hadn't told Hepburn about it in any of my reports. When they landed on the island and found nobody around, Hepburn and his men might assume I'd left the island.

We could die here, just as my cousin intended. It was the most likely outcome.

"Nick!" Ellie's voice, coming from one of the deepest recesses of the cave, jolted me. "I think I've found something."

"What?"

"I'm not sure. There's a slab of rock here that looks similar to the one at the cave's entrance. It's at an odd angle, though, as if it's been jolted by some great force. Didn't you say there was an earthquake on this island some decades ago?"

"Yeah, that's why the rich old recluse who used to own Granddad's villa abandoned the island. The epicenter was at sea, but the quake was close enough to the island to do a lot of damage."

"I think there's an opening behind this slab. It's barely visible, but I can feel air currents moving. I'm going to investigate, if I can get up enough courage to squeeze through this narrow cleft."

"No!" I managed to lurch to my feet. "Are you crazy? Whatever it is, you have no idea whether it's safe. Wait for me. I'm coming."

I stumbled after her in the dark, my head aching, my legs about as responsive as stilts. I found the recess just in time to see her disappear through what, from my perspective, looked like solid rock. "Ellie!"

A moment later I heard her cry out. Fear slammed through me. Fuck! Damn it to hell! I imagined one horror after another—a steep drop-off, a poisonous snake, rotting skeletons, the face of the devil himself.

I forced my useless, aching body through the same narrow slit where she'd disappeared. The thought of losing her had kicked my stomach into my throat.

"Ellie!"

All was silent now. My heart was pounding at a rate that would have rivaled hers at the height of one of her panic attacks. I rounded a mammoth stalagmite and saw her flashlight beam shooting like a laser into the darkness. I stared, and then I, too, made a hoarse sound.

She was there, quite safe, standing still in the small circular alcove of an inner cave. The ceiling shimmered with light as our flashlight beams were caught, captured and thrown back by a thousand twinkling facets of quartz that arched overhead. In the middle of the alcove, rained upon by the brilliant crystal light, were several gleaming objects of varying sizes: Bowls, vases, a large caldron, several ceremonial drinking cups, bracelets, earrings, diadems and other jewelry. Most of them were tipped over at various angles, but they were roughly grouped around a beautiful three-foot-high statue of a golden dolphin twisting as he leaped out of the sea into the arms of a young man so perfectly proportioned he could only be a god.

"Fuck me. I don't *believe* it. My grandfather was right. You've discovered the fucking treasures of Troy."

She pointed to the statue. "Altinyunush Adasi—Golden Dolphin Island," she said, the awe ringing in her voice. "It was a true name for this place, after all."

Chapter 40

ELLIE

Nick insisted on examining the "treasure" with me, even though it was obvious that he was feeling rocky. "So close and yet so far," he said as he gingerly brushed dust from the golden dolphin and scrutinized the beautiful object with the flashlight. "My grandfather will leave this island without a clue that only a few feet of stone separated him from his greatest discovery."

"How do you suppose they missed finding the inner cave?" I asked him.

"It's well-hidden. It's probably a sacred shrine, dedicated to the gods. Whoever left the items here in the first place didn't ever want them found."

"I couldn't see the opening. I only found it because I'm so desperate to find a way out. I was following something that felt like a draft."

He laughed hoarsely. "Leave it to Nigel to seal us up in a cave that's concealing priceless artifacts."

"I'm glad they didn't find it," I said fiercely. "These things should be on public display in a museum, not pirated into illegal collections."

"It's nice, finally, to be able to agree with you."

"Do you suppose all this is really from Troy?"

"I'm no authority on metallurgy. The golden treasure Schliemann found at Troy actually dated from an earlier epoch than Homer's city. That stuff was more primitive than this, though. The dolphin is very finely executed. Did the Trojans of the Homeric epoch have the skill to do such work? I don't know. It'll have to be evaluated by the experts."

"If the experts ever get a look at it." If we die here, I was thinking, Nick and I would take this secret with us across the silent borders of death.

When Nick put a hand to his head and swayed slightly, I started panicking again. Not for myself, though. It was him I was worried about. I grabbed him, and he leaned on me. "Please. You need to lie down."

His lips had whitened. "My blasted head aches, that's all."

"You're supposed to be resting. Are you dizzy? Nauseous?"

"Yeah. A bit." He sat, looking weak and frustrated because of it. "I probably have a slight concussion. I had one a few years ago, and this is what it felt like. I must have cracked the back of my head on the rocks when Nigel knocked me down."

My fingers felt for and found the lump just below the crown of his head. Another horrible series of what-ifs ran through my mind. What if it's a serious head injury? What if he loses consciousness? What if he dies?

Stop it! Shut up, dumbass brain!

I helped him settle so he was leaning against the wall of the inner cave. If only there was a blanket to cover him with. It wasn't damp, but the air was cool. I could feel a draft on my legs and ankles. If only we weren't so thinly dressed.

I've got to get him out of here. There has to be a way.

"Close your eyes and rest, but try not to go to sleep."

"Aye aye, doc."

"Nick—"

He touched my hair gently. "Relax, darlin'. I'm not dying of a brain hemorrhage, if that's what you're worried about. I have a hard head. I'll be fine. I'm going to meditate for a while and try to gather my strength."

"Will meditating help?" I asked doubtfully.

"Can't hurt. Jeff, one of my friends from home, swears by it. It's very calming. If we're stuck in here for any length of time, I'll teach you how to do it."

"Okay. I'm going to look around a bit more and see what else there is to discover."

"Please don't disappear through any more mysterious passageways."

"I won't. I promise. Rest."

It didn't take me long to find the tunnel. I'd become increasingly convinced of its existence by the air currents flowing around us. And every now and then, I got a tangy whiff of the sea.

So I poked around stalagmites, shone the flashlight into recesses and crawled on my hands and knees on the cold, rough floor of the cave, seeking the source of the draft. I was confused by the way the airflow was distorted by the irregular shape of the cave, but at last I identified the one deep recess through which the currents seemed to be moving.

There I found a crack less than two feet high. Lying on my stomach, I stared into blackness, beaming my flashlight into what appeared to be a low, narrow horizontal shaft. The drafts assaulted my face. But I could see no light, nor any other indication, apart from the cool, fresh air, that the shaft led to the outside world.

"Nick." I knelt down beside him and touched his shoulder. Nick lifted his head from his arms. His face was white and his mouth was set in a tense attempt at a smile. He probably felt even worse than he looked. He wouldn't complain because he wouldn't want to worry me.

I swallowed hard. I was choked up; I tried to hide it. I couldn't let him see me weep for him.

"I'm not asleep." He spoke so defensively that my heart jerked. "I'm okay."

Sure you are.

"I think I may have found a way out." I described the air currents I'd been following. "There's some kind of tunnel. It looks as if it's man-made. Maybe the people who stashed the treasure here carved a secret entrance for themselves. I can smell the sea every now and then, so I think it must lead out of the cave."

"Can you see the other end? A light of any kind?"

"No, but maybe the shaft curves." I paused, adding in a voice that shook, "I thought I might crawl in and see where it goes."

Nick's eyes came fully open. "I'll do it."

"No. You're hurt. Besides, it's narrow. You'd have to slide along on your stomach. You've got a concussion and maybe a couple of broken ribs. You can't do it."

"Neither can you. You're claustrophobic."

"I want to get out of here. I want to get *you* out of here." I firmed my spine and lifted my chin. My insides were mush, but I mustn't let him see that. "I'll do whatever it takes."

"Let me see this tunnel."

I gave him my hand and helped him to his feet. He tried to hide his unsteadiness from me. His weakness hardened my resolution. I could do this. Couldn't I?

Nick squatted beside me and examined the tunnel with our flashlight. He sniffed the air. "You may be right," he conceded. "But it's black as the devil and there's no way to know whether it's safe. Or even how far you'd have to crawl. The source of the draft might be nothing more than a small hole like the one in the roof of the outer cave." He turned back to me, his expression grim. He shook his head decisively. "It's too dangerous, Ellie."

I was briefly relieved. Too dangerous. Not likely to save us. Good—I wouldn't have to crawl into that hole. "But what alternative do we have?"

"We can return to the outer cave and wait. We can hope Metin's free to come after us. If something's happened to him, Hepburn might find us. If neither of those things happens and we're really desperate, we can attempt this. By that time maybe I'll be better."

"And maybe you'll be worse. Maybe we'll both be so weak and dispirited that we won't have the energy to escape. We don't have much water, and we've got no food. There are no blankets to keep us warm at night. We can't wait, Nick. If we wait we'll die."

His lashes came down and curtained his eyes. He must know I was right. His headache would probably get better with each passing hour, but broken ribs wouldn't heal overnight. How cold did it get in this place at night? We could die of hypothermia if we couldn't keep warm.

What if the damn shaft actually did lead out? Wouldn't it be foolish not to investigate it?

"Let's give it a couple hours," he said. "Maybe I'll start feeling better after I rest a bit. I was the one who got you into this mess. Broken ribs or no, I'll be the one to take the risk."

"No. I'll go."

"Ellie, it's dangerous! We have no idea how stable the tunnel is. If you crawl in there, disturbing things, the whole shaft might collapse. I have no tools, nothing to dig you out with—"

I quivered at the image but kept my head high. "Suppose you go in and it collapses on *you.*"

"Then I'll be dead, which is probably exactly what I deserve."

"And I'll be trapped here, alone in the dark and waiting to die. I couldn't bear that." Involuntary tears filled my eyes. "I can't just sit here and do nothing."

Nick swore, then caught his breath. Dammit! I could see that breathing too deeply hurt him.

"Anyway, your shoulders are too wide," I dropped to my hands and knees and measured the opening to the shaft with my hands. "Look—I'll barely fit myself."

"And if it gets narrower?"

"I'll come back."

"Oh, God, Ellie!"

"There's really no choice, is there?" The truth was, if I was doing this, I had to do it now. If I waited, more hellish images of everything that might go wrong would flood me and I'd dissolve into a state of helpless anxiety. I had to act, and I had to act now.

"Let me try this. If I sit here and think about it I'll chicken out. But, hey, if I succeed, I'll probably never be claustrophobic again. If I get through this, I can get through anything."

He caught me to him and held me hard. "Shit, Ellie. I love you."

The tears fell faster then. I didn't know if he meant it, but it gave me courage. "I love you, too." I lifted my face for his kiss. It was fierce and tender. His hands moved gently over me, as if memorizing my body.

"If we get out of this, you and I are going to be together, *hayatim*. I mean—" He stopped, looking vulnerable in a way I'd never seen in him before. "If that's what you want."

"You think I'd crawl through a dark, eighteen-inch-wide tunnel for the sake of anyone else?" I grinned. "Only for you, master."

He rolled his eyes, and then hugged me. "If we get out of this, I'm gonna fucking thrash your ass for even suggesting such a crazy stunt."

I kissed him one more time, and turned to begin my journey into the night.

Chapter 41

ELLIE

There was barely room to crawl. I had to slither along on my stomach, one hand holding the flashlight, the other reaching out in front of me and feeling for obstacles. My light revealed the inner walls of the shaft to be quite solid-looking. The sides were smoother than nature could have made them. Someone had hewn this tunnel out of rock, hundreds, perhaps thousands of years ago. It had to lead somewhere.

Calling back my findings to Nick, I began to move a little faster. I could see no exit—there was nothing but gloom and darkness ahead. I concentrated on propelling my body forward, trying not to think about the possibility of a cave-in.

After several excruciatingly slow minutes of forward motion, I noticed that my light seemed to be glancing off stone ahead. Oh, no. Could someone have constructed a tunnel only to abandon it after a few yards? But the air still smelled fresh. Crawling a few more feet, I saw why. The tunnel did not end; it took a sharp turn to the right.

Again I called back and explained. My voice echoed oddly and Nick's sounded faint as he replied, pleading with me to be careful. I clung to the sound of his voice. I stuck my head around the corner, hoping now to be able to see some daylight. But there was nothing. The shaft continued as black and forbidding as before.

This was depressing. And scary. Rounding the bend made me feel as if I was cutting myself off. Separating from him even more dramatically. I thought about earthquakes, like the one that had shaken this island in the past. I pictured the tunnel convulsing as the earth moved and hundreds of meters of dirt and rock above my body crashing down and burying me. Faltering, I paused, not sure I could go on.

Don't quit now. That's sea air you can smell in here. There must be a way out.

Getting around the corner was no easy task. I had to jackknife my body, and in the process I scraped my breasts and my belly on the rough stone. Worse, the tunnel seemed to grow narrower, and for a few moments as I negotiated the turn, I got stuck. My heart, which had been remarkably well behaved so far, leaped into panic-alert. Sweat burst out under my arms and along my spine. Terror swept over me.

"Ellie?" Nick yelled.

I wriggled my hips and pulled free. Maybe the sweat that had blossomed on my skin actually helped. But Nick would never make it through the tunnel. He was too big. "I'm fine," I said. My voice was shaking and squeaking. It was hard to swallow because my mouth was so dry. "I don't see anything yet, but I'm going on."

I few minutes later, I thought I saw something move ahead of me in the darkness. Visions of snakes halted me, but I determinedly pushed that idea from my mind. If anything did live in here, it would hear my noisy approach and get the hell out of my way.

I came to another bend in the shaft. This time I hesitated. I was panting from the effort of dragging myself along, and my knees and palms were growing numb. If I got stuck I'd be in a real fix. Too wide-shouldered to get past the first turn, Nick wouldn't be able to reach me. I'd be doomed to lie here, trapped, watching helplessly as my flashlight got dimmer and dimmer until it went out, leaving me to die alone in the dark.

For the first time since Nigel had sealed the entrance to the cavern, I felt my will and courage fail me. Tears squeezed out of my eyes and carved a ragged path through the grime on my face. *I can't do this. I've tried my best, but I just can't go on.*

My flashlight flickered. I remembered that Nigel and his men had been burning the flashlights all morning. This one was running out of power. How much time did I have before it died altogether? Not enough to waste feeling sorry for yourself, Ellie, my girl, I thought.

Determinedly scrunching myself up as small as possible, I took a steadying breath and ventured slowly around the second bend. As soon as I did so, the quality of the darkness changed. Pressing my flashlight against the rock to hide its feeble light, I squinted into the gloom. Ahead of me, like a star shining in the velvet depths of night, a light gleamed. It looked blue. Sky or sea? I didn't care which.

I shouted the news back to Nick and launched myself toward it, praying it would be large enough to provide me with an exit. I couldn't judge distance well in the tunnel, but presumably the smallness of the aperture meant that the light was still far away.

It was not. I had to crawl no more than five yards before I came to the end of the shaft. The smell of fresh air was dizzyingly strong here, but even so, the opening was no larger than my fist.

For several seconds, I stared from a yard away, unable to accept that my odyssey could end in failure. It didn't make sense. The tunnel was large enough—just—for a person to crawl through. Surely it required a more substantial exit than *that.* Through the circular hole I could see the blue sky. The irony of it appalled me. Only a few inches of rock separated me from light, life, and freedom.

"I will not cry," I said aloud. "There's got to be a way out."

I ran my faltering flashlight beam over the stone around the aperture and noted that it looked different from the other walls of the shaft. Moving closer, I checked it with my fingers and realized why. What I was confronting was not a solid wall of rock, but a tightly packed mound of stones. Hope leaped in me once again. Whoever had constructed the tunnel had walled it up to conceal it from the outside.

Putting down the flashlight, I tried to shift the stones around the opening. My hands were quivering. At first the stones wouldn't shift at all, and I was afraid they'd been mortared. But I finally felt one loosen. I dug at it until I was able to push it out, enlarging the aperture to the size of two fists. I pressed my face to the opening and looked out.

Before me was the most beautiful sight I'd ever seen—the blue arc of the sky and, just beneath it, the sun-drenched sparkle of the Aegean Sea. And straight ahead, almost on a direct line from me, I could see the trim, clean-lined prow of the *Voyager,* gracefully floating on the silken sea. "Nick!" I shouted, hearing the joy in my own voice. "I made it! I'm on the other side of the mountain, on a cliff overlooking the bay where *Voyager* is anchored. I can see her!"

Ignoring the cuts and bruises on my fingers, I continued to widen the opening. "I'm going to climb down and swim to the boat. If Metin's there, I'll get him to help us. If he isn't, I'll radio the mainland for help."

"Dammit, Ellie! If Nigel catches you he'll kill you."

"I'll be careful, I promise. Are you okay back there? How's your head?"

"My head is fine, and you are amazing. I fucking love your ass! But please be careful."

My spirits were soaring. I no longer knew what fear was. Even the prospect of climbing down an extremely steep and rocky slope to the sea didn't faze me. I had crawled through my own personal vision of hell and survived the experience. Nothing, not even a devil like Nigel, was going to stop me now.

The swim to the boat through the cool water was a welcome change to the harsh, sweaty work of crawling through the tunnel. I was cautious, breast stroking as noiselessly as possible. When I reached the yacht, I hauled myself up the built-in metal ladder at the stern and jumped lightly over the side. I stayed perfectly still for several moments, listening. There was no sound.

I slid open the main hatch and went below. On tiptoe, I checked the various compartments. They were empty. Damn. What had Nigel done with Metin? I thought about the young man's handsome face and quick smile and prayed he was still alive.

The last door I approached led to a tiny storeroom. As I opened the door—a little less cautiously now, since the boat seemed deserted—I was grabbed from behind. I stiffened and would have cried out had a hand not clapped across my mouth. Then I heard the mutter of a masculine curse, and I was released.

"Allah be praised. I thought you were dead."

I whirled. "Metin! You scared me."

"*You* scared *me*. I thought you were one of them, come back to finish me off." He held up one wrist, which still had a coil of rope knotted around it. "They knocked me out, the dogs, bound my body and left me in here about an hour ago. Fortunately I have a hard head and strong teeth." He showed me where the cord had been gnawed through. "I was coming to search for you and Nick when I heard someone board the yacht. What happened? Are you okay? Where's Nick?"

"He's hurt. Nigel beat him badly." I quickly explained our ordeal in the cave. "You've got to help me get him out of there."

"Okay. No problem."

I looked at him doubtfully. "But there is a problem. Nick can't crawl out the way I did. His shoulders are too wide, and he's hurt. You and I are going to have a hard time clearing the entrance to the cave alone."

"Then we will get help," Metin said confidently. His white teeth flashed in his swarthy face. "You think I would let those swine escape after all the time I have invested in their capture? The first thing I did upon freeing myself was radio for assistance. The Turkish Shore Patrol are on their way."

"Thank God!"

"Nick will not be pleased. He hoped to keep his grandfather out of prison. I was ready to help him with that—why not—one must have respect for the old, even if Sir Avery was a little crooked. To trap Nigel was the important thing. But now—" He shrugged. "I don't know what will happen now."

Whether or not Nick's grandfather went to prison was not my immediate concern. "We need blankets, bandages, medicine, water. A couple of new flashlights. If we can't move the stone, I'll crawl back in through the tunnel and wait for help to arrive."

"I will come with you."

"You can't. Like Nick's, your shoulders are too broad."

"Then we will move this stone of yours. Come, Ellie *hanim.*"

Chapter 42

ELLIE

The hot afternoon sun beat down upon us as we rowed into shore, unloaded our supplies and began the trek around the promontory to the excavation site. As we scrambled over the arid ground, I stared at the cliff towering above us, trying to take in the fact that I had crawled through a narrow tunnel in the bowels of this jagged rock pile, propelled myself through silent darkness and escaped safely into the light. I stretched, reveling in the warmth of the sun dancing upon the bare skin of my arms and legs. If it weren't for my anxiety about Nick, I might actually have felt good.

We were nearly at the site when Metin, who was leading the way along the narrow track, stopped. He looked back at me, laying a finger across his lips. I listened. I heard the swell of angry male voices, moving toward us from the direction of the compound.

"Quickly, get behind these rocks," Metin ordered. I obeyed without hesitation, responding to the cool note of authority in his voice. We were both speaking Turkish since I no longer had to hide my knowledge of that language. My Turkish was better than his English.

No longer did Metin look like a fisherman's kid with a lust for adventure. Instead he'd transformed himself into a Mediterranean bandit, armed from head to toe with handguns, knives and a deadly-looking object that was, he'd informed me, an automatic rifle. He was also carrying a crowbar and an oar from the yacht's lifeboat, which he intended to use as a lever at the cave entrance.

We crouched out of sight just a few yards from the sealed entrance to the cave. Through a chink in the rocks, I had an unobstructed view of the men who were approaching from the other side of the excavations. "It's Sir Avery," I whispered. Because of his crippled legs, the elderly archaeologist rarely visited the excavations. It would have been impossible to push his wheelchair over the rough, stony ground.

But they were carrying him. Mustafa, the cheerful, burly cook, and Erdal, Sir Avery's longtime companion, between them were cradling him in their strong arms. Beside them were the other men loyal to Sir Avery—Ahmet, Engin, the leonine Aslan, and a couple of others. They were armed. One of them had Sir Avery's folded wheelchair.

Also present, looking disgruntled, were Nigel and Sinan. Sir Avery was holding a gun upon them, just as he had earlier held one upon Nick.

I stared, puzzled. What had happened? I remembered that Nick was friendly with most of the workers at the compound and that Sir Avery's workers outnumbered Nigel's by a considerable margin. Had Nigel been unable to convince them all to do things his way?

The small procession halted in front of the boulder that now blocked the entrance to the cave. "Open it," Sir Avery growled. "You sealed it, now roll away the stone. They better be in there, and alive, Nigel."

I looked at Metin. "I guess Sir Avery didn't wish us dead."

I was all for showing ourselves, but Metin wouldn't allow it. "We will wait. In the meantime, they will do the heavy work for us."

It took the efforts of several men to shift the large boulder. I wondered what Nick must be thinking if he could hear the sounds of the cavern being unsealed.

At last it was done. At his command, the men lifted Sir Avery and prepared to carry him into the cave. "We will follow," Metin said. He cradled the rifle in his arms. His face was set, but his eyes were gleaming with a kind of pleasure I supposed that only men of certain macho tendencies could truly share and understand.

"You're not actually going to shoot anybody?"

"We shall see."

"May I have one of your guns?"

He raised his eyebrows. "Do you know how to use firearms?"

"Yes," was all I said.

When he hesitated, I reminded him that the odds were against us. He gave me a pistol, and briefly explained its action. I familiarized myself with it quickly. I was amazed at how calm I felt. I'd done the hardest thing by crawling through that narrow tunnel. Anything ahead of me seemed almost trivial in comparison.

We waited several minutes, and then silently followed the men into the cave, crawling silently through the entrance and remaining deep in the shadows. As the cool, black darkness closed once again around me, I heard Nigel cursing. "They were right here. Here, in this spot. Both of them. They've disappeared."

"What do you mean, disappeared?" Sir Avery said. "Put me down, for God's sake," he ordered the men who were carrying him. "There, on that flat rock. Watch Nigel. I no longer trust him."

"This is a fool's errand," Nigel snapped. "We could be safely away from the island by now. You can come out now, coz," he said more loudly. "It seems the old man wants you alive, after all."

Where was Nick? I hoped he hadn't fallen unconscious again.

He must still be in the inner chamber of the cave where the treasure was. When they could not find him here, would they continue to search until they discovered the narrow passageway that led to the gold?

"Nick?" Sir Avery called. "Where are you, my boy?" He was answered only by the echo of his own shout. "By God, Nigel, if you've been lying to me..."

"They must be here somewhere, Avery *bey,*" Sinan said, sounding genuinely distressed.

"They must have escaped," somebody suggested.

"They were here," insisted Sinan. "There on the floor of the cave. Nick was hurt. He could not have escaped."

"How badly hurt?" Sir Avery's voice was thin and hard.

"Nigel beat him," Sinan admitted.

Sir Avery swore. "Is this true, Nigel? You claimed you hadn't harmed him."

"I didn't hear you berating him for beating me."

"You've killed him, haven't you?" This time Sir Avery's voice was low, broken, barely audible. "And Ellie. You've killed them both."

"I should have," Nigel said. "They're in here. Look harder, you fools."

While they searched, Metin and I edged forward, our weapons at the ready. The stalagmites near the entrance gave us plenty of shelter.

"This tale of sealing them in the cave was fabricated in order to lure me away from the compound, away from the boat, so the few men who are still loyal to you would have the chance to steal some of the artifacts," Nick's grandfather said. "You probably planned on sealing me in the cave."

"No," Sinan protested. "We left them here. They were alive."

"Shut up. I'm weary of your lies." Once again, I heard the sound of a gun being cocked for firing. My eyes had adjusted to the dim light, and I could see Sir Avery's drawn face. "I never wanted Nick hurt. I was angry with him, yes, but one uses words when one is angry. Words, not fists or guns. You've never learned this basic lesson of civilization, have you? You're corrupt, Nigel. Your grandmother warned me often enough. So did Nick. I should have listened."

"I kicked him a few times, that's all. The clever bastard is in this cave somewhere, listening to this conversation and laughing his head off."

"You are a liar, a thief and a murderer. I begin to understand why Nick was so determined to stop you."

"But you're not a murderer, old man," Nigel said unpleasantly. He took a menacing step forward. "So put the gun down."

Instead, his grandfather raised it. "Any man can kill if he is pushed far enough."

I touched Metin's shoulder. We needed to intervene now.

But Nick beat us to it. Just as Metin and I were about to make our presence known, he emerged from the narrow crevasse that led to the treasure.

"I'm here," he said in a clear voice. "For once, he's telling the truth."

"Nick!" Sir Avery swung around, and even in the gloom, I could see the relief that marked his craggy features. His mouth worked speechlessly for a second before he managed to gasp, "Thank god."

Holding his ribs, Nick walked unsteadily into the center of the cavern where his grandfather sat. He reached down and clasped Sir Avery's hand. Even through the darkness, I could see that the old man was overcome with emotion.

"When your cousin came back without you, I realized what a fool I'd been to think he'd leave you unharmed."

"He'd have killed us if Ellie hadn't stopped him."

"He tried to get me to leave the island with him. He claimed you and Ellie were tied up on your boat, and that by the time you worked yourself free, we would be far away from here. But I couldn't leave, and Sinan finally confessed the truth."

The archaeologist's throat sounded choked up. I felt pretty weepy myself. During the time I'd spent with Sir Avery and

Nick, I'd seen the unacknowledged depth of the affection between them.

Nick stooped beside his grandfather so their eyes were on the same level. "You should have trusted me. I've been trying to get you away from Nigel and save your scrawny ass."

"What a touching scene," Nigel mocked. He seized the moment to dive toward his grandfather. He moved smoothly and fast, and his grandfather was not expecting it. Nigel wrested the gun from Sir Avery's hands and swung it toward Nick, snarling, "Die, asshole."

Time slowed. There was no doubt in my mind that Nigel was going to kill Nick. I couldn't allow that. I acted without thinking. I steadied the gun Metin had given me, took aim, and squeezed the trigger.

Metin fired at approximately the same moment, and Nigel went down.

In the next instant, I stood staring at my own hands in shock, not quite believing what I had done. Sweat broke out on my brow. Nick was swaying but standing. Nigel had recoiled, obviously from the impact of bullets, and fallen. I could see blood.

Was he dead? Had I just killed a man?

Nick swayed a little more, and I realized there was blood on him, too. I dropped the gun. I could hear Metin calling out orders to the others, but the meaning of words didn't penetrate. Sir Avery was anxiously asking questions about his grandsons. I ignored him.

On legs that barely seemed capable of holding me, I ran to Nick. He grabbed me and held me to him with his right arm, but his left arm hung by his side.

"I think I'd better sit down, *canim*," he said, as his legs folded beneath him. We sank to our knees together on the cave floor.

Chapter 43

NICK

She kept surprising me. When Ellie burst out of the shadows, pistol in hand, I was dumbfounded. I was sure I was dead this time, but she had saved my life twice. She'd shot my fucking cousin, although not before he got one bullet into me. My arm. Unless he'd hit a fucking artery, it wasn't gonna kill me.

It took me a few seconds to realize that Ellie wasn't the only one who had fired. Metin, looking like a Middle Eastern Rambo, appeared beside her. He assessed my condition swiftly and efficiently, and then checked on Nigel. From the groans issuing from my cousin's fallen body, I concluded he wasn't dead.

"One bullet wound in the right shoulder, another that's grazed his left hip," Metin announced. "If you were aiming for his balls, Ellie, you missed."

She didn't seem to be listening. She was clinging to me, trying to stop the bleeding in my left arm. We were both sitting on the ground. I glanced down at myself, noticing that if it had hit me about three inches to the right, the bullet would have pierced my heart and I'd be history. The shot wouldn't have gone wide, either, if Nigel hadn't been winged in the shoulder while firing. Yep. My cousin wanted me dead.

"Is he gonna live?" I asked Metin.

"Looks like it. We will need medical assistance for both of you, though."

Fuck medical assistance. I felt great. "You rock," I told Ellie.

"Ssh. You're shot."

"Flesh wound, no big deal." It was beginning to hurt. I felt like a battered wreck. Why had I ever thought I could do stuff like this? Who the hell did I think I was, Indiana Jones?

"I was so afraid for you," I confessed to her. "I can't believe you crawled all that way through the darkness. I wouldn't have wanted to tackle that tunnel, and I've never had an anxiety attack in my life."

"All I cared about was getting back and making sure you were okay."

"You just saved my life. Again. Fuck, Ellie. You're amazing."

"I love you," she said.

I shook my head, stunned. She'd said it before, but it seemed much more real this time. She had crawled through a narrow black tunnel and shot a guy for me. She must mean it. Something welled up in me, strong and a little bit scary. I hoped I wasn't going to start bawling or something. My eyes were stinging. Must be the concussion, right?

Truth was, I loved her too. I hadn't known her long, but damn, somehow or other she had slid into my heart.

I'd forgotten about Metin, who was efficiently cleaning things up. From somewhere he produced a couple of pairs of handcuffs, which he snapped on the wrists of Nigel and Sinan. Then, still waving his weapon, he herded everyone toward the entrance of the cave. "You will all come with me," he ordered. He proceeded to pull out an official-looking I.D. stamped with the star and crescent that symbolized the Turkish nation.

While I blinked at him, stupefied, Metin continued, "I am an agent of the Turkish Customs Bureau, working undercover. I regret to inform you that I must arrest the lot of you—except Ellie—for crimes against the Republic of Turkey."

"Metin?"

"Sorry, Nick," my friend, associate, and sailing partner returned, not meeting my eyes. "That includes you."

Chapter 44

ELLIE

"I'd like to have a chat with you, Metin," said Nick.

The three of us were in Nick's bedroom at the compound, where I was taping his ribs. A helicopter had arrived on the island with the Turkish authorities, who had already rounded up Nigel and his cohorts and taken them back to the mainland. Metin and several other agents had been assigned to clean things up here, and both Sir Avery and Nick had been left in their custody. Nick had insisted that he was too weak to travel and his grandfather too elderly and frail. Metin backed him up, while at the same time making it clear to everyone that both men were still technically under arrest.

Weak though he was, Nick was not behaving like a chastened criminal, I noted. He was treating Metin the same as ever, despite the younger man's change in status. "Rob Hepburn threatened to put a man on me," he went on. "That man was you?"

"You could say so. Our agency is cooperating with Mr. Hepburn, although I do not personally know the man."

"Jeez." My lover's tone was a cross between annoyance and self-deprecation. "And here I thought I was livening up your uneventful life by giving you a much-desired taste of adventure. What a blind, trusting amateur I am."

"I'm truly sorry, Nick," said Metin who now admitted to the age of twenty-five and several years' experience as a customs agent. His eyes looked anywhere but at his erstwhile employer's face. Although Nick had initially been furious with him for his betrayal, I could tell he was most of the way toward forgiving him now, simply because Metin looked so miserable. "I was only doing my job."

"I know, and I can't really blame you. You did it damn well. I certainly never suspected."

"I'm sure Hepburn will make a deal to get you off," Metin said earnestly. "My agency owes his several favors. You won't be prosecuted, Nick."

"If there's a deal to be made, I'd rather make it directly with you."

"And is there?"

"Maybe. I presume, since you've shown no interest in the subject, that Ellie didn't happen to mention the discovery we made?"

I hadn't, of course. The hidden cache of ancient treasures was a secret known only to Nick and myself. "Nope," I said. "I was preoccupied with getting you safely out of the cave."

"What discovery?" Metin asked.

"The treasures of Troy exist, my friend. Jewelry and gold objets d'art, of rare beauty and ancient workmanship. My grandfather was right." Nick paused a moment to let the news sink in. "There's loot on this island, all right, and it's been hidden for nearly three thousand years. Ellie and I are the only two people alive who know where these treasures lie."

"In the cave?" Metin guessed.

"Did you see any indication of that?" Nick scoffed. "Be sensible, Metin. We would have found the stuff long ago if that's where it was."

I blinked over this blatant lie.

"I don't think I'm going to give you any further hints," Nick continued. "Let's just say that somewhere on the island is a collection of extraordinary artifacts, including the golden dolphin after which the island was named. But they are well concealed and will remain so."

"Unless?"

"Unless the government of Turkey is prepared to deal justly with me."

Metin grinned, his dark eyes sparkling. "You devious dog. What do you want?"

"You know what I want. What I've been working all these months to achieve. My grandfather's freedom. He's too old and ill to spend his remaining days in prison."

"And your own freedom? Surely that, too, is important to you?"

"Well, yes, of course," Nick acknowledged with a smile.

"How do I know you're telling the truth about this?"

"I'm not lying, Metin. The treasures exist."

"I believe you. Still, if you found them, so can I. I can order a troop of men to comb the island until they turn up. Then you will have nothing to deal with, Nick."

"You can do that, yes." Nick met Metin's eyes implacably. "But I don't think you will. You owe me something, at least, for the entertainment I've provided you with during the past six months."

Metin flushed. "It was more than entertainment! You have been my friend."

"Yes, I thought so, too."

"I had a job to do," the young man repeated mechanically. "I haven't always liked it, but there was no choice."

"Metin." Nick's voice was gentler now. "We are friends still, as far as I'm concerned." He extended his hand. "You are my brother, my *kardesh.*"

Metin grasped his hand and held it hard. "I will go downstairs and consult with my superiors."

"I'd appreciate that," said Nick.

"He's in a quandary, I think," I noted as I wrapped the last piece of tape around Nick's chest, hoping I was doing it properly. We could hear Metin bounding down the stairs. "He's proud of having accomplished what he set out to do, yet he's sincerely fond of you."

"I know. Poor Metin. I wonder if he's tough enough to last at this job."

"Will he make the deal?"

"If his superiors don't balk, yes, I'm sure he will. He doesn't want to see me go to prison. He knows it wasn't loot I was after. I'm not too worried about myself. The Turkish government isn't unreasonable. Once the facts come out, they'll be lenient."

"It's Sir Avery you're worried about."

Nick nodded, his expression grim. The old archaeologist had been philosophical about his probable fate, but Nick was taking the prospect of his grandfather's incarceration very hard.

"It'll be all right," I soothed him. "Metin will fix things. I have a feeling everything's going to work out okay."

"*Inshallah.*" God willing.

I helped him into bed, and then sat beside him on the mattress, stroking his golden hair. "It's odd about Metin, isn't it? I've always thought of him as a kid. But he's older than I am. When I made it safely to the yacht and asked for his help, I had no idea he would return with me to the cave and arrest you."

"How could you know? I spent six months in virtual seclusion on the yacht with him and I had no clue." He looked up at me and grimaced. "Some undercover agent I turn out to be. You'd built up this fantasy of me as a rough, tough criminal, with lethal talents in the martial arts and the brain of a corrupt intellectual. So how do I end up? Beaten to a pulp by my cousin, rescued from death by a woman, and outwitted by a kid!"

"You did that kick-ass thing with your feet while your hands were tied behind your back. And your amorous talents are considerable," I teased him.

"Yeah, well, do I look like I'm capable of hauling you into bed? The only thing I'm going to be able to do right now is sleep."

I put my arms around his shoulders and kissed—gently—the sore spot on the crown of his head. "I must love you very much, because I want you to sleep. I want you to rest and get better. You can worry about impressing me with your devastating sexual prowess at some later time."

He smiled. "With that as my incentive, I'll start resting immediately."

"I'd rather see you human and vulnerable than that cold, controlled scary guy you seemed to be when first we met."

"Mmm," said Nick, closing his eyes.

He was nearly asleep when Metin burst into our room. "You've got your deal, Nick. We'll trade the gold for you and Sir Avery."

Nick jerked back to a sitting position, rubbing his eyes and swearing.

"There's one condition, though," Metin added with a grin. "If you steal so much as a gram of the treasure before you turn it over, we'll toss you into the deepest, darkest prison Turkey has to offer."

Nick groaned. "Don't worry, Metin. I swear to you I'm going straight from now on."

"And you'll accept full responsibility for that sly old fox, your grandfather?"

"My grandfather will doubtless spend his declining years writing a book about the treasures of Troy. Yes, I promise you, his relic-stealing days are over."

Once again Metin clasped Nick's hand. "Then it's a deal."

"What about Nigel?" I asked.

"He's going to hospital first and then to a secure lockup," Metin said. "He can expect a stiff sentence. Our judges are harsh with thieves who ravage Turkey's cultural and historical heritage."

"With any luck, he'll be imprisoned for a long time." Nick's expression was one of pure satisfaction. "Rob Hepburn will probably suggest that the Turkish authorities search his boat. They're likely to find all sorts of evidence there."

"We'll coordinate with Mr. Hepburn on Nigel," Metin said. "I believe he is wanted by several agencies of several nations, but we will try to ensure that The Republic of Turkey has the first shot."

I was glad now that I hadn't succeeded in killing Nigel. My bullet had only grazed his hip, probably because my arm had been wobbling as I'd fired. I wasn't sure how I'd have felt about killing a man. Even though the creep had deserved it, ending his life would probably have haunted my conscience.

But I had no trouble at all envisioning Nigel rotting for a few decades in a Turkish prison.

Chapter 45

ELLIE

The sun was high in the late April sky on the day I finally visited the ancient city of Troy. Nick and I sailed *Voyager* up the coast from the Aegean port city of Izmir, where the Golden Dolphin Island discoveries were being dated and appraised by experts. I felt more at home on the yacht now; Nick had taught me to crew for him.

I was at the helm, delighting in the responsiveness of the yacht as it skimmed over the bright water near Truva, the site of Troy. Nick came up behind me and placed his firm hands on my waist. I leaned back against him, tossing him a grin over my shoulder. Although the weather was warm in the Aegean region, the wind was strong, so he had changed his usual jean cutoffs for the sexy black leather trousers I'd discovered that first morning in his cabin. With a loose white shirt and the gold stubble of the beard he was beginning to grow, he looked more like a pirate than ever.

I felt his breath against my scalp as he leaned over and whispered, "You're almost home, Helen of Troy."

"She was Helen of Greece, actually. Not until after she was abducted did she become known as Helen of Troy."

His hands slid down my arms and clamped my wrists to the wooden wheel of the yacht. "So? You've been abducted, too. You're still my prisoner, *hayatim.*"

I laughed. "Am I complaining?"

"Haven't heard one word of complaint lately, though in the beginning you sure spit fire at me."

"In the beginning I was frightened of you, Nick."

"I'm sorry for that, but I'm not sorry for the way it turned out. Those old-time heroes were no fools. Abduction is a great way of getting a woman. No awkward texting while trying to wrangle a hook-up, no plotting the chick's seduction over an expensive dinner, no distressing scenes when the boredom sets in. When she begins to get on your nerves, you just grab the wench and toss her overboard."

"Jerk!" I laughed, turning on him with a mutinous expression.

He kissed me on the throat, where I was still wearing my rope collar. I'd grown fond of the thing. Nick had woven it himself, and I thought it was much nicer than those leather slave collars they sell online. "Knew I could get you spitting fire again without much effort." He took the helm himself. "Get your camera. I think it's time you finished your assignment for that website back in Boston, don't you?"

"I took some great exclusive photos of the treasure," I reminded him. "Not to mention all those lovely shots of the artifacts you crooks stole. Or didn't steal."

"Coming about," he warned, bringing the bow across the wind. "Mind the sail, will you, crew? We're gonna bring this boat in for a landing on the ancient Trojan shores."

Actually, since the site was a couple of miles inland, we had to hike a bit before we came to the ruins of the fabled city. And, after the wondrous inner chamber of the cave on Golden Dolphin Island, Troy was a bit of an anticlimax. The Turks had erected a replica of the Trojan Horse near the entrance to the site, but nothing was left of the city itself except some grassy mounds and the rough stone walls that marked the various levels of the excavations.

"How the mighty are fallen," I said sadly as I focused my camera and photographed what little remained of Homer's "holy citadel." Hand in hand, we walked around the deserted grounds. "There aren't even any tourists here."

"No," Nick agreed, slipping an arm around my waist and squeezing. "We have the place all to ourselves." He pushed aside the hair at the back of my neck and nuzzled me. "Very tempting. Why don't we stroll over to that grassy mound and rest for a while?"

"Rest?" I laughed.

"Yeah. I feel a headache coming on. Concussions take a while to get better, you know." He feigned a look of lassitude and his hand moved up to brush across my breast. I felt my nipples harden instantly. "I need a lotta rest."

"Stop. Someone might see us."

"Who? The ghost of King Priam?"

"Think of it," I said, swiping his hand away. "Lots of people died here."

"Lots of people made love here, too, *canim*." He took my hand and led me toward the grassy mound in question, which was sheltered by a scrubby bush. He dropped to his knees and pulled me down beside him. "It's time, fair Helen, to show me what it took to launch those thousand ships. Your namesake must have had something more than a pretty face going for her to start a war that lasted ten years and destroyed one of the greatest cities in the ancient world." He wrapped his arms around me and delivered a series of devastating kisses. "I'm going to fuck you in this ancient spot."

"We really shouldn't," I said as he laid me back in the stubby grass and brought his golden body down on mine.

"Shame on us."

"It's not what I had in mind when I, uh—" I squirmed a little as he raised my skirt and treated me to the wicked enticement of leather against my bare skin "—planned this pilgrimage."

"No? Well, pet, your Dom doesn't give a shit about your plan at the moment; it's time to follow mine."

I laughed. He'd already taught me quite a bit about his kinky lifestyle, and I'd enjoyed every minute. Still, I protested a little, just for fun, as I felt my panties slip away. "Don't."

"Don't?" he repeated, chuckling softly. "Wrong response, slave. Say 'yes, master, harder, master.'" He stroked me until I grew slick and hot and ready.

"Yes, master," I whispered.

"*Seni seviyorum*," he told me. I love you.

"*Ben de seni seviyorum*." I love you, too.

Somewhat later, when we sat up and rearranged our clothing, I stretched and said, "You know, with my claustrophobia
and all, I never thought I'd be so relaxed in the presence of anything vaguely resembling excavations. I asked my mother when
I called her from Izmir why we'd never talked about that pyramid we were trapped in. She said she thought I'd been too
young to remember. She felt guilty when she heard how anxious
I had been, and for how long."

"So the idea of puttering around in archeological excavations
doesn't scare you anymore?"

"Not after I faced crawling through that tunnel. I think that
burned my fear away."

"It's always better to face things. To acknowledge the bad
stuff in life."

I suspected he was referring to his own stuff as much as
mine. There was still a lot I didn't know about the man who was
now my boyfriend, but he was slowly opening up to me.

I hugged him hard. "I love you so much."

"It doesn't matter to you that I'm just an ordinary archaeologist, specializing in archaic linguistics, rather than some sort of
badass criminal?"

"Not at all. I left home hoping for an adventure, but I got rather more than I'd expected."

"We can still have adventures. Let's just try not coming so
close to getting ourselves killed."

"I'll raise a glass to that."

He wound a long lock of my hair around his fingers and said,
"We make a good team, don't we, you and I?"

"The best."

"I'm asking you to stay with me, Ellie."

I laughed. "Wow, you're asking? You're not ordering me to stay with you? How times have changed!"

"Imp. There'll be punishment coming for that." He slapped my ass. I sighed. It felt good. "But we'd better return to the yacht first, before we get arrested again."

"Are you kidnapping me?"

He rose to his feet, swooped down, and dragged me to my feet. "Don't even think about trying to escape. I'll be tying you to my bed when we get back to the boat. No way I'm ever letting you go."

Well, hey. That sounded good to me.

THE END

AUTHORS NOTE

If you want to meet some of Nick's friends, check out Linda's previous romance, *Blazing Nights* or her short story, *A Kiss is Just a Kiss*. Other stories about this circle of friends will be released over the next few months in *Nocturnal* (Max's story) and *The Dangerous Hero* (Stephen's story). Jeff's story, current untitled, will follow.

Linda's website: http://www.lindabarlow.com

Linda Barlow is the bestselling author of 23 novels, with more on the way. She lives in New England with her kinky spouse (who sleeps during the day, which has often made her wonder if he's a vampire) and their equally enigmatic and nocturnal cat.

Her novel *Leaves of Fortune* won the Rita Award from Romance Writers of America, and *Fires of Destiny* was a finalist for the same award. She loves reading, writing, computer games, and dark chocolate.

Linda lived and worked in Turkey for several years, and keeps up her Turkish by watching her beloved Turkish soap operas on the internet. She has visited the ancient site of Troy on the Turkish Aegean coast. But Golden Dolphin Island and the lost treasures of Troy are the products of her very active imagination.

www.ingramcontent.com/pod-product-compliance
Lightning Source LLC
Chambersburg PA
CBHW050921250626
47155CB00001B/322